W9-AQR-305

Mint Chocolate

MURDER

Also by Meri Allen

THE ROCKY ROAD TO RUIN

From St. Martin's Paperbacks

Mint Chocolate
MURDER

ICE CREAM SHOP MYSTERY #2

By Meri Allen

St. Martin's Paperbacks

NOTE: If you purchased this book without a cover you should be aware that this book is stolen property. It was reported as "unsold and destroyed" to the publisher, and neither the author nor the publisher has received any payment for this "stripped book."

This is a work of fiction. All of the characters, organizations, and events portrayed in this novel are either products of the author's imagination or are used fictitiously.

First published in the United States by St. Martin's Paperbacks, an imprint of St. Martin's Publishing Group.

MINT CHOCOLATE MURDER

Copyright © 2022 by Meri Allen.

All rights reserved.

For information, address St. Martin's Publishing Group, 120 Broadway, New York, NY 10271.

www.stmartins.com

ISBN: 978-1-250-26708-5

Our books may be purchased in bulk for promotional, educational, or business use. Please contact your local bookseller or the Macmillan Corporate and Premium Sales Department at 1-800-221-7945, ext. 5442, or by email at MacmillanSpecialMarkets@macmillan.com.

Printed in the United States of America

St. Martin's Paperbacks edition / August 2022

10 9 8 7 6 5 4 3 2 1

DEDICATED TO LIBRARIANS EVERYWHERE—
Underpaid, underappreciated, and underestimated
guardians of the world's knowledge, you encourage
and grow generations of readers. Thank you.

AND TO YOU, DEAR READERS—Characters
are words on a page that only come to life when
you read them. Thank you for spending a few
hours of your precious time with me and Riley.

Xo Meri

Acknowledgments

Many thanks—and a double bourbon—to Luci Zahray, aka the Poison Lady, for her invaluable help with venom and poisons of all kinds. I'll never look at wallpaper the same way again.

Bill and Charlotte, my ice cream dream team, for whipping up all the treats and keeping our fridge stocked with good things. Laurie, for all the bee info. Ginny for the scoop on photos and photography. Jessy and David for encouragement and cheering. To the talented Barb Goffman, the wonderful friends in Writers Who Kill, Cozy Mystery Crew, Stiletto Gang, and Sisters in Crime who keep me thinking like a writer.

And special thanks to Alice, who inherited me and helps me keep it cozy.

Wherever you go, you take yourself with you.

—Neil Gaiman

Chapter 1

After spending ten hours on my feet at the ice cream shop, I longed for a hot bath and a few hours curled up with an Agatha Christie paperback, a glass of pinot noir, and a cuddle with my cat, Rocky. But as the old New England saying goes, there's no rest for the wicked. I have a nine o'clock meeting with Maud Monaco, the mysterious and reclusive director of Moy Mull, Penniman's artist colony.

A former model who inherited a fortune after her European nobleman husband died, Maud wanted a fantasy ice cream social to celebrate the opening of a special exhibit at Moy Mull's summer art festival and hired me to work with her caterer to invent specialty flavors for the event. Well, she'd sent an employee, Prentiss Love, over to the shop to hire me. Now I'd get to meet Maud herself. I had to admit, I was intrigued and maybe a bit nervous and puzzled. The gallery opened tomorrow night and she wanted a tasting now? I sighed. No one said no to Maud Monaco.

So instead of sinking into a warm bath, I grabbed a slice of leftover pizza from the fridge, took a quick shower, and threw on a breezy shirtdress in navy blue linen. I brushed aside my too-long bangs and dug through my closet for something to improvise as a hairband.

Rocky, my all-black rescue cat, padded into the room and gave me a plaintive yowl as I tied on a silk scarf I'd picked up at a flea market in Rome. "I'm sorry, I promise you a big cuddle when I get home." He flashed me an injured look and stalked off with a flick of his tail. He'd been neutered two weeks before and still hadn't forgiven me for that, plus the indignity of the cone.

I dashed outside and gave a quick wave to the Fairweather Farm's employees closing up the stand across the lane. The farm's fields rolled to the horizon and warm lights burned in the windows of the sprawling farmhouse. I drove down the lane, passing the small purple building that housed Udderly Delicious, the ice cream shop I managed. The shop's parking lot was full, every picnic table surrounded by families enjoying the warm night air.

As I turned onto Fairweather Road, I took a deep breath. From what little I knew of Maud Monaco, nothing should surprise me. Nothing about this woman was ordinary. I was a librarian before I took over the shop, so I'd done my research on her. "Exotic, Enigmatic, Elegant" was the headline on the *Penniman Post*'s article about Maud when she bought Moy Mull, the former estate of an eccentric millionaire who loved the Scottish Highlands and wanted a castle of his own. His eccentricities included not allowing any guests to sleep under his roof, so several guest houses dotted the estate. Maud's friends found Moy Mull a welcome escape, and since her friends were artists, she rented them cottages on the property and converted the barn into an art gallery and studio space. Her friends told their friends, and before she knew it, Maud had an artists' colony.

The setting sun provided a warm, burnished glow to the spreading branches of oaks and maples. Cool air streamed in the window of Sadie, my loaner Volkswagen station wagon, as she strained up the one hill between the shop and Moy Mull. My company car. "Come on, Sadie, this is no time to give up the ghost." I patted the dash.

Two pier lanterns on tall stone pillars bracketed a narrow lane lined with laurel bushes. I drove between black iron gates topped with sharp spikes that could be swung shut to close off the drive. Just past the entrance, the road forked around a gate house, gray stone with a moss-covered black tile roof. A man stepped out, holding a clipboard. Though he wore khakis and a polo shirt embroidered with the double MM monogram, his solid, squared shoulders and ramrod posture made me think he was ex-military.

"Good evening," he said. "Name please?"

"Riley Rhodes."

He didn't bother to check the clipboard. He pointed at me. "Chunky Monkey."

I laughed, then sighed, then laughed again. The first time this happened, it took me a moment to remember that Chunky Monkey was a flavor, and not a warning to lay off the ice cream. Since I'd been running Udderly Delicious, people greeted me with their favorite flavors.

The guard continued, "That pecan crumble on top is great."

"I made a fresh batch today," I said.

"I'll be by." His face resumed its impassive expression. "Please park in one of the service spots at the back of the castle and follow the lighted path to the kitchen entrance. Don't block the portcullis—that's the fancy gate on the entrance to the garage. You'll see the coat of arms over the door. Have a good night." He nodded toward the house.

I thanked him, not mentioning that I knew what a portcullis was. Visiting castles on trips—what my dad called collecting castles—has always been one of my favorite things to do. I followed the narrow, twisting gravel road up to the castle. I was still getting used to being referred to as the ice cream-shop lady. My best friend, Caroline Spooner, had inherited the shop two months ago when her mom, Buzzy, passed away, and asked me to run it for her, since she worked for an auction house in Boston. The timing had been right. I'd needed a place to land after leaving my job as a librarian for the CIA (yes, the Central Intelligence Agency, not the Culinary Institute of America). I didn't know if I'd stay. Penniman, Connecticut, was my hometown and my father still lived here, but I hadn't since I finished high school seventeen years ago. Penniman was the epitome of New England Charm—it had a town green, a covered bridge, and the crowds of leaf peepers in the fall to prove it—but it was so quiet, so peaceful, maybe too quiet for someone like me who'd lived in Washington, D.C., for the past ten years. Still, I'd promised to stay through the season. The shop would close for the winter at the end of October. Until then, this request by the mysterious lady of the manor was a bright spot. I needed to stretch my creative muscles, and the contract I'd signed had a solid number of zeroes, which would help the shop's bottom line.

Ice cream, Riley. They only want you for your ice cream.

Sadie's 1970s vintage engine complained as she climbed to Moy Mull, each turn of the road revealing another a glimpse of the quirky building.

Moy Mull wasn't a dream castle with white marble walls and fairy-tale spires. Moy Mull was modeled on a real medieval castle, thus the walls were built of roughhewn local fieldstone and cement, gray and weathered. There was a four-story tower with crenellations at one end, a broad porch overlooking rolling hills on the other. The narrow, mullioned windows above caught a glint of sunset red and it was easy to think of an archer standing there, demanding to know if I was friend or foe. Instead of balls and princesses, Moy Mull brought to mind narrow passageways and dungeons lit by torchlight. Fortification instead of Decoration. Fortified, not Disneyfied.

The original owner, Benjamin Franklin Clitheroe, named the castle Moy Mull, but some locals still referred to the quirky building as Clitheroe's Folly.

I drove past the portcullis, where spotlights illuminated a shield above the lattice gate, the shield bearing an ornate golden script double M over crossed paintbrushes, one tipped with sapphire, one with ruby paint, and waved as the driver of a van with Creative Caterers stenciled on it passed me. I guess I wasn't the only one called into Maud's presence. I recognized Bitsy Bittman, caterer to New England's elite. I'd developed the ice cream flavors for Maud's party, and Bitsy's job was to invent creative ways to serve them. I couldn't wait to see what she came up with. I parked in a spot marked Service and unloaded a cooler packed with samples of some of the most creative flavors I'd ever made.

My footsteps crunched on the gravel of the well-lit path marked with a discreet sign that read Kitchen. Might as well say Servants' Entrance.

Before I could knock, the kitchen door swung open on Prentiss Love, a slight, bald man with big brown eyes, glasses with thick black frames, and personality with a capital P.

He gave me a saucy wink. "Hello, Riley, I was just saying I could use some dessert!" He waggled his bushy eyebrows and took the bulky cooler from my arms as I stepped into the kitchen. "Welcome to Moy Mull, Maud's humble abode, where I serve as the major domo, chief cook and bottle washer, and ice cream tester par excellence."

I gave Prentiss a quick curtsy, then entered.

The kitchen was long and narrow, with a slate floor, low ceiling, and a wall of windows; despite the presence of shiny stainless steel appliances, I felt as if I'd stepped back in time. There was a fireplace at the far end of the room, where a Black woman with a full Afro sat at the head of a gleaming oak table where three bowls were set on woven place mats.

"Have you two met in person?" Prentiss plunked the cooler on a counter and unpacked my samples as the woman rose to greet me. I'd seen Maud shopping in town, but had only spoken to her on the phone in connection with this job.

Slim and at least six feet tall, Maud Monaco wore jeans and a white silk button-down tunic with a wide neckline that highlighted her elegant collar bones and long neck. Her graceful posture and unhurried movements brought to mind the term "lady of the manor." As she approached, light shimmered on a gold pendant of a bee that hung from a chain around her neck, a gold belt that cinched her tiny waist, and hammered gold discs on her ears. She shook my hand, her smile brilliant and welcoming.

"How nice to meet you in person, Riley. I'm dying to taste the treats you've whipped up for the festival." Even Maud's voice was beautiful, rich and deep. It was easy to see why Penniman village had embraced the reclusive former model. I'd seen Maud's magazine covers from her teen years, when she'd been one of the first Black cover models, and I marveled that she hadn't seemed to age in the past three decades.

"I can't wait for you to try them." I started to remove the lids on the pints I'd brought, but Prentiss shooed me to the table.

"Prentiss, spoons if you please." Maud resumed her seat.

"Yes, your highness." Prentiss set an ice cream scoop and a handful of spoons next to a crystal water pitcher and three glasses. "Napkins." He spun back, set three damask napkins on the table, sat next to Maud, and rubbed his hands together.

"Shall I do the honors?" I asked.

"If you don't, I will." Prentiss scooted his chair up to the table. "I'm positively drooling. I know you worked with Bitsy to develop the menu for the social and you have my complete trust, but you must know Maud is a complete control freak. She can't leave anything to chance, even ice cream."

I blinked, taken aback by the playful way Prentiss talked to Maud. I thought he was an employee? Maud gave Prentiss a less-than-queenly eye roll.

I stifled a laugh. "Let's start with the most delicate flavor first." I scooped a small portion of the six flavors I'd brought into each bowl. "Cherry vanilla with Luxardo cherries poached in bourbon and cinnamon; rhubarb crumble; pumpkin spice—"

"My fave!" Prentiss exclaimed, taking the pint from my hands.

I laughed and continued. "Amaretto laced with bitter chocolate with almond biscotti crumble; pear and stilton; and this one we call Unicorn: blue, pink, and white stripes of light cream with a bubble-gum flavor."

"Sprinkles?" Prentiss asked.

I pulled a jar of matching sprinkles out of my bag.

"You're prepared," Maud said, taking the tiniest taste of each flavor. "I like that. You've done such a wonderful job."

We tasted in silence, Maud with a cat-got-the-cream curve of her lips, Prentiss with a broad, kid-in-a-candy-shop grin. Maud sighed and took a big scoop of the chocolate. "These are fabulous."

Prentiss licked his spoon. "Magical, ambrosial! Well, you can tell. Maud took seconds and Maud never takes seconds."

"Oh, one more thing! The gift, Prentiss!" Maud said. "I wanted tomorrow's exhibit opening to be special, thus the fantasy ice cream social. Bitsy's run with the theme and hired some kids to serve in costume."

I stiffened. Did Maud expect me to wear a costume? That was not in the contract.

Prentiss stepped out of the room and returned with a tote bag embroidered with the Moy Mull logo.

Maud took out a royal purple chef's jacket and turned it so I could see that Udderly Delicious was embroidered on the breast pocket. "For you and your staff to wear at the festival. What do you think?"

What I thought was that my staff and I usually wore T-shirts printed with cartoon cows and really bad cow puns. Looking at the charm offensive in front of me, both Prentiss and Maud beaming, even if I had wanted to say no—and I didn't—I knew resistance was futile. "My staff will love them."

"And your badge." Prentiss handed me a high-tech badge with a computer chip hanging on a yellow lanyard. "This gives you entry to the castle and the Barn Gallery. It knows who you are. Just press it against the readers by the door."

Maud said, "Now, there is one more thing, and of course we'll adjust the fee."

One more one more thing? I tried not to let my surprise show.

Prentiss put a paper in front of me, the copy of the contract I'd signed a month earlier. Now there was an addendum.

I remembered this was a woman with deep pockets and cleared my throat. "What did you have in mind, Maud?"

"I'm planning a very special dinner party for the board of the Moy Mull Art Foundation on Sunday night to celebrate the end of the festival. A small gathering, thirty or so. I'd like some ice cream that"—the light glinted on a ruby the size of a half dollar in the ring on her left hand as she waved it—"feels like Scotland."

"Scotland," I repeated.

"It's a Scottish theme to go with the castle. Bitsy's doing a traditional Scottish feast with haggis and everything." Prentiss made a gagging gesture. "I'm going to the party as Scotland's greatest export."

"Whisky?" I asked.

Prentiss laughed. "Close. I'm going as Sean Connery in his white-dinner-jacket look from *Goldfinger*, red carnation and all."

I recalled cranachan, a traditional dessert I'd enjoyed in front of a roaring fire on a foggy night at an inn at the foot of Edinburgh Castle. I'd made it many times—it was simple and elegant. "I've got an idea."

"Marvelous! I hope this will cover everything." Maud pointed at the generous fee she'd added. It would cover everything and more. I nodded.

"Oh, and one other thing . . . just a teensy change of plans. Now, you know I'm including the treats you and Bitsy have dreamed up in the new Moy Mull cookbook. The photographer would like to get some publicity shots of you and your staff and the owner—is it Carol?"

Change of plans? "Caroline Spooner," I said warily.

Maud nodded. "On the farm and in the shop kitchen."

Prentiss stood, gathering our silverware and empty bowls. "I'll let you ladies discuss business while I clean up." He carried everything to the sink, squirted soap, and ran the water.

All of Maud's "one more things" were making my head spin.

"My photographer is coming from New York later tonight and would like to do the shoot tomorrow morning. I hope the short notice won't put you out." Maud smiled.

Having a photo shoot in the ice cream shop kitchen was not convenient. Did it matter? Maud's smile was one of a person who always got her way.

"That's fine but Caroline won't be there tomorrow," I said. "She's coming back late on Saturday."

"I'll make sure we do her photo later," Maud said.

A mountain of soap bubbles surged over the lip of the sink. Prentiss laughed and swore.

I remembered all the zeroes on the check. "No problem at all."

Chapter 2

The next morning a *thud* woke me before my alarm. I batted at a soft tickle of fur on my ear and peeled open an eye. Rocky had knocked my Agatha Christie paperback to the floor. He seated himself next to me on the bed and swished his tail into my face just as my alarm rang.

"How do you do that?" I groaned. "You always wake me seconds before my alarm goes off."

Rocky settled next to me, allowing me to stroke his soft black fur. I'd found him a few months earlier when I first moved into Caroline's farmhouse. He'd lived outdoors since birth and had the battle scars to prove it, but now his fur was sleek and shiny, and his copper eyes bright. He'd lost the tip of his left ear in a fight, but now, instead of sending me into a panic, I thought it gave him a rakish look. I sat up and stretched. I'd have to get going if I wanted a run before I started work and Maud's photo shoot.

"Just make me another ice cream flavor. Something that's never been done before, and Scottish, in two days," I muttered. The request, well, command from the Mistress of Moy Mull was over the top, but I welcomed the challenge. My travels had taken me all over the world and I loved using all that international inspiration in my ice cream recipes.

Maud was used to getting what she wanted. I'd realized last night that Maud had summoned me to her castle because it would've been easier for me to say no to her requests in a phone conversation. She knew her personal magnetism plus the cachet of meeting the Mistress of Moy Mull at Moy Mull itself would make it hard for me to say no.

I sighed. "I could use a personal assistant like Prentiss. Want the job, Rocky?"

He considered me, yawned, then jumped to the floor.

"Guess not. Let's get going."

If anyone was a major domo around here, it was me. I threw on running gear and hustled out the bedroom door, jerking to a stop, still expecting a white Persian cat to dart out of the bedroom across the hall like a fluffy, bad-tempered, heat-seeking missile. The other resident feline, Sprinkles, stayed during the work week in Boston with her other minion, Caroline, and each weekend they returned to Penniman. Caroline's mom, Buzzy, had adopted Sprinkles when Sprinkles was kicked off the show-cat circuit for bad behavior. Sprinkles hadn't adjusted to Buzzy's absence and wasn't adjusting well to her new home in Caroline's Boston apartment. I didn't miss the claw marks, but I knew Rocky missed his playmate. He'd been out of sorts, prowling throughout the house, watching me with accusing eyes, and staring in that unnerving cat way at the spot where Sprinkles' bed had been.

I put Rocky's breakfast on the faded yellow linoleum kitchen floor, filled his water bowl, then put on my running shoes.

I stepped onto the broad porch of the Spooner family's two-hundred-year-old white farmhouse. How strange life was. Here I was living in Buzzy's farmhouse, running the ice cream shop where Caroline and I'd worked in high school.

Across narrow Farm Lane spread Fairweather Farm's gently rolling fields and orchards. I could hear tractors in the orchards, where the hands were hard at work bringing in heirloom apples, Ida Reds, Cortlands, and Macouns, and picking early pumpkins.

September was my favorite time of year on the farm. The sun brightened the sky where some maples were turning russet red as I turned north up Farm Lane.

The scent of rich earth rose as I ran to a crossroads where a path cut west to the centuries-old Fairweather family cemetery and east past a small cottage. A barn had stood beside the cottage for decades but had recently been torn down, and we planned to plant the turned earth with sunflowers come spring. I took a deep breath and resumed my run, passing two properties with For Sale signs. As I looped onto Town Road, my footsteps pounding the tar, my thoughts turned to Maud Monaco and Prentiss Love.

Maud. A woman who was used to getting her way. Tall, statuesque, mysterious.

Prentiss. Her wish was his command. Short, nebbishy, funny. What an odd pair.

Her major domo. I laughed. For the woman who has everything. Who wouldn't want a major domo? I thought of my own to-do list for the weekend: deliver ice cream to Maud's ice cream social at the Barn Gallery tonight, set up and manage a booth at the arts festival tomorrow, and create a Scottish-themed dessert for her board-of-directors dinner on Sunday night . . . all on top of my usual duties running an ice cream shop. Kids had returned to school, but that didn't mean business had slacked off. September was a beautiful month in New England and the fall leaf peepers were already out in full force to watch the trees mellow into orange and crimson hues. I'd made plenty of fall-themed flavors to

tempt them: pumpkin spice, apple crumble, caramel cappuc-
cino. Warm fall days were some of our busiest—ice cream
was a temperature-driven business.

I turned off the road onto a twisting dirt path through a
thick stand of trees that led to the orchards and would loop
me back to the farm. The shade was welcome, and I breathed
in the cool air. Oaks and pines gave way to apple trees, and
I watched my step, looking out for the slippery drops, apples
that had fallen from the tree. I powered up a steep embank-
ment, pushing my max heart rate. At the top I slowed at the
farm apiary, two dozen hives in a field with a small shed.

The softest buzzing emanated from the hives as two figures, dressed in white bee suits with netted veils, hats, and
thick gloves, bent over them. One set a bee-covered frame
back into the wooden hive while the other saw me and slowly
raised a hand. I stopped while she walked over to me, remov-
ing her hat and shaking out a wave of golden hair.

"Hi, Riley, we just finished checking the hives." Willow
Brightwood was the eighteen-year-old daughter of the farm
managers, Darwin and Pru. Quiet and artistic, Willow was
working during a gap year between high school and the start
of art school next year. She whispered, "Everything around
bees has to be slow and quiet. Luca says it's important to keep
the bees tranquil." Luca Principato, a twenty-year-old from
Italy who was doing the farm's organic farming internship,
hadn't been at the farm long before he'd captured Willow's
heart. The feeling was mutual. They were rarely seen apart.

"Definitely," I whispered, matching her low tone, though
we were far from the hives. "I don't want to get stung."

Luca joined us. "Good morning, Signorina Riley."

"Hi, Luca."

He pushed back his veil, revealing a broad, handsome face,
a shock of long dark brown hair, and deep brown eyes with
lashes I'd kill for. Why did guys always get the best lashes?

"You come for honey to make ice cream?" Luca's gentle accent told of his home in the north of Italy. He also had the Italian male's effortless style, the *bella figura* I'd seen when I lived in Rome. He'd come to the farm as an intern, but when Willow's father learned of his interest in beekeeping, he'd asked the young student to revive the moribund apiary. Now it was thriving and there was enough honey to sell at the farm stand.

"How are your bees doing?" I asked.

Luca waggled his hand side to side. "Bees can be testy this time of year. Bees in fall, they are protective because they're stockpiling their food for the harsh winter. Still, we're getting beautiful honey."

"Wonderful." Willow sighed.

I didn't think she was talking about the honey. "I could use some," I said. "Can you spare a couple of jars?"

"Your wish is my command." Luca gave me a little bow.

"Thanks." It was good to have a major domo.

"I'll see you later," Willow said. "I'm working this morning."

"May I come too?" Luca said.

Willow and Luca were a two-for-one deal. With the distraction of the photo shoot, I could use the extra help. "Definitely. By the way, the cookbook photographer will be in the shop this morning, in case you're wanted for something back in Italy."

Luca laughed. "No worries."

"I thought the photos were going to be taken at the festival?" Willow said.

I shook my head. "Maud wants some shots at the shop and farm."

"Senora Maud has many hives. She's"—he hesitated, then said—"an accomplished beekeeper."

I wondered what he'd been about to say. "I didn't know

she kept bees." His words brought to mind the gold bee pendant Maud had worn last night.

"She invited Luca to see them when she heard he was bringing back our apiary," Willow said.

I wiped sweat from my brow. "I'd better get ready for my closeup." I waved and headed home, thoughts of the accomplished Mistress of Moy Mull soon drowned out by my to-do list.

After a quick shower, I dried my hair smooth and slicked on some mascara and lipstick. That was as far as I usually went, makeup wise. Since this was a cookbook shoot, I was pretty sure the focus would be on the ice cream, not me.

Rocky sat in the doorway, keying in that something different was happening as I looked through the purple chef's jackets Maud had given me. I blessed Maud for her foresight. A chef's jacket meant I didn't have to think about what to throw on over my jeans. I found a medium and put it on, turning side to side in front of my full-length mirror. Who knew a purple chef's jacket could be so flattering to my emerald green eyes and black hair? Rocky tipped his head, giving me a critical once-over, then slinked over and rubbed against my ankles.

I hung one of the size-small jackets in Caroline's closet and closed the door. If the Mistress of Moy Mull wanted us in uniform, the lady would have us in uniform. As I headed out, I caught sight of the contract I'd left on the kitchen counter. I flipped it over and scanned the paragraph about the photographer, Adam Blasco—the name rang a bell—and his assistant, Vye. Hmm, just Vye? I'd meant to do some research on them (see: former librarian) but I hadn't had a chance.

As I hurried down the lane to Udderly, I recalled a long-ago visit to an edgy art museum in New York City. Blasco's work had been exhibited in one of its galleries. I had vague memories of unsettling, life-sized images of half-naked models. His work included many techniques, like unusual exposures or the addition of painted highlights to create one-of-a-kind works. I recalled a particularly disturbing work that included slashes made by a box cutter.

Why on earth was an avant-garde photographer like Adam Blasco taking photos for a cookbook?

Chapter 3

As I entered the shop kitchen, I added "paint shop sign" to my mental to-do list. The second *d* in "Udderly" was practically illegible. And yes, the original owner, Caroline's dearly departed mom, had been a fan of terrible puns. Terrible puns, the color purple, and cows, which accounted for the dozens of ceramic cows that filled the shelves in the shop's tiny office. She also liked inspirational quotes. One wall in the shop kitchen was covered with black chalkboard paint where Willow had drawn sunflowers and pumpkins and a new quote in honor of the Moy Mull Art Festival: *"Art washes away from the soul the dust of everyday life."/Pablo Picasso*

Two women were already in the kitchen doing prep work, and the mouthwatering, rich scent of hot fudge suffused the room. "Flo and Gerri, I come bearing gifts." I set the bag of chef's jackets on the counter.

Flo Fairweather and Gerri Fairweather Hunt were sisters, stalwarts of the Penniman community, especially the Penniman Historical Society. Many called them the Graver Girls because of their involvement with a genealogy group called Finding Your Dearly Beloved. They were both retired educators, but that's where the similarities ended.

"Gifts? How wonderful! What's the occasion?" Petite Flo

Fairweather was a widow who'd retained her maiden name with her husband, Francis Florio's, blessing. ("Too many *F*s!" she'd declared.) She exuded the sweet energy of her former profession, kindergarten teacher, but had a twinkle in her eye—especially where men were concerned. She wore crayon-bright primary colors that set off her white curls and merry blue eyes.

Geraldine "Gerri" Fairweather Hunt, the older, many-times divorced sister, wore her hair dyed black and styled in a bouffant. She had a booming voice and forceful personality—many called her a battle axe, but never in her hearing. She'd been the revered, and feared, principal of Penniman High, and her raven dark eyes never missed a trick.

"I heard you were up at Moy Mull last night," Gerri said, laying aside a mixing spoon.

This sort of thing had ceased to surprise me. Penniman's gossip network was second to none.

I filled the sisters in on my visit with Maud Monaco, then took two chef's jackets out of the bag. "Since you two are working at our booth at the festival, you get one of these." I handed them each a chef's jacket, grateful that Maud had given me a range of sizes. Flo slipped on her size small, making exclamations of happy surprise. I watched with trepidation as Gerri tried on her extra-large, but the jacket buttoned over her ample bosom and broad shoulders.

"How did I know it would be a purple day?" Flo had dressed in purple jeans and an Udderly Delicious T-shirt with a cartoon cow eating a cone (*Moove It to Penniman!*) and had purple laces on her white tennis shoes.

"Perfect!"

Gerri swiveled side to side, stretching her arms out. "I'll do my nails purple tonight to match. I like this professional look. I'm feeling very Julia Child." She hesitated. "Should we wear the jackets for the shoot? I want mine pristine."

"I'll ask. The photographer will be here soon."

Flo hung her coat on the coat pegs by the door. "I'm so excited about the festival. Maud always outdoes herself at these things. What's the photographer's name?"

"Adam Blasco, and his assistant's name is Vye." I tied on an apron. Gerri was right, making ice cream could get messy.

"Vye what?" Gerri turned back to the hot fudge. "Is it short for Violet?"

I shrugged. "Just Vye. V-Y-E."

"Unusual name." Flo gathered ingredients for our waffle cones.

"Isn't it? There's a book character named Eustacia Vye," I remembered out loud. "In *The Return of the Native*."

"By Thomas Hardy," Gerri intoned. "She comes to a Bad End."

"I'd rather be called Vye than Eustacia," Flo said. "Maybe it's a nickname."

Through the broad front window I saw a silver SUV pull up. I hurried to the front door and observed the new arrivals as they exited the vehicle.

A woman in her twenties wearing a brown plaid flannel jacket and ripped jeans jumped from the driver's seat. Her tousled pixie-cut hair was dyed a shimmering peacock blue, and as she turned I could see that the hair to the left of her part was shaved close to her skull. She slid aviator sunglasses to the top of her head, tipped her head back, and inhaled deeply. For a moment her eyes closed and her shoulders relaxed. Then she shook herself and pulled a canvas duffle from the rear seat.

Her passenger, a middle-aged man in a black leather moto jacket, black skinny jeans, and black high-top sneakers, exited the car. He squinted as he put on sunglasses and settled a black leather driving cap on his buzz-cut salt-and-pepper hair. He exuded an intense nervous energy as he scanned his surroundings. His lips turned down and he shut the car door with a definite push.

"All black clothes. Expensive sunglasses. Impractical footwear. That's got to be him." I unlocked the front door. "Good morning. Welcome to Penniman. I'm Riley Rhodes."

The woman hefted the duffel bag to her shoulder, and her gold nose ring gleamed as she shook my hand. Despite the heavy black eyeliner, a scatter of freckles on her round face and warm doe brown eyes made me think of friends from the Midwest—open, honest, kind. "Hello, ice cream artist. I'm Vye," she said, then pointed to the man behind her. "This is Adam Blasco."

"Nice to meet you, Vye." I extended my hand. "Hello, Adam."

Adam shook, his hand as pale as his unshaved face. His glasses slid down his nose, and I could see his watery brown eyes were bloodshot. His demeanor didn't exactly scream morning person. It was closing in on 10 a.m. and his pale skin had me thinking he was one of those people who didn't roll out of bed until past noon. I wondered why he scheduled the shoot for the morning, then wondered if Maud had scheduled the shoot for morning.

"Hey. Nice to meet you." He jerked his chin toward the side of the shop, where I caught sight of a black tail rounding the corner. "Who's your familiar?"

"Rocky, my rescue," I said. "He has to know everything that's going on."

"Adam loves cats," Vye said.

"Do you have one?" I said as I ushered them into the shop

"Not anymore. I travel too much." Adam's head swiveled. "Let's see where you make the ice cream."

Right to the point. "This way, please."

Vye exclaimed, "Isn't it charming, Adam?"

Adam rubbed his forehead and muttered, "Charming. Cute." The way he said the words was not a compliment. I wondered if he was hungover.

Vye pasted a determined smile on her face and kept up cheerful patter, compensating for her boorish boss.

Gerri and Flo greeted the newcomers, and soon even Adam couldn't resist the cheerful charm of a woman who had taught kindergarten for forty years. He surveyed the kitchen, taking test photos and experimenting with angles, while Vye set up large umbrellas. "To diffuse the light," she explained.

"Shall we get out some ice cream?" Flo asked.

"We're not shooting the actual ice cream here," Vye said as Adam pursed his lips and stalked around the room. "Ice cream melts too fast in the lights. For food shoots, the stylists usually whip up some cement-like goop that only looks like the ice cream, because it won't melt under the lights. Nobody would eat it in a million years. Today, we're here to capture you and Udderly."

Flo grinned and Gerri raised her chin as if to accept this as her due. "Shall we don our jackets?" Gerri held up the new purple jacket.

Adam glanced at the jacket. "No. Too formal." Gerri raised her eyebrows but put the jacket back on the rack.

Adam turned to me as if he'd just noticed me. "Nice eyes. Good chin. Strong. Stubborn. I like strength." His stare was so frankly appraising that a blush crept up my cheeks.

Before I could think of what to say, Willow and Luca pushed open the kitchen door. "I'm so sorry, I didn't know you'd started," Willow exclaimed. "Is it okay if we watch from out here?"

"Crowded in here," Adam muttered, but then he did a double take, and focused his attention on Willow. "Come in. Do you work here, too?"

Willow nodded.

I introduced Willow and Luca.

"Willow's our resident artist," Flo said. "She did the wonderful artwork on the chalkboards."

Willow blushed. "I'm going to art school next fall."

"She's very talented." Luca beamed at Willow.

Adam joined them. "Tell me about the chalkboard."

While they chatted, I watched Vye set up equipment and take test shots on her digital camera.

"How can I help?" I asked. "What are you going for?"

"Let's make it look like a day in the life, only better. I have a list—we need you alone, you with staff or customers, the shop, the farm, cows—"

"Cows?" I asked.

"I'll do those," Vye said. "Adam's not an outdoor person. To him outdoors is what he has to walk through between his apartment building and the car service."

I laughed. "I guessed."

Vye lowered her voice. "He's a New Yorker, through and through. Adam only likes farms if they're falling down—textures interest him, weathered wood, rusting machinery, decay, that sort of thing."

"Rusting, weathered, decay . . ." I said, and thought again that he was an odd choice to shoot a cookbook.

Vye smiled. "He's an amazing photographer. I think you'll be happy with the photos. Maud wants to use these shots in social media for promo, and some may be in the book itself."

Adam and Vye conferred and scoured the shelves for props. They grouped me, Gerri, and Flo behind the big wooden worktable in the center of the room so the blackboard wall was behind us. Vye found some of Buzzy's oldest Pyrex bowls in golden yellow and harvest orange, whisks, cow figurines, and several jars of homemade preserves, and arranged them on the table in front of us. We generally used industrial-sized stainless-steel bowls, but I could follow Vye's thought process of the image and feel they wanted: homey and homemade.

Adam showed Willow and Luca how he adjusted the camera and lights, and we all pretended to whip up ice cream. The blackboard made a colorful backdrop as Adam took shot after shot. I hadn't realized what a hambone Gerri was and almost felt sorry for her as Adam's attention zoomed in on her younger sister instead.

I could tell Adam and Vye were pleased, and we were soon done.

"You're a natural, Flo," Vye said.

"I did forty years of class pictures." Flo poufed her white curls. "You have to act fast with kindergartners."

Willow turned to Vye. "Would you like a tour of the farm?"

"Sure," Adam said. "Vye, pack this up, okay?"

A red flush crept up Vye's neck. "Sure."

"I can show you the apiary," Willow said. "The view from the top of the hill there is beautiful."

"Apiary?" Adam said.

"You know, bees," Luca said. "Where we get the honey."

"Nope." Adam jutted his chin toward the barn. "How about here by the wall of the barn. By those bales of hay." I saw what he saw: the texture of the weathered wood, the rich red, the contrast with the pale yellow of the bales.

"You can meet Hairy," Willow said.

Adam smiled. "Of course."

As they went out, I turned to Vye. "Hairy's her goat, Hairy Houdini."

She snorted. "That's something I want on film."

Willow, Luca, and Adam left, and I helped Vye break down the equipment while Flo and Gerri returned to prep work. Vye had seemed so cheerful, but now her lips turned down and she kept throwing glances out the window toward the barn.

When we finished packing the equipment, Vye and I headed to the barn, where Adam had settled Luca and Willow on a bale of hay. Then he asked Luca to stand aside while he shot Willow. I sensed a wariness growing in Vye. She was more than attentive to Adam's requests—she anticipated them, always ready with a lens or adjustment. But I realized that she was no longer watching Willow and Luca, she was watching Adam.

No, Vye was watching Adam watch Willow. He was positively oozing charm and good humor, and I could see Willow warm to him, relax, grow comfortable. Luca, too, sensed the attention to Willow, and his expression flashed between pride, protectiveness, and jealousy. He moved closer to her.

Good boy, I thought.

Adam spoke with Luca and Willow with growing animation, gesturing with his camera. There was a tire swing behind the barn and the three of them headed toward it. I couldn't make out what Adam was saying, but Willow laughed.

"Do you need so many photos?" I asked.

Vye smoothed her hair. "I'll let you in on a professional secret. We take so many photos because people who aren't professional models need time to relax. Sometimes Adam will shoot more than a thousand frames. We'll use only four or five, but that's enough."

"How long have you worked for Adam?" I asked.

"Five years." Vye's voice was soft. "He helped me get into art school." She avoided my eyes as I had a flash of insight, a flash to a young photographer who needed a recommendation to get into school. A girl Willow's age. Had there been a price to pay? Did Vye see history repeating itself?

"Would you like some ice cream?" I asked.

She raised her eyebrows and I saw a flash of her earlier good humor. "Rocky Road?"

"Of course."

Chapter 4

At five o'clock, after loading coolers of ice cream, Flo and Gerri shooed us out of the shop and Willow, Luca, and I headed to Moy Mull. Sadie's circa 1978 engine labored mightily, but still I sped. Ice cream melts fast.

Willow read from an email on her phone: "Volunteers serving at the Fantasy Ice Cream Social Opening Reception of the Adam Blasco: Dangerous Beauty Art Show, please check in at the castle upon arrival. You will receive your costume and access badges with a red lanyard. Then proceed to the Barn Gallery space for further instruction from the caterer."

It was a ten-minute walk from the castle to the Barn Gallery. Moy Mull's original barn had been incorporated into a sprawling art space that included a gallery, studios, offices, and a catering kitchen. "Just help me get the ice cream into the freezer in the Barn Gallery kitchen first and then I'll drive you to the castle," I said.

Sadie's air conditioner was loud but not terribly effective. Luca shrugged off his sweatshirt and tucked it into a bright yellow backpack covered with souvenir patches of places he'd traveled. I felt a pang seeing so many spots I'd visited on my own travels. Luca saw me look. "I know you love to travel, Signorina Riley. You must come visit me next summer," he said.

"I'd love to."

"Luca and I are already planning a trip," Willow gushed.

"You must see Rome," Luca said, "and—"

Their excited chatter faded to background noise as I stopped at Moy Mull's gate and showed the guard my badge. He waved me in.

I parked at the service entrance for the Barn Gallery and after we unloaded the ice cream, I drove down the gravel lane to the castle and dropped Willow and Luca by a table with a sign reading volunteer check in. A tall, muscular man with wavy brown hair in a blue button-down shirt sat there handing out badges with red lanyards.

I found a spot between two Creative Catering vans and parked. Stepping from the car, I heard a buzz of activity as caterers hustled boxes from their vehicles into the kitchen. Overhead, from a balcony, languorous jazz music streamed.

Just before I got to the kitchen door, it slammed shut. I pressed my badge to the reader, heard a tiny click, and went inside, where four caterers worked, all dressed in black pants, white shirts, and bowties in the signature fuchsia pink of Bitsy's company.

A beefy man with black hair and a neatly trimmed beard in a Creative Catering jacket set down a flat of strawberries and hustled over. "Hey, you're Riley from the ice cream shop, right?" We shook hands, his hand warm, his smile broad. "My fiancée has been raving about your ice cream. I'm Barry Esposito, Bitsy's right-hand man."

"Nice to meet you. I love working with Bitsy." I looked around. "Why are you working here and not in the kitchen in the Barn Gallery?"

"Bitsy needs to do some last-minute baking," Barry said.

"Much better facility here. This place was a hotel at one time and there's a whole other commercial kitchen down the hall. Bitsy has some staff working there, but she likes to work in this space." He spread his hands. "Who wouldn't? It's a freaking castle."

A short, curvy woman with blond corkscrew curls burst into the kitchen. "Riley!" she exclaimed as she gave me a hug. Bitsy herself was dressed in a black and gray tartan kilt, a white top, and black flats, and had an adorable black tam-o'-shanter with a fuchsia knitted ball perched at a saucy angle on her curls. "Saucy" was the word for Bitsy, a dynamo in pink. Her outfit was cute, but after working with her for a short time, I knew she was an organized and driven entrepreneur.

"Guess what?" Bitsy's big blue eyes sparkled. "I was catering a do in Newport and when I told the hostess I was from Penniman, she asked about Udderly. You're on the map!"

"Newport!" I said. "You're getting around. How exciting."

Barry threw an arm around her shoulders and kissed the top of her head.

She pinked and playfully pushed him away. "Hey, watch the tam! I know, Newport, right? I started baking cookies for bake sales at Penniman High and now I'm catering galleries and Newport mansions. Well, Barry's been a huge help. He's invested in me, time and money and . . ." She blushed. A chef waved Barry over and he excused himself.

"I could go on." Bitsy bustled over to an oven, sliding on an oven mitt as she spoke. "But Barry's really helped push me into a bigger league. And now my recipes are going to be in the Moy Mull cookbook with that famous photographer!" Bitsy took a tray of lady fingers from the oven, the buttery sweet scent making me swoon. "I can't wait for you to try the finished products." Bitsy gave me a shrewd look. "You're helping serve tonight, right?"

"Um." I hadn't planned on it. With the shop covered, I'd

hoped to get back home to my book and a quiet evening with my feet up.

"It'll be fun," she said. "You'll get to see the famous Adam Blasco photos too."

"And you'll get to sample these amazing treats." Prentiss joined us, inhaling the heavenly scent. When Bitsy turned back to the oven, he snatched two lady fingers from the tray, tucked them into a napkin, looped his arm through mine, and pulled me to the back door. "Riley will catch up with you at the social," he called, then lowered his voice. "I'd like to disappear for a while before Maud finds me anything else to do. Want a tour of the castle?"

"Sure!"

We hurried into the gravel service parking lot. "I thought we were touring the castle?" I said.

"We'll go in the back door. This way we avoid all the traffic in the kitchen. And Maud."

Past the vans and my car was a back entrance, a heavy oak door studded with black iron nails. The door was flanked by massive metal trellises covered with the thick canes of climbing roses. The soft jazz music I'd heard earlier was gone. Prentiss pressed his badge to a card reader next to the door. "Maud takes security very seriously," Prentiss said as we stepped into a hallway and the heavy oak door closed behind us. Though the walls were lined with large, carved doors, the low ceiling, beige paint, and hazy fluorescent lighting of the hall were disappointingly reminiscent of a department store bargain basement.

"Welcome to Moy Mull. Don't worry it gets better. Hang on, I need to check the mail." He stepped into a room next to a small sign that read Security Office. Spare, angular modern furniture clashed with mahogany wainscoting and a wall of old-fashioned wooden mail cubbies. High-tech computers and screens topped two desks, and one wall was covered with an array of screens that flashed with shots of the castle's exterior.

This setup was beyond simple security. Maud wasn't just security conscious. Between the high-tech surveillance and the guards at the gate, I wondered if Maud had had threats, maybe even a stalker.

Off this room was another, smaller room stuffed with old metal filing cabinets and a huge antique rolltop desk. Prentiss followed my gaze as he dumped some junk mail into a recycling bin. "That desk has been here since old Ben Clitheroe built the place. This room used to be the office for the castle. That desk weighs as much as a car. It's too heavy to move, so it's been stored there forever." He offered me a lady finger. I accepted and almost swooned at the buttery sweet flavor of the still-warm treat.

He ate his, made a chef's kiss gesture, then tossed the napkin in a wastebasket. "Bitsy can bake." He waved me back into the hallway.

"Let's get to the good stuff. This lower level's not that exciting." He led me down the hall, pointing at doors as we went. "Cloakrooms, dungeon, TV parlor, darkroom . . ."

I pulled up short by a room with an ornately carved oak door. It had a doorknob with an intricately etched design of thistles and lyres. "Wait a minute, you have a dungeon? The sign on the wall says Conference Room."

"Believe me, I felt the same way when I first came to the castle. Dungeon? I'm so there!" Prentiss sighed. "It's not that fun. Talk about a wasted opportunity. What I could do with a dungeon." He shrugged, then pushed open the heavy door and flipped on the lights. "I guess some of it is cool."

The first thing I saw—a magnificent, massive fireplace at the far end of the room, the mantle six feet tall—was breathtaking. The effect was ruined by a motel-quality painting of some ducks over it and fluorescent lights buzzing overhead.

The windowless brick walls had been painted a depressing greige. A long conference table flanked with twenty chairs and some audiovisual equipment ran the length of the room. There was a side table with an eighties-era push-button telephone and two sad, dust-covered artificial plants. A dried floral arrangement on the conference table dropped a bud as we watched.

"That is one disappointing dungeon," I said.

"They did keep the chains!" He pushed aside a rolling white board, revealing rusted chains attached to the wall with iron fittings. I smiled at Prentiss's excitement, but remembered colleagues in my previous workplace who'd undergone interrogation training—and worse. The low ceilings, lack of windows, and restraints—even though antique—gave me a less-than-pleasant sense of claustrophobia.

"I saw pics of the original room, it had wonderful rough brick walls. But when it was a hotel, they transformed it into a conference room," Prentiss said. "Well, still used for torture, as you can see."

I shook off my musing and laughed as we exited. He shut the door firmly behind us. "It's a strange lock. You need a key to lock it from the inside and outside. There's only one key after all these years, so it's never locked."

"I would not enjoy being locked in there," I said.

"I want to show you the really cool stuff, the stuff the hotel had the sense to leave alone." We headed up a tightly turning staircase to another hallway, where we dodged one of Bitsy's staff carrying a tray of cookies. We stepped into a dark paneled dining room, long and narrow, the walls covered in hunting scenes, the space dominated by a spectacular hearth at one end. Light streamed through a tall stained-glass window at the other end, a scene of a long lake surrounded by green hills. "There's a spotlight outside that comes on at dusk, so we can see the stained glass even at night. Maud thinks of everything."

I turned to the magnificent fireplace, the mantle crowded with sterling loving cups, silver candlesticks, and framed photos, many engraved. "Did the hotel have all this on display?"

Prentiss shook his head. "Maud hired a historian to help her put together an exhibit about the castle. He found tons of stuff packed away in the attic, and Maud's busy putting things back as they were when Ben and Oona lived here."

I searched my memory. "There was a second wife, right?"

"Alma. A Jazz Age brunette," Prentiss said. "She cleared the decks of anything that was Oona's, judging from all the stuff in the attic."

Above the massive fireplace was a portrait of a stout man in a kilt. "Old Ben Clitheroe, and"—Prentiss pointed to a carved wooden shield hanging over a buffet table—"every lord of the manor must have his own heraldic shield." I stepped closer to examine the shield, recognizing the same motifs I'd seen engraved on the lock downstairs: two thistles and two entwined hearts flanking a lyre.

He flung open double doors at the end of the room and announced, "The great room."

We stepped into an airy space with a broad staircase in the same dark mahogany as the paneling on its walls. The ceiling soared two stories and I could see more artwork along the walls of the upper floors. "And you must meet"—Prentiss pulled me across the cavernous space to another fireplace—"the Lady of the Manor." Above the fireplace was a life-sized portrait of a woman wrapped in a fur coat, well, "draped" was more the word. One sleeve fell from her shoulder, revealing a plaid skirt and riding jacket with a cameo pin. Her gloved hand held a sprig of heather and her vivid red hair curled beneath a tam. A lake gleamed sapphire in the background.

"Oona?" I said. "I thought the second wife took down all traces of wife number one?"

"Again, found in the attic. Maud loved it and wanted to give Oona her due as first lady of the manor. We're adding it to the display when we open the house to the public next year."

I spun in a slow circle, taking in the stunning space. "Spectacular. All of it. I feel like I'm in a Robin Hood movie. But—" I shook my head as we crossed to the staircase. "It doesn't seem very much like Maud."

Prentiss shrugged. "When you live in a castle you have to give people castle."

A woman descended the stairs, a tanned leg flashing through the thigh-high slit in her tight black dress. Like Maud, she was impossibly thin and tall and beautiful. Blond hair fell like curtains from either side of her center part, where dark roots contrasted with the bright gold color. One hand gripped the banister, the other held a half-full glass of red wine, and both hands sparkled with rings set with multicolored gems.

"Prentiss, when is the elevator going to be fixed?" she moaned. "This place has too many stairs."

"Hello, Dree," Prentiss said with forced politeness. "Next week, maybe? You know how these things go. Historic house and all."

"Haunted historic house." She sipped her wine. "Nobody told me about the ghost until I got here."

"No such thing." Prentiss turned his face away from her and rolled his eyes.

"That's what you say." Her heavily lidded pale green eyes shifted to me. "Hi, I'm Dree." The planes of her face were taut, but I'd put her in her late forties or fifties, with the deep tan and freckles of a sunworshipper.

"Hi. I'm Riley Rhodes."

"If you're staying here, stay away from Oona's room," she said. "I'm serious, Prentiss, it's haunted. I moved my things to one of the rooms downstairs."

"Uh, which one now?" Prentiss's voice took on a shade of exasperation. "I'll have to tell the housekeeping staff."

Dree drifted past us. "The one with my stuff. They'll figure it out. See you at the party. Gotta go pay homage to the great Adam Blasco." She waved and walked unsteadily through the great room.

Prentiss pinched the bridge of his nose. "Dree Venditti. She worked with Maud back in the day. If only the cottages weren't all full. She's driving me to take up yoga." He took a deep breath. "Come on up." We climbed to the third floor, where he led me down a quiet hallway covered with richly colored oriental rugs to double doors carved with the same thistle-and-lyre motif I'd noticed downstairs. "Maud's suite."

Dismay shot through me. "Prentiss, should we be up here?"

"Housekeeping sees it all the time." He shrugged. "Maud's always with her bees. I want to show you something."

Chapter 5

He opened the door to a jewel-box room with cream silk wallpaper, overstuffed gold-upholstered sofas, floor-to-ceiling gold drapes, and caramel, pink, and peach velvet pillows. We crossed a deliciously soft cream carpet to open French windows. Prentiss peeked outside and we stepped onto a large balcony.

"See?" He swept his arm high, like a magician who'd completed a marvelous trick. Over the gently rolling hills to the west the descending sun cast a pink and orange wash of watercolor across the sky. "Sunsets here are fabulous."

"It's beautiful," I sighed.

"My room faces east, so I don't get this. I come here for a mental health break at the end of the day." He leaned his elbows on the stone rail.

A spicy sweet scent made me turn, and I marveled at the height of the old climbing rose. I looked closer and noted the metal lattice was anchored to the stone wall with heavy rusted nails. The thick canes of the plant had to be a century old, and a few bloodred blooms still clung among the thorny stems. "Must be gorgeous when it's in full bloom."

"These are very old roses, brought from Scotland with Oona," Prentiss said.

Music flowed again and I leaned out over the rail to see past the rose vines, to a matching balcony on the other side. An insect buzzed by my head.

"Be careful!" Prentiss waved away the insect and I saw it was a wasp. "There was a wasps' nest in there. We had it removed yesterday but I still see some of the buggers. Maud went on and on about how it had to be cleared before Adam got here because he's allergic to bee stings."

I breathed in the sweet rose scent. The balcony over-looked a walled garden on the other side of the gravel parking area. Within the wall of gray stone, subtle landscape lighting illuminated a lovely small cottage.

"Maud's own secret garden and her she shed," Prentiss said.

"It looks like something from the Cotswolds!"

Some she shed. The cottage was constructed of warm yellow stone, storybook style, with steep gables and a slate roof, the whole thing covered in ivy and roses. There was even a dovecote behind it. I expected Hansel and Gretel to skip down the slate path and through the gate at any moment.

On a rise beyond the cottage, through another iron gate in the stone wall, I saw a tall figure in a white bee suit moving slowly along rows of hives and I remembered Luca talking about visiting Maud's bees.

I jutted my chin. "Her apiary?"

"Yes," Prentiss said, "and the lab where she processes her cosmetics, wax, and honey, too, the cutest little lab in the world."

"Cosmetics?" I watched Maud pass through the gate into the garden, closing it firmly behind her.

"She uses products from the bees, propolis and venom, that have healing properties." Prentiss rubbed his fingers to-gether. "You wouldn't believe what rich people will pay for a tiny pot of goop that promises to keep them looking young."

I considered Maud's smooth complexion. "Whatever she's using, it works."

"Well, there's the little matter of the portrait in the attic," Prentiss said.

I laughed.

Prentiss continued, "The stuff she uses, you can't mass produce. It's very specialized, bee spoke. Yes, I did say bee spoke. So sue me."

I laughed again. "You and my dad would get along—he never met a bad pun he didn't like. How long have you worked for Maud?"

"Longer than I haven't I worked for Maud." Prentiss looked over the garden. "When she started modeling in Chicago I was a twenty-one-year-old roadie for a band you never heard of. They went nowhere but they made a music video—remember those? And needed some girls to dance in the background. I asked my cousin if she had any friends who were interested, and she asked Maud, who was in her algebra class. The band only picked her because she had her Catholic school uniform. Stunning then, but didn't know it; self-conscious about her height, can you believe it? So she did the video, and some modeling agencies in New York saw it and next thing you know they're trying to track her down and want to talk to her manager. That"—he shrugged—"turned out to be me. Next thing I know she's on the cover of all these magazines and I'm an agent."

He glanced at his watch. "Before we go, you've got to see the dressing room." He tugged my arm and led me into a room with rows of dresses, a wall of shoes, and floor-length mirrors flanking an ornate marble fireplace, its lintel decorated with a row of carved roses. "She knocked some rooms together when she renovated. This was the lady of the manor's dressing room. Well, it was the lady of the manor's room when Alma was here. Oona had a lovely suite at the front of the house. I'd always heard Oona was a simple girl, but the room is fabulous."

I remembered what Dree said. "Is Oona the ghost? Or Alma?"

Prentiss shrugged, "I think the stones came pre-haunted from Scotland. I tell you, though." He shivered. "Honestly, I've heard the odd noise, especially when I'm in the TV parlor watching *Jeopardy!* But it's just old houses."

His phone dinged with a text. "Duty calls. Hey, did someone say you used to be a librarian? We have a library here. I'll introduce you to Tony Ortiz; he's the historian who's putting together the history of Moy Mull exhibit for next year. Maud's taken him under her wing. His office is in the library."

Chapter 6

Down the hall from Maud's suite, two suits of armor stood guard at a heavy, carved oak door with a brass plate that read Library. Prentiss opened the door and stuck his head in. "Tony, you in there?"

A muffled voice answered, "Yes, on the phone."

"I have a fellow librarian here. Riley Rhodes. Show her around, will you?" He gave me a smile. "Gotta run, see you at the opening!"

I stepped into the welcoming hush created by shelves of books and thickly carpeted floors. The library's interior glowed with polished and intricately carved oak bookcases and a large worktable. Open French doors centered on the back wall were framed with shelving lined with hundreds of books. There were even two parallel rows of shelves in the center of the room, shoulder height, topped by leaded-glass Tiffany-style lamps. At the end of each row was a curved wooden chair with a pretty needlepoint seat.

An arm, clad in a sleeve of brown corduroy with a professorial leather patch on the elbow, waved from a doorway into what appeared to be an office. The rest followed, a guy with tortoiseshell glasses and a tumble of wavy brown hair.

"Be with you in a sec," he said, then stepped back to finish his conversation.

I went to the balcony that overlooked the same view as Maud's suite. Below, the small gravel service parking lot buzzed with activity and I glanced at my watch. I was playing hooky in the most magical place, an old library inside a castle. This evening had turned into an unexpected adventure. I wanted to check out my booth and make sure everything was ready for tomorrow's festival, but that wouldn't take long. I'd enjoy this moment before I had to dive back into work.

I inhaled the scent of the lush rose vine, which blocked the view of Maud's balcony and ensured privacy. I turned back to the magnificent room, marveling at the leather-tooled spines of the books. Behind the glass doors of one cabinet I saw rows of old books by Dickens, Thackeray, Bronte, and Poe. I knew, from having a dad who owned a second-hand bookshop, that I was looking at thousands of dollars' worth of collector's items.

"Yep, first editions." The man I'd seen earlier at the volunteer check-in emerged from the office and held out his hand. "It's a miracle the previous owners didn't toss them all and make this space another conference room. I'm Tony Ortiz."

His large hand enveloped mine as we shook. Tony's tweedy jacket and tortoiseshell glasses said "professor," but his broad-shouldered, muscular build and strong grip said "bodybuilder." His hair curled over his collar, and he pushed back a hank that fell over his forehead, revealing a surprisingly handsome face with a strong nose and chiseled jaw. If he were a college professor, his class would be packed with students more interested in his dreamy eyes than history.

"Riley Rhodes. Sorry to bother you."

"Not at all. I'm finishing paperwork before I head over for the opening. How may I help you?"

"Prentiss was giving me a tour," I said. "I'm a librarian, well I was, so I always check out libraries."

"Prentiss mentioned you. I heard you worked in the D.C. area. For a three-letter agency? Bet you did a lot of very interesting research"—Tony smiled, his teeth brilliant white—"but if you told me about it you'd have to kill me."

"That's correct." A joke I'd heard a thousand times, but I laughed politely. But the truth was, there was stuff that I couldn't ever divulge, especially the occasional missions I'd undertaken as an asset. Those days were behind me after the disaster of my last mission.

My eyes fell on an oversized coffee-table photography book, *Elegant Despair: The Women of Adam Blasco*. The cover, a photo of Adam, was marred by several garnet-colored, circular stains.

Tony followed my glance and folded his arms. "One of Maud's"—he hesitated—"guests borrowed this, and housekeeping retrieved it from her trash."

I remembered Dree and her wineglass.

We shared a glance and Tony said, "Maud asked me to order another copy. I was going to toss this copy. If you'd like to take it, you're welcome to it."

Meeting Adam and Vye had piqued my interest in the photographer's work. "Thanks, I'd like to take a look."

The phone in Tony's office rang. "I'd better get that. See you at the reception. Feel free to come by any time."

Through the open door of Tony's office I saw another spectacularly tall fireplace like the one downstairs and more shelves stuffed with old books. I could spend hours exploring this castle.

I gathered the heavy book into my arms and made my

way down to the second floor, where evenly spaced, numbered doors reminded me that this building had once been a
hotel. The walls were lined with hunting scenes, landscapes
in ornate gold frames, and sepia-tinted old photos. There
were several cozy little nooks with carved wood and richly
patterned paper that the owner of the hotel had had the good
sense to leave alone.

I returned to the ground floor, crossed through the great
room and dining room, and stopped to admire a marble
sculpture in front of open Juliet windows. I heard a door
slam and looked up to see Vye and Adam taking equipment
out of the SUV. Vye was by the rear hatch of the SUV, her
arms crossed.

"What's eating you?" Adam said.

His vicious tone made me rear back against the long
green velvet curtains.

"Adam, you have to stop." Vye's voice trembled.

There was an edge on Adam's words. "What are you
talking about?"

"You know exactly what I mean," Vye said. "That girl.
Willow."

"Afraid of a little competition?" Adam said.

Vye's voice wavered, with fear or anger, I wasn't sure.
"It's not competition with an eighteen-year-old who draws
pictures of cows and sunflowers."

"Listen, I want to help her. If I can use my influence to
help a young artist . . ." His tone hardened. "Besides, you
know what our arrangement is."

"All I'm saying is, I can't do this anymore. It's over. I'm
leaving."

There was silence. I peered around the curtain. Vye stood
with her shoulders hunched, her arms wrapped protectively
around her stomach.

"Leaving?" Adam's voice dripped sarcasm as he grabbed her arm. "And then what will you do? Shoot weddings? Baby pictures?"

Vye jerked away. "I can't do this anymore!"

"You need me, Vye."

"Don't remind me. I hate that." Vye spun and stormed off.

Chapter 7

Witnessing the fraught exchange between Vye and Adam unsettled me. I rushed through the kitchen, barely seeing Bitsy's cleanup crew. I tossed the heavy book onto Sadie's passenger seat, and the next thing I knew I was parked next to the dumpster in the employee parking lot behind the sprawling Barn Gallery. I took a deep breath. Vye was an adult. Adam was an adult. Who was I kidding? I was never the type to stand by. I couldn't stand by. I'd try to find Vye later, see if she was okay.

The buzz of conversation and the soft music of a jazz ensemble carried on the cool night air. There was a tea garden, centered on a replica of a Japanese pagoda, behind the Barn Gallery, and I could see colorful paper lanterns glowing there. I was eager to see the enticing scene Maud had created, but first I had to check my booth for the festival tomorrow. I jogged back down the gravel drive, dodging art lovers heading to the gallery from the field parking lot, and crossed onto the broad lawn between the Barn Gallery and the castle.

The canvas of the tents and booths that lined the paths glowed ghostly white in the growing dark. The booth for Udderly was one of the closest to the gallery, so I didn't have to go far. I stepped inside, marveling at the tent. Because

Udderly was at the festival at Maud's behest, she'd provided a medieval-style tent with a pointed roof and crenellated trim. Inside, two coolers hummed, ready to keep my treats cold tomorrow.

I hurried back to the Barn Gallery and stopped at the end of a long line of art lovers to read the sign posted near the front entrance.

ADAM BLASCO. DANGEROUS BEAUTY.
Opening reception: Friday, 7–10 p.m.
Gallery talk by Adam Blasco: Saturday, 11:30 a.m.
Talk by Professor of Photography J. F. Kaplan on
    Adam Blasco's Influence and Influences: Sunday,
    5 p.m. Reception: 6 p.m.
Moy Mull Art Foundation Dinner: Sunday, 7 p.m.
    Invitation Only

A security guard gestured to me from a side door. "If you'd like to come in this way." He held the door open. "Press your badge to the reader." I did as he instructed, then gave him a puzzled look. "You have the yellow lanyard," he explained. "That gets you in everywhere."

"Thanks." I had no idea that I'd been given a magic ticket. The entrance to the exhibit was closed off with a red velvet rope and the lights were off, but a face loomed out of the darkness: the iconic closeup of Maud Monaco, her skin smooth and lustrous as moonlight. Adam hadn't captured an expression, he'd captured many: flirtatiousness, serenity, confidence. Her beauty couldn't be denied; no wonder she'd caught the eye of a prince.

Not far from Maud's portrait, Max Truwitt, the gallery manager, and a security guard conferred over a computer tablet. Max looked up and waved. "Hey, Riley!" Max, a retired banker who raised racehorses, was a regular at Udderly. He was a handsome man with a mane of dark hair with the touches of silver at the temples people called distinguished.

"Good luck, Max." I smiled and hurried toward the hall off the lobby.

Behind me, Max and the guard opened the doors and the crowd surged in as I hurried to the catering kitchen. The noise level was high as Bitsy's team whirled through prep, and she waved when she saw me. "Leave it to Maud, right? Ice cream for an opening reception."

I slipped on an apron. "She said she didn't want the typical wine and cheese."

"Yeah, that can get old." Bitsy waved a spatula. "But ice cream's tricky. Can't have it melt all over the carpet. Can't have it drip on some trust fund baby's boots. Can't have sticky fingers when writing thousand-dollar checks for the art." She nudged me with her elbow. "Not that I'm complaining."

Barry set down a stack of trays and kissed her cheek. "Not with the check Maud wrote."

A young caterer carried a box in the door. "These badges don't work." I noticed he wore a red one.

Barry waved the yellow badge he had stuck in his shirt. "I have to badge everyone in and out every time they go to the van. The security team won't let us prop the door. Hang on, I'll be right there."

Bitsy turned to me. "Our challenge. We must serve everything immediately so nothing melts. Maud wanted fantasy, so we will give her fantasy." She walked me to the table where two of her staff were assembling trays of treats.

Bitsy's ice cream creations were truly works of art. I

sighed at the enchanting variety: a fragile white-chocolate
teacup filled with my chocolate/amaretto/biscotti ice cream
and drizzled with raspberry sauce; a mini sampler of delicate pizzelle cones filled with three kinds of ice cream and
tied with a fondant ribbon in Bitsy's trademark fuchsia pink;
a cookie shaped like a mini artist's palette topped with four
scoops of ice cream in different colors, made with the tiniest
doll-sized ice cream scoop I'd ever seen; ice cream "tacos,"
the waffle-cone taco dyed in blues, greens, and pinks, and
each stuffed with a different flavor and topped with sprinkles,
bits of candy, or edible flower petals.

Bitsy pointed with a wooden spoon the way a fairy god-
mother would magick a pumpkin. "One palette is a chocolate-
covered graham cracker and the other is a gluten-free almond
cookie topped with a thin layer of almond paste." I popped
one in my mouth. *Heaven.*

Several volunteers from the farm greeted me as they
hefted trays and headed into the gallery and the garden. Flo
and Gerri had dressed in Shakespearean garb. "From the
Penniman Players Scots play," Flo said. Willow wore Ophelia's gauzy white mad-scene dress with daisies tucked in a
long braid.

"Riley, where's your fantasy outfit?" Gerri said.

I'd hoped no one would notice.

"You're not getting out of this that easily." Bitsy reached
into a box and plunked a dried flower wreath on my head.
"Wedding reception leftovers."

I got a kick out of how broadly the term "fantasy" had been
interpreted. Luca wore a polyester vampire cape; a few of
the farmhands wore butterfly wings; and there was a fair
representation of steampunk from Bitsy's crew. One guy was
dressed as Tarzan in a leopard loincloth. Well, we all have
our own idea of fantasy.

September in New England could be tricky weather-wise but we'd been blessed by a weeklong warm spell of soft beauty just as the oaks started to change color, and the evening was cool enough that we didn't have to worry about the ice cream melting too quickly. What a relief.

Just as I started my second pass in the garden, a guy in jeans and a flowing poet's shirt stood at the entrance to the tea garden and began playing a pan flute. The music drifted above the chattering crowd and fell as a magic incantation that cast a hush on chattering partygoers. A troupe of dancers in wispy pastel dresses entered, carrying Chinese lanterns on tall poles. Then the strains of a bagpipe wailed from behind the pagoda in the center of the garden.

Maud made an entrance, in what can only be described as a mythic Scots warrior dress with tiny pleats, a long plaid scarf over her left shoulder, and gold cuffs on her arms. Her trademark bee pendant swung on a chain at her chest.

"She's magnificent," Bitsy sighed. I had to agree but, as Maud was surrounded by admirers, I had to wonder about her relationship with Adam. She was stealing the spotlight. Inside, black-and-white photos in a unique but staid setting of wood floors and beige walls. Outside, a party that swirled with color, magic, music, and fantasy. Maud hosted Adam's party, but this outdoor celebration was all Maud.

For an hour I was too busy to think about Maud, or Adam and Vye's ugly fight. We raced trays of treats from the kitchen to the gallery and the garden where revelers crowded around, exclaiming with delight as they sampled the imaginative delicacies. Many took photos and posted them to social media. That, too, was probably part of Maud's plan.

In the garden, I saw Willow serve a group, and when she tucked her empty tray under her arm and headed back to the kitchen, Adam stepped in front of her. He held up his camera and leaned toward her, whispered in her ear with a charming smile. She glanced back at the door to the kitchen, her expression uncertain, but at another word from Adam she nodded and followed him down a shadowy path.

Chapter 8

Adam in general set off my inner alarm bells, but Adam turning on charm really set off my alarm bells. Then I chided myself. Calm down, Riley. Willow was eighteen, old enough to take care of herself. But across the crowd, I saw Luca crane after them as they disappeared deeper into the garden. A group wanted him to take their photo and then they took his. All the time, I sensed his attention pulled toward the path where Willow and Adam had disappeared. When Luca's tray was finally empty, he put it down and pushed through the crowd. *Uh-oh*, I thought. Though I, too, had the same instinct to go after them. What was I, an old lady chaperone? I couldn't help it. There was something about Adam that I just didn't trust.

A guest took the last ice cream taco from my tray, and I also made my way through the crowd. The pagoda, hung with dozens of softly glowing lanterns, sat in the center of a maze, and the paths leading from it twisted into many quiet corners. In one was a swing hanging from the branch of a sturdy oak, and there I found them, Willow on the swing, arranging her gauzy white dress. Adam had hung a Chinese lantern, and its glow illuminated her face from the side, a haunting image of loveliness. Unlike what I'd seen of Adam's work, he was capturing something of Willow's uncomplicated joy.

A short distance away, a tree branch trembled, though there was no breeze. I watched a shadow materialize into a solid shape, then disappear. Was it Luca? I couldn't be sure if it was a man or a woman. A devotee of Adam Blasco, watching the master at work? Or some voyeur?

Was *I* a voyeur? No, I was the chaperone. I waited.

Adam snapped some photos, his camera on a tripod, his camera bag open at his feet. Willow perched on the swing, her expression uncertain one moment, then laughing the next.

After a few minutes, Adam reached around Willow's neck and pulled her long braid forward, letting it fall slowly through his fingers to her shoulder.

Footsteps pounded down the path as Luca ran up to Adam. "What are you doing?" he shouted.

Willow jumped off the swing. "I'm having my photo taken!"

"No, you, Adam," Luca shouted. "Leave her alone. You look like you're . . ." He pushed Adam aside, into his tripod, and the camera tumbled to the ground.

"You idiot! That camera cost a fortune! Watch what you're doing, we're working here." Adam swore and bent to gather his equipment. Luca sidestepped and ran to Willow, but she pushed him away.

"Luca, I'm having my picture taken! Stop being so jealous!" She stormed off, and I stepped deeper into the shadows as she passed by me. Luca put his face in his hands, his shoulders slumped. He muttered something in Italian, called "Wait, Willow!" and started after her.

"Don't follow me!" she shouted.

He froze, then ran down the path in the opposite direction. The dark form had disappeared into the trees. I hurried back to the party, leaving Adam swearing as he examined his camera.

What had just happened? Adam had created a lovely setting for a photo, but still I was glad Luca had broken the spell.

I tried to compose myself as I hustled back to the kitchen to replenish my tray.

"These people are absolute locusts. I've never seen people eat so much in such a short period of time," Bitsy complained, then laughed and gave me a fist bump. "The ice cream's a hit. We're opening the bar now, and serving champagne to loosen up the crowd so they'll open their pocketbooks for the art."

My nerves still jangled after witnessing the altercation between Adam and Luca. I needed to stay busy. "I'll help."

I took off my wreath and walked through the exhibit, scanning for Willow and Luca but I didn't see them in the crowd. I took a tray of champagne and offered it to the guests. The guy in the loincloth and a fairy chatted in front of Maud's photo, and they each took two flutes of champagne. My tray emptied quickly, and I could sense the alcohol changing the atmosphere of the room. The gallery was crowded, almost claustrophobic. I watched Dree Venditti chat with Max Truwitt. She whispered in the gallery manager's ear and toyed with the sky blue lanyard of his security badge, but kept looking over his shoulder. I wondered who she was looking for.

By the entrance was an alcove with a sign posted: Early Work. Over 18 please. A man dressed as an intergalactic warrior swooped up the last two flutes of champagne on my tray, so I moved inside the alcove to check out the art. The black-and-white images were all of young women, their emaciated bodies bent, their eyes shadowed, their cheekbones hollow. Many sprawled on pavement, in gutters, or on wrinkled, dirty sheets, and the techniques Adam had used to develop the photos distorted the images further. A group parted in front of me, whispering.

"It makes me think of that trend in the nineties? What was it called, heroin chic?" "They look drugged, don't they? Do you think he drugged them?" "It's how he made his name." "Mucho dinero for these early prints." "I don't know that I'd want this on my wall." "Ugh. Degrading." "Absolutely amazing. I have to have one."

Tony Ortiz stood by the entrance to the sequestered work, in front of a portrait of a young woman in a clearing wearing a torn, muddy dress. It was titled *Redwood*. Tony turned to me. "These older works made his name, but I think his new work is better than anything he's done."

We walked together out of the alcove and stood by Maud's portrait. "Say what you want about him, Blasco's got talent." Tony reached out for a waiter's tray, leaving his bottle of beer and taking two champagne flutes. He handed me a glass. "Congratulations, the ice cream was a success."

"I'll drink to my partner, Bitsy." I raised my glass in the direction of the kitchen, then we clinked glasses. Maud stood across the room, glowing in a group of admirers, Adam at her side. "Maud looks happy."

"Because she's always the star." Tony lifted his glass toward her portrait.

"How long have you known Maud?" I asked.

"I met her a few years ago when I was organizing an exhibition at a museum in Newport," Tony said. "She and her husband liked to take their yacht there and they were a big part of the social scene, gallery and museum events. Her husband was a real-life prince, but he treated everyone like a friend. When he died, she fell off the radar. Then a few months ago I ran into her again and she asked me to come to Penniman to mount an exhibit about the history of Moy Mull. It's fascinating. I've found some great stuff about the building: blueprints, floor plans, even letters from Mr. Clitheroe to his builders."

Adam looked over at us, did a double take, abruptly left the group, and joined Tony and me. He squinted at the younger man. "We've met, right?"

Tony shook his head and adjusted the heavy tortoiseshell frames of his glasses. "No, I'm sure I would've remembered. I work for Maud. My name's Tony Ortiz. I admire your work."

Adam tilted his head and stared at Tony with discomfiting intensity. "I never forget a face." He held an empty champagne glass, and I wondered if he was drunk.

Tony laughed. "I have one of those faces."

As Adam continued to stare, Tony glanced at me with a can-you-believe-this look and he quickly finished his drink. "Will you excuse me? I see someone I have to talk to."

I followed his gaze through the gallery entrance to the lobby. No one stood there. I guess he wanted to escape Adam's unnerving scrutiny. I didn't blame him. I gave Adam a quick nod and also excused myself. I stepped behind a group inspecting a row of fashion magazine covers, then turned back to Adam.

He stood, his arms wrapped around his thin frame, his black sneaker tapping the floor, in front of one of his early works, a portrait of a girl with chiseled, almost rawboned features, her face surrounded by long matted hair reaching past her bare shoulders. Her chin was raised, defiant, but her eyes were afraid, unsure, pleading. A fine spray of brown paint spattered one half of the work.

That was the difference, I thought, between art and decoration. Photographs could be well composed and aesthetically pleasing. Adam's work spoke. There was a force in them, power. His photos pulled you in, attracted, repulsed, made you think, made you uncomfortable.

I shuddered and turned away. As I did, Dree pushed past me, sloshing champagne as she joined Adam.

"I've been calling you for weeks," she hissed. "We need to talk."

"Hello to you too, Dree." Adam sighed.

She placed her hand on his upper arm and squeezed. "Let's talk outside."

Adam winced. "Are you going to make a scene if I don't?"

Dree's lips curled and she leaned close, whispering in his ear. He swore but allowed Dree to loop her arm through his as the two of them headed outside.

What was that about? I hesitated for just a moment, then followed them.

Chapter 9

I set my tray on a table in the lobby and stepped outside into the cool night air in time to see Adam and Dree disappear into the tea garden. I hurried after them, cursing the sound of my footsteps on the gravel, following them down paths lit with low landscaping lights and Chinese lanterns. Up ahead, I saw Dree pull Adam into the shadowed interior of the pagoda in the center of the garden. I skirted behind it, grateful for the cover provided by the surrounding laurel. I had to stay out of their sight, and avoid being caught eavesdropping by Bitsy's cleanup crew, who were sweeping through the garden, clearing left-behind plates and glasses, and breaking down those tall stand-up tables used for cocktail parties. I stood as still as I could, afraid that the sound of my footsteps would alert them to my presence.

"Two minutes, Dree. If you didn't notice, there's a reception in my honor and I'd like to get back." Peering between the leaves, I saw Adam pace.

"Adam, you know I'm persistent." Dree's voice was a purr. "And I will persist. I want you to know that right away. Didn't you get my letters, my emails?"

"Yes." Adam's voice was harsh. "There's a reason I didn't answer. It's not happening. Never."

"Come now. It's a simple favor."

"Not so simple, Dree. You don't understand what you're asking."

Dree's voice dripped poison. "Because you're the great Adam Blasco?" She lowered her voice. "I had a conversation with a friend who told me something very interesting." Her next words were a murmur and I strained to hear.

Adam stopped pacing and replied in a such a low voice I couldn't make anything out beyond "money" and "castle" and "darkroom."

One of the caterers carrying a trash bag appeared at the end of the path, so I hurried away in the other direction, keeping to the shadows. Ahead of me, Adam stormed out of the garden onto the drive toward the castle. Behind me in the still night air, I could hear Dree's throaty voice as she sang an unsteady string of lyrics about black magic.

So, Dree was shaking down Adam. What was the favor Dree wanted? I watched Adam's figure disappear into the distance and wondered how one man could be the focus of so much animosity and drama.

I hurried back into the lobby, retrieved my tray, and served a few more rounds of champagne. Maud and some admirers stood by her portrait and accepted congratulations as the crowd streamed out. Max and a petite woman wearing bright blue designer glasses with silver blond hair pulled into a ponytail were surrounded by a chattering group. They toasted each other and he gave her a kiss on the cheek. Many of Adam's works had red stickers on their labels, indicating that they had sold. It looked like Max and the gallery had a lot to celebrate.

My cell buzzed with a text from Willow. CAN WE GO? I'M WAITING WITH SADIE.

I said good night to the catering crew, grateful that this wasn't my rodeo and I didn't have to clean up. Bitsy hugged me. "I can't wait to do another ice cream social. Don't forget, I'll help you out at the booth tomorrow."

"Great. See you then."

I crossed the parking lot to my car. Willow sat cross-legged on Sadie's hood, bent over her phone as she yanked daisies from her braid.

"Where's Luca?" I asked.

Willow got in the car and slammed the door.

Uh-oh. I got in and started the engine.

She stared straight ahead, arms crossed, and muttered, "I don't care."

I wasn't going to worry about Luca. His biggest danger walking back to the farm was getting hit by a deer. "Don't you want to change out of that costume and get your clothes?"

Her head fell back against the seat rest and she groaned. "I left my stuff in the cloakroom at the castle. I can get it tomorrow." Maud had hired Willow and a few other farmhands to dress up in medieval costumes and move through the festival crowd on Saturday. "Right now I want to go home."

"You sure?"

She nodded, checked the phone screen once more, then tucked it away.

I pulled out of the parking lot. "So how many times has Luca texted you?"

She exhaled. "About twenty. Riley, I didn't do anything wrong, did I? I mean, Adam offered to take my picture, and with me going away to school, I thought it would be nice to give to Mom and Dad, him being a famous photographer and all. Luca thought Adam was making a pass."

The images from the eighteen-and-over part of the gallery swam into my mind, and I pushed them away. I couldn't imagine anything like that developing from the sweet scene I'd seen in the garden. But had Adam's other shoots started like Willow's? Sweet images until Adam crossed the line?

Or was there some venom in the photographer that poisoned the images he took?

"I bet the photos will be beautiful. Luca was being . . . protective, maybe?"

Her chin jutted. "I can take care of myself."

A memory surfaced, the figure in the trees. Was it a partygoer charmed by the scene? A fan enamored, not believing his luck to watch his idol at work? My stomach lurched. Or could it have been Vye, watching a too familiar scenario play out? *Oh, Willow*, I thought, *sometimes it's nice to have someone watch out for you.*

That night I sat in bed, a cup of cocoa on my nightstand, Rocky purring by my side. Caroline texted: I HOPE I DIDN'T MISS TOO MUCH!

I was too tired to go into it. I texted: I'LL FILL YOU IN TO-MORROW. CAN'T WAIT TO SEE YOU. I hesitated then added, AND SPRINKLES.

Chapter 10

The next morning at Udderly, I loaded Sadie with ice cream for the festival booth, tubs of the "stalwarts" (vanilla, chocolate, strawberry) and a sampling of our rich fall flavors—maple walnut, apple pie à la mode, and pumpkin spice, lots of pumpkin spice. Bitsy would supply cones in pastel "unicorn" colors, taco-shaped waffles for our ice cream tacos, and a rainbow of specially colored sprinkles and toppings.

Across Farm Lane, shoppers jammed the just-opened farm stand, eager to buy pumpkins and apples from the orchard. Willow marched out of the farmhouse, letting the screen door bang shut behind her. Warily I got into Sadie. Willow joined me, slammed the door, and folded her arms.

"Where's Luca?" I asked, treading carefully. "Isn't he working at the art festival?"

Willow pursed her lips and shrugged. From behind the barn across the road, I saw Luca pushing a glossy yellow bike, complete with bell and basket on the front.

Willow followed my gaze and huffed. "Mom lent him her bike."

I started the car. "Shall we go?"

She chewed her lip as I let the car roll slowly down the road. "No! Please pull over, Riley."

Willow lowered her window and stuck her head out of the car. "Hey dork, you want a ride?" she shouted at Luca.

Luca set the bike against the barn, ran to the car, and got in the back, his words coming in a rush. "Yes, I was a dork. Can you forgive me?"

Willow turned in her seat, her eyes locked on his.

I pulled back onto the road, keeping my eyes forward as the two shared a silent look.

"I suppose," Willow said slowly. Out of the corner of my eye I saw her smile. "Took you a long time to get home last night."

"I had a lot of thinking to do." Luca's tone carried an apology.

Within moments their chatter filled the car. *Ah, young love.*

"Where's your backpack?" Willow asked.

"I forgot it at the castle last night," Luca said. "I left it in the cloakroom."

A few minutes later I backed the car up to the tent and they helped me load ice cream into the freezer case at our booth. In the bright morning light, we marveled at the tent Maud had provided. Along with its crenellated trim, it sported a flag with Moy Mull's double M logo from its peaked roof.

"It looks like she bought it at Ye Olde Wizarding Campground," Willow said, giggling.

I checked that all the equipment was at the ready and glanced at the time.

"Do you want me to drop you at the castle so you can get your costumes on?"

Willow took Luca's hand. "No, we want to look at the booths before my shift and before the crowds get too big. See you later."

They were once more "we." Equilibrium restored. "Will you need a ride back to the farm later?"

"No, thank you," Luca said. "We're going back at noon to work at the farm stand. Some friends will drive us."

I moved Sadie to a small field designated for exhibitor parking, where volunteers waved us into spots. One was a woman wearing the red Moy Mull Art Festival T-shirt over a swirling tartan skirt, chunky lace-up Doc Martens, a purple floral head wrap, and lavender glasses—the police station secretary, Tillie O'Malley, aka the loosest lips in Penniman.

She leaned on Sadie's hood. "Hey, how are you? I heard your fancy ice cream was the hit of the gallery opening."

"Good. How are you?" I grabbed my purple chef's jacket from the back seat and looped my ID over my head.

"Look at you, all official," Tillie said. "You got the lucky yellow badge that gets you inside the castle."

"Coming by for an ice cream later?"

"I'll be there! I hope you have pumpkin spice." Her eyes glowed. "I live for pumpkin spice."

Oh-kay. "We have it. See you later." As I walked back to the booth, Prentiss hurried by, carrying a stack of four cardboard boxes. "I'm late, I'm late, for a very important date!" The box on top slipped off and tumbled to the ground.

I picked it up. "Let me help."

"Would you? Lifesaver," Prentiss said. "These are heavier than I thought. The printer shipped these programs to the castle office instead of the gallery office and we need them for Adam's talk."

I took another box from his arms and jogged alongside. I'd only seen Prentiss looking cool and collected, but now sweat beaded his upper lip, his pale yellow linen jacket was wrinkling, and his chunky stylish glasses were fogging up.

"I have a million and one things to do before Adam's talk

at eleven thirty. Why don't I have the golf cart? Maud took the golf cart. I need the golf cart! People at the opening last night ran off with all the programs. That's what we get for having such an icon. A controversial icon, to boot. Well, it means more attention and bigger crowds. All to the good. Ka-ching, ka-ching."

"Where's Maud?" I said as we jogged toward the Barn Gallery.

"Yoga in the morning," he gasped. "Bees in the afternoon. Dealing with Adam in the middle."

Dealing with Adam? "Have they known each other long?"

He laughed and shot me a surprised look. "Honey, they were married!"

I stopped short. "What?"

Prentiss grinned. "Actually stopped you in your tracks, didn't I? The marriage didn't last longer than a few months, but yeah, they were officially husband and wife. So help me God, I'm not making that up. Vegas wedding. She was a teensy bit not quite legal and had to get a letter from her folks. Elvis and I were witnesses."

Maud, the supermodel, and Adam, the creepy photographer, had been married?

"Yeah, you know the old story, the sculptor who falls in love with his creation," Prentiss said. "What was that play called?"

"*Pygmalion.*" I trailed Prentiss up the Barn Gallery steps, stunned by this news.

He stopped at the door and shifted his boxes to his hip so he could scan his badge. "All this scanning." He rolled his eyes. "Give me the good old days when a sleepy security guard who knew me could wave me through *and* get the door for me."

I barely heard Prentiss as I processed the information about Maud and Adam. We went inside and he dropped his two boxes onto a table, then took a handkerchief from the pocket of his linen blazer and mopped his brow and head.

I placed my boxes next to his. Dozens of folding chairs and a podium were set up in the expansive lobby space, as well as several tables with flower arrangements.

"Thank God I had the foresight to have the caterers set up last night," Prentiss said as he sliced the boxes open with a box cutter. "When I finish, I'm sitting down for Adam's talk, snoozing behind my sunglasses, and then I'm going to your booth to eat my weight in ice cream."

"Good plan." I pulled programs from the box.

"Please set these on the tables by the entrance door," Prentiss said. "I'll put some over there by the podium."

I stacked my programs on a long table covered by a cloth in Bitsy's trademark fuchsia pink. The speaker's podium was set up directly in front of Maud's photo. Adam would have Maud looking over his shoulder as he spoke. I thought of cartoons with an angel on one shoulder and a devil on the other. Maud had certainly been good to Adam, hosting this exhibition. Or, I mused as I fanned the programs across the table and emptied the box, had *he* been *her* angel? Her professional life had taken off when his iconic photo of her was published. She had Adam's photo to thank for her career. Had marriage to him been the price?

Prentiss ran back to me. "Maybe I'll switch up my schedule. Do you have pumpkin spice ice cream?"

What was it with pumpkin spice?

"Right this way."

Chapter 11

I should've known. As soon as I handed Prentiss his ice cream cone, a line of volunteers and booth exhibitors formed. When Bitsy joined me just before ten, when the gates to the arts festival officially opened to the public, there was a line a dozen deep of people wanting ice cream. It felt like a regular Saturday at Udderly, except the customers were more artsy. I was relieved when Flo and Gerri joined us, Flo in leggings printed with purple cows, and Gerri accessorizing her purple chef's coat with one of her trademark flowing scarves.

I'd shown everyone how to make ice cream rosettes, an easy technique that made the cones look extra special, especially with the pastel-colored unicorn ice cream. Bitsy's colorful cones, waffle "tacos," and specialty sprinkles were a hit. Pumpkin spice was a huge seller, as expected, and I was already thinking that I'd need to get more from the shop before the end of the morning.

The freezer hummed, and I fanned myself as Willow and Luca walked by, Willow costumed as a Scottish lassie, Luca wearing the same red Moy Mull Art Festival T-shirt I'd seen on Tillie. As I watched, a couple asked them to pose in their selfie. Maud was a marketing genius.

The scent of spiced apple cider drifted from a neighboring booth and the Rotarians fired up their hot dog grill. Rows of booths filled with artists and artisans—knitters, potters, glass blowers, portrait painters. All of Penniman's artistic community were represented.

A flash of yellow caught my attention and I turned my head to see Prentiss rush by. Bitsy and I raised a hand in greeting but he didn't stop, instead pushing toward the Barn Gallery, his cell phone to his ear.

Bitsy brushed a stray lock of blond hair from her forehead. "He's in a rush."

I saw Vye cut through the crowd, her expression grim.

"Vye, what is it?" I called.

Vye ran over and showed me the time on her phone: 11:25. "Adam's supposed to do his talk at eleven thirty, but Maud called me and said he's not at the gallery."

Bitsy said, "Oh, he's probably lost in thought taking pics somewhere. Isn't that what these artistes do?" She greeted a customer.

Vye's chest heaved. I put a hand on her shoulder. "Vye, what is it?"

"He's not answering his cell and he always answers his cell." Her worried eyes shimmered with tears. "Would you mind coming with me to his cottage?"

I turned to Bitsy, Flo, and Gerri. "I'll be right back."

"We've got this," Flo said.

"This way." Vye ran behind the tent and I followed her onto the gravel drive.

"He told me to set up the laptop with the presentation at the barn thirty minutes before the talk, but he hasn't shown," Vye said. "I've been looking for him everywhere."

"Was he staying at the castle?" I asked.

"No. Ivy Cottage. Back this way." I jogged alongside Vye as she took off down a gravel path that skirted the back of the tea garden.

Vye's breath came in ragged gasps and her steps slowed. "I'm so out of shape. Adam told me this cottage is the farthest you can get from the castle. And it's getting so hot." She pulled the thin cloth of her black tank top from her skin and bent to take a breath.

We fast-walked as the path curled into a clearing with a little stone cottage, far from the noise and bustle of the fair. I remembered that Maud and Adam were exes, and wondered how amicable their divorce had been. It must've been amicable or why else would she host his show? But if it was amicable, why put him so far from the castle?

Vye dashed up the steps and knocked. "Adam? Adam?" The silence grew as her worried eyes met mine. I turned the knob.

The door was unlocked. Before I could say a word, Vye pushed it open. We stepped into a quiet room with a queen bed, its silky navy blue duvet smooth. She rushed through into a small bathroom. "Adam!"

"The bed's made," I said.

She came back, panting. "He didn't sleep here. He never made his bed. He's got to be . . . somewhere."

There was a small weekender bag on a chair by the door. "That's right where I set it yesterday."

"Did he have anything else on his schedule this morning?" I asked.

Vye ran her hand through her hair, panic making her words tumble. "He was supposed to be at the Barn Gallery, that's all. He didn't have a schedule in his working life. He worked when something inspired him and then he'd work for hours and collapse. If he had something else planned for this morning, he didn't tell me."

I made my voice quiet and soothing. "Could he have driven somewhere? Maybe gotten a flat tire? There are places here that don't have good cell coverage. Is the car still here?"

"He doesn't drive, remember? The car's parked behind the castle. That's where I'm staying." She jerked open the closet, ran into the tiny kitchenette. "I don't see his camera bag." She pulled up. "There's a darkroom in the castle."

Vye's phone rang. "Maud."

While she talked, I peeked into the bath, scanned the kitchen, opened the refrigerator. It held small bottles of orange juice, water, and yogurt. I checked the trash. Empty. There was a small bar by the door with crystal glasses upside down on little paper doilies. It looked like nothing had been touched, and I wondered if Adam had come back here at all last night.

Vye pushed the phone into her pocket, and ran her hand through her hair again. "I told Maud about the darkroom. She's going to have someone check it. In the meantime, she wants me to do the presentation in Adam's place."

I squeezed her arm and looked her in the eye. "You can do this. Come on."

"I guess I have to." Vye's tone, so frantic and worried, now simmered with anger. She slammed the door as we left. "I'm going to kill Adam."

As we rushed to the Barn Gallery, I tried to encourage Vye, tried to summon all the pep talks from all those old movies about the young understudy who goes on for the established star and becomes a star herself, but Vye's expression was so blank I could tell she wasn't listening. Turmoil and fear radiated from her along with the scent of sweat and sandalwood.

The lobby was full of the standing-room-only, restless crowd that had already waited over a half hour for the speaker. I caught bits of chatter as we pushed toward the podium, where Maud waited. "Where is he?" "Probably passed out in a gutter somewhere." "He's been sober for years." "Well, there are addictions and then there are addictions." "I got him to sign my catalog last night. I'm going to eBay it."

Maud wrapped an arm around Vye, her smile wide but steely. "Thank you for stepping in, Vye."

Vye startled at Maud's touch and threw me a panicked look. I squeezed her arm, giving her a smile that I hoped would inspire confidence.

"You know the work better than anyone," Maud said.

An expression I didn't expect twisted Vye's open face, one of derision.

"Yes, I do," she said. Vye tapped the laptop and put up the first slide, a photo of an arid landscape under a vast sky. Maud stepped to the microphone and gestured for silence.

"Adam Blasco is unable to join us this morning, but I have a wonderful surprise. His assistant, Vye, who is a talented photographer in her own right, is here to speak to us about Adam's work. Believe me, she knows his work better than anyone on the planet. And"—Maud turned to Vye—"I have no doubt that one day we'll be collecting her work as avidly as we do Adam's. Please welcome her warmly to Moy Mull."

Chapter 12

An hour and a half later at the ice cream tent, Prentiss said, "When I get my hands on him, I'm going to kill that wormy little hipster." He swore at such length that Gerri pursed her lips and cleared her throat.

Prentiss shrugged and reached for a second pumpkin spice cone. "Sorry, ma'am, I'm from Chicago."

"How did Vye do?" Flo asked.

"You know, for being thrown into the deep end like that, she did well—though it took a while to shake off her nerves," I said. "But she knows photography and that came through."

Prentiss pressed a napkin to his lips. "The problem is people paid to see Adam, and there was no Adam. Gotta keep looking for him. I'll try the other cottages. Maybe he got lucky last night." He ran off.

"Adam's disappeared?" Flo said.

"And he's not answering his cell phone," I said.

"Do you think he went back to the city?" Gerri asked.

I shook my head. "He doesn't drive."

Flo said, "Maybe he called a car service?"

"He reminded me of the Bender boy." Gerri lowered her voice. She and Flo shared a significant glance. "Remember him?"

"Who's that?" I said.

"He ended up in jail." Gerri tsked. "Started in third grade, writing bad words on Post-it Notes and sticking them on little girls. Always peeking into the girls' restroom. Eventually he set up a camera in the girls' locker room. That's what got him sent to reform school."

A customer took a maple walnut ice cream taco from my hands and said, "Maybe Adam heard the Weeping Lady."

"The Weeping Lady?" I said.

"Oh, you know that old story," Flo said.

I restocked napkins. "I haven't thought of it in years."

"What's the story?" another customer asked.

Flo waved her scoop toward the castle. "When we were in high school and the hotel was closed, we used to come up here and party, and people would whisper about the curse of the Weeping Lady."

I smiled at the image of Flo "partying."

Flo turned to Gerri. "Let me think, was the ghost Oona, the wife of Ben Clitheroe, the man who built Moy Mull?"

"It wasn't Oona," Gerri corrected. "Oona ran off with the chauffeur."

"That's right, the story goes back before that and sometimes the old stories blend." Flo warmed to her tale. "Well, when he built Moy Mull, old Ben Clitheroe brought over some stones from a real-life castle in Scotland. He even brought Scots stonemasons to work on the castle. The stones were haunted and unbeknownst to him, the stones carried a ghost across the Atlantic. The ghost was the Weeping Lady, betrayed by her husband, murdered, so he could marry his mistress. The story goes that on the wedding night, the new wife heard weeping and discovered the old wife's name carved into the windowsill of her bedchamber. The sight drove her mad and she jumped from the top of the tower.

"The legend says that if you stand on top of the tower,

on the night of a full moon—" Flo gestured dramatically to the castle.

"Naturally," I said.

"If you hear her crying, you're doomed to fall off."

I laughed. "With all the drinking that went on up there, I'm surprised nobody ever did fall off the tower."

"Did you go up there?" Gerri peered at me over her sunglasses, and I remembered she'd been principal of Penniman High School.

I blushed. "I wasn't part of that crowd. But I dated a guy from my cross-country team who dared me to climb up the stone wall by the front entrance." At Bitsy's surprised look, I explained. "The stones of the exterior are uneven and make pretty good hand- and footholds. I made it to the top of the porch and sat down to wait for him. It was a pretty easy climb." I shook my head. "My date didn't make it more than two feet. I waited for him for an hour before he gave up and drove off in embarrassment. I had to call Caroline to drive me home."

"So when you heard crying, it was your boyfriend." Flo chuckled.

I laughed, but my date had been too embarrassed to speak to me for months after that.

Farther down the row by the Supreme Pizza tent, a stocky woman caught my eye. She wore a green army coat covered with patches, sunglasses, and a black watch cap pulled over her ears. A lock of blue hair curled at the nape of her neck. Vye, in a disguise that called attention on this unseasonably warm and sunny day. She bought a slice then skirted out of sight behind the tent. When I finished serving a customer, I said, "I'll be right back."

Vye sat cross-legged in the shade of an oak behind the tents.

"Hiding out?" I said.

She shuddered and took off her jacket and hat. "Giving

that talk was terrifying, Riley. I thought I'd pass out. I hate public speaking. It was so far out of my comfort zone."

I sat near her in the warm grass as she folded her slice in half and took a bite. "They say all the good stuff happens at the end of your comfort zone. What matters is, you did it."

She snorted but relaxed against the tree. "It's over. I don't know what I said. I just talked about the photos."

"I couldn't stay for the whole presentation, but what I saw was great. Prentiss said you did a good job."

"You're both being nice. But it wasn't hard." She raised her chin. "I took most of those pics. Most of Adam's later work is mine."

My shock must have been plain. That explained her expression this morning when Maud said she knew the work better than anyone. "Does Maud know?"

"No one knows. I don't want to get into it now." She finished her slice and licked sauce from her fingertips. "I've never told anyone that before. I should help look for Adam, but I'm kind of drained."

"Understandable," I said. "Maybe some ice cream would help."

Her eyes brightened. "Pumpkin spice?"

I was still surprised by Vye's revelation as I went back to the ice cream tent, served Vye an extra-large cone on the house, and waved as she melted into the crowd. All the European museums I'd spent hours in were full of work by master artists' apprentices. The phrase "From the School of" appeared on thousands of paintings by aspiring artists toiling in the workshops of their more-famous mentors. Still this rankled. Adam kept this talented young woman in the shadows while he took credit for her work. It was yet another reason to loathe Adam Blasco.

"Take a break," Flo said. "We've got this."

"Go see if they've found Adam," Gerri said. "I'm dying to know where he's gone."

"Thanks." I pulled off my purple chef's coat and tucked it away under one of the tables. "I called the shop and asked them to send over more pumpkin spice."

"Thank goodness," Flo said. "We'll have a riot if we run out."

I joined the crowd, a slow-moving river of people flowing through the booths. So many beautiful things caught my eye—a scarf in luscious shades of green from the llama farm, tiny landscapes depicting Penniman's covered bridge, the scent of handcrafted lavender soaps. But the question grew more insistent—where was Adam Blasco?

I recalled the shadowy figure I'd seen last night when Adam was photographing Willow. Who was that? And I recalled Vye's words about Adam's schedule. He'd go off and work on whatever project intrigued him.

I wondered if Adam had gone to the darkroom to work on Willow's photos.

The castle loomed ahead against a vivid blue sky. As I approached, I saw Maud standing by the rear door by the rose trellises, speaking to a security guard.

"Any luck finding Adam?" I asked. "Has the darkroom been checked?"

"The darkroom was the first place I looked," Maud said. "He left his bag in there." We followed behind the security guard into the castle, then stopped in the hallway as he went into the security office.

The tiniest line appeared between Maud's brows. "That man always has his phone glued to his hand. At first I thought he just wasn't answering Prentiss, but then I called. Adam always answers my calls." She pinched the bridge of her nose and squeezed her eyes shut. "I've asked my team to scour the security tapes to see if they can spot him."

"When did you see him last?" I asked.

"At the party last night. After the party, I went to my she shed, and yes, I know Prentiss calls it that. I had some things to attend to. Then I came back here around midnight. All was quiet. I didn't see another soul."

Prentiss emerged from the office. "I've asked Tony to check the attic."

Maud rolled her eyes. "Adam has no interest whatsoever in old stuff in attics. *Cherchez la femme*, that's Adam."

"What's left to search?" I asked.

"The cloakrooms?" Maud shrugged. Prentiss and I got the message: Maud Monaco didn't search cloakrooms, nor their adjoining bathrooms. There was a shallow room off the hallway, lined with coat hooks full of volunteers' jackets and backpacks, with two restrooms on either end. Prentiss looked in the men's room, and I the women's. Both were empty.

Maud said, "Prentiss, did anyone search the dungeon?"

Prentiss ran over and turned the knob. "It's locked." He and Maud exchanged frowns.

"What is it?" I asked.

"It's never locked." Prentiss twisted the ornate knob. "Never."

"You need the key to lock it or unlock it." Maud banged on the door and rattled the ornate handle. She raised her voice. "Adam, if you're in there, I swear to God I will kill you. How dare you miss that talk! After all I've done for you!"

The security guard stuck his head out of the office.

Prentiss ran past the guard into the office, where I saw him open a carved wooden cabinet mounted on the wall by the mail cubbies. He grabbed a key from inside and ran back. "There's only one key. If this doesn't work . . ." He nudged Maud aside and put the key in the lock. "Maud, you can stop yelling. The walls are three feet thick and this door is solid oak. If he's in there, he won't hear you."

Maud's nostrils flared as she stalked with her hands on her hips.

As Prentis turned the knob and opened the door, Maud pushed in front of him, stumbling slightly as she went through and flipped on a light.

Maud screamed, the sound ringing in the hallway. Prentiss hurried in with me right behind. Both of them had stopped just inside so I moved past them until I could see what they were looking at—Adam's body.

Maud fell to her knees with a gasp. Prentiss knelt, too, flinging his arms around her so quickly he almost knocked her off balance.

Adam was sprawled on the stone floor, so still I knew he was dead. He wore the same clothes I'd seen him in Friday night. I stepped to the side of the shocked group to see better. Adam's face was turned to the side and grotesquely swollen, the mottled flesh of his cheek hanging over the neck of his tight black T-shirt. The side of his face against the stone floor was purple. One arm was curled against his chest, the other extended from his body, as if he'd been reaching for something when he died. His glasses were askew and a lens broken, an abrasion on the bridge of his nose.

Maud heaved a breath and cried out, "A bee!"

I followed her line of sight to Adam's outstretched hand. It was slightly curled, and the tiny body of a bee lay next to it, as if Adam had gotten careless and dropped it.

"Was he stung?" Prentiss said.

The security guard pressed forward and crouched next to Adam. He tried to find a pulse, but I could've told him it was a useless gesture. He rose and hurried into the hall, speaking into his radio. Maud stretched out her hand toward the bee, but Prentiss pulled her away.

Chapter 13

I'm not sure how long we stayed in the dungeon with Adam's body, but the next thing I knew, a police officer escorted us out and into a small parlor next door. I sat with Maud while Prentiss ran to the kitchen to make her a cup of tea. Before we left, I'd scanned the dungeon. The room was as I'd seen it when Prentiss had given me my tour, except that two chairs had been overturned and the table had been pushed a few inches out of place.

My mind whirled with questions. There were no windows. How did a bee get inside? Were Adam's injuries inflicted by an attacker? Or were they from his last efforts to get help, scrabbling against the lock and falling as he tried to open the heavy door? The lights were off. Had Adam turned them off at some point, or did a killer turn them off to make people think the room was unoccupied? I imagined Adam's struggles to breathe as his allergy triggered anaphylaxis, but pushed the thought from my mind and ran my hands over the worn fabric of the sofa where I sat next to Maud. She sat frozen, her expression blank and her body still except for one hand that worried the bee pendant at her breast.

As Prentiss returned, carrying an ornate tray with a silver teapot and three delicate china cups, cream, and sugar, the sound of sirens and emergency vehicles flowed from the hallway. He set the tray on the coffee table and I poured tea for Maud. He reached into a bar cabinet, took out a small bottle of whiskey, and poured a splash into all the cups. "Won't hurt."

I pressed the cup into Maud's hands. She murmured thanks as she took it, but the cup rattled against the saucer. She took a sip, then stood and paced across the rug.

The room was decorated in Ye Olde Rec Room: gold and green plaid rug, wood paneling, dusty book-of-the-month selections and a yellow row of old *National Geographic* magazines lining bookcase shelves flanking a large-screen television. Shelves on the other wall were filled with games and puzzles that were surely missing pieces and a battered Ping-Pong table had been pushed against the other wall.

I thought how incongruous it was that we were having what looked like a tea party as the police and EMTs ran into the building to attend to the dead man in the next room. I heard heavy equipment belts jangle as the experts walked briskly down the hallway.

I sipped my tea, felt the whiskey burn. The combination of strong black tea and whiskey was fortifying, but the low-ceilinged room and thought of Adam's dead body on the other side of the wall set off a wave of anxiety that drove me to my feet, and I, too, started to pace. I wanted to get outside in the fresh air. I knew who would be coming, who I'd have to talk to, and I rubbed my temples.

Prentiss knocked back his whiskey-enhanced tea then poured another cup. I had the feeling that Prentiss and Maud had a lot to say to each other, but now they studiously avoided each other's eyes, my eyes.

I pulled out my phone, thinking I'd text Flo and Gerri to let them know what was happening, but I had no signal.

"Cell service down here is terrible." Prentiss nodded to a push-button phone in the corner. "You can use the house phone. Dial nine and you'll get an outside line."

I pressed the buttons and called Flo.

"I heard sirens," she said. "What's going on up there at the castle? Are you okay?"

I quietly told her what was happening.

"Holy smokes! Promise to tell me everything when you get back."

An officer arrived to take statements. I'd expected Jack Voelker, the new chief on the Penniman Police Department, a sharp guy but inconveniently Caroline's boyfriend. But the guy who took our statements was young enough to make me think he was a recent graduate of the police academy. He had a slim runner's build, dark hair in a buzz cut, and careful printing. He didn't introduce himself, but his name tag read Ruiz.

When Maud went to the office to talk with Officer Ruiz, both Prentiss and I hovered just inside the TV-parlor door, sipping our tea. "Look inconspicuous," Prentiss whispered. An officer left the darkroom, stuck his head in the office, and said to Ruiz, "I found his bag."

They all walked down the hall to the darkroom, and we heard Maud say, "Yes, he had a severe allergy to bee stings."

"Did he carry an EpiPen with him?" I whispered to Prentiss.

He nodded.

Maud returned and Officer Ruiz asked me to join him. He didn't go far beyond the basics, asked me for my contact information, then told me I could go. From his cursory questions, I could see the direction of his thinking—Adam's death was an accident.

But my mind whirled as I left the castle. The police seemed to think this was a severe reaction to a bee sting. Yes, he was allergic, allergic enough to carry an EpiPen. But . . . the door. The lock. No windows in the dungeon. The bee. Maud's shocked face.

I took a deep breath. Maybe I was the one seeing shadows where there were none. With so many ways to die, I never even thought of being stung. I'd been stung plenty of times when I was a child—a consequence of spending a lot of time running the farm with Caroline—but the one-in-a-million, struck-by-lightning bad luck of being killed by a bee sting made me shake my head.

My thoughts were interrupted as I passed a knot of security clustered by the kitchen entrance. As I passed, I heard a voice shriek, "What do you mean I can't go in? I'm telling you, I left my badge in my room. How many times do I have to tell you, I'm a guest. Just ask Maud. Cripes, I have a headache, can you turn off that blasted squawking radio?"

In the center of the group stood Dree, wearing the same black dress as last night. Well, someone had had an interesting night. She caught sight of me and to my surprise waved wildly. I glanced behind me, thinking she was waving at someone else, but there was no one there. Puzzled, I raised a hand but didn't stop. As I passed, the kitchen door opened and Prentiss let her in. I couldn't wait to hear that story.

Back at the booth, Flo and Gerri crowded me. "Everyone's talking about the cops up at the castle! What happened?"

I filled them in with what I knew.

Gerri's brow furrowed. "A bee sting? Inside the castle?"

I remembered Adam at the farm, demurring from visiting the apiary. "He knew Maud kept bees. He had an EpiPen in his camera bag."

"So he didn't have it with him when he needed it." Gerri tsked at this bad planning.

"Well, when word gets out, his photos are going to be worth a lot of money," Flo said. "Isn't that what happens? Artists are worth more dead than alive."

A customer cleared his throat and I turned to serve him a cone. After he paid, I turned back to the sisters.

"I wonder if Vye knows." No matter her feelings for Adam, he'd been her employer—more than that, her mentor. Who'd used her. How complicated. Poor thing.

"How did the bee get in?" Gerri said. "I've been to meetings at the dungeon room and there are no windows. Someone must've been careless and left the doors open."

I shook my head. "They removed a wasp's nest Thursday. One must have gotten in." Wait. Wasp. Bee. Maud had said "bee." Maud kept bees. She'd know the difference.

"Oh, critters do these things. We've had squirrels in the attic. Gerri, remember when the skunk got into the kitchen?" Flo greeted another customer.

"How can I forget?" Gerri said. "You forgot to shut the breezeway door. It took a dozen tomato juice baths to get the smell out of Mr. Cuddlesworth's fur."

As they talked, my thoughts wandered back to the discovery of Adam's body and something else I'd seen.

The door was locked. Why did Adam lock the door? How did he lock the door? Prentiss said you needed a key to lock the door even from the inside, and there was only one key. Where was it? I hadn't noticed one in the dungeon.

And what brought Adam to the dungeon in the first place?

Chapter 14

The festival ended officially at seven, but we ran out of ice cream at 6:45. Gerri and Flo helped me pack up, and I drove back to Udderly. Out of the frying pan into the fire—the parking lot was jammed. I took a deep breath as I parked at the house and hustled down the hill and into the shop kitchen.

Teen guitarist and aspiring rock god Brandon Terwilliger bopped at the sink as soap bubbles flew. He wore headphones, as usual, his passion for music as great as his passion for making ice cream flavors that baffled me but were highly prized by the adolescent population of Penniman. He grinned and saluted me, soap bubbles flying off his fingers. This was also progress. After working together for the summer, he could meet my eye and speak to me without blushing. Actually, sometimes I had a hard time getting him to shut up. I was an only child and my male cousins lived out of state, so I didn't understand the male of the species, especially the music-loving teenage male.

"Hi, Riley." He shook his shaggy brown hair out of his eyes.

"Hey, Brandon. No football game tonight?"

"Next weekend." Brandon was the drum major of the Penniman High School Panthers. "Guess what? I'm working on a new Halloween flavor. Marshmallows for teeth, blackberry jam for blood, pistachio-green base. Gerri said it's a bloody mess and I think that's the name, don't you? I'll call it Bloody Mess."

Dear God. I had to laugh. Brandon's excitement was infectious. "How does it taste? Flavor is key."

He considered. "I have to fine tune it, I guess. I put in too many marshmallows. I'll work on it."

"Sounds good."

More soap bubbles flew as Brandon readjusted his headphones and went back to his dishes. He was my best cleaner. He'd make a spouse very happy someday.

The bright kitchen, the flying soap bubbles, always raised my spirits, but tonight something churned, something that bothered me beyond Adam's death, something I'd seen. I grabbed a waffle cone and stuffed it with pumpkin spice ice cream. If you can't beat 'em, join 'em. I savored the spicy blend of cinnamon, nutmeg, and ginger, the rich mouthfeel of the cream. Our blend was full of farm-fresh pumpkin, which is full of vitamin A. Pumpkin spice ice cream is practically health food.

Pru Brightwood, Willow's mother, came into the kitchen carrying an empty basket.

"How's it going, Pru?"

Pru was a midwife who managed Fairweather Farm along with her husband, Darwin. Between delivering babies, she also helped at Udderly. I don't know when she slept. She wore her pewter-colored hair in an almost waist-long braid down her back, and favored earth-toned jumpers and colorful woolen socks she knit herself. She brushed ringlets from her forehead and filled the basket with waffle cones. "Whew, the crowds have been crazy. As you know, the art festival brings in a ton of people. Line's been out the door all day. Farm stand was busy and the pumpkin patch too."

"Same at the festival." I hip-checked Brandon aside so I could wash my hands. "We went through every bit of ice cream."

She nodded. "Brandon helped me make more pumpkin spice and apple crumble and now he's making . . . something green." She smiled, friendly crinkles forming at the corners of her cornflower blue eyes. She and Willow shared the same lovely shade.

She pulled me into a corner and lowered her voice. "Is it true? About the photographer?"

News traveled fast in Penniman. "Yes. Supposedly Adam died from a bee sting."

"Anaphylaxis? How awful." She gave me a shrewd look. "Wait a minute. You said 'supposedly.'"

"There's a lot about it that doesn't make sense," I began.

"Hey," Brandon called. "There's a tour bus in the parking lot!"

It was all hands on deck until we served the last customer. Tomorrow would be just as busy. I'd agreed to Saturday only at the art festival because I didn't have enough employees to staff the shop for the whole weekend, but hoped that tourists would now visit the shop after trying ice cream at Moy Mull.

I filled Pru in on what I'd seen at the castle as we closed up the shop. As we walked up Farm Lane, warm light flowed from the kitchen window of the Brightwood's sprawling farmhouse across the road.

"Have you seen Willow and Luca today?" I asked.

She yawned. "Too busy. I saw them both head home for dinner. Together. I think they patched up whatever they fought about yesterday. I know he came in pretty late last night, well after midnight. She never said what they fought about."

I made a noncommittal sound; I didn't want to get into the scene between Luca and Adam. "I'll see you tomorrow."

I'd driven home after the gallery reception last night with Willow shortly after ten. It hardly would've taken Luca two hours to walk back to the farm from Moy Mull. I wondered, Where had Luca been last night?

Rocky materialized out of the shadows as I ran up the kitchen steps of the Spooner farmhouse. Mentally I catalogued the food that was left in the fridge—pickles, a jar of mayonnaise, a bottle of white wine—and prayed there was some peanut butter left in the jar. I hadn't had a chance to buy groceries all week. A small rental car was parked in the drive. The kitchen door was flanked by two bright yellow mums that hadn't been there this morning, and they glowed in the porch light. A country-music love song twanged through the door and the rich aroma of spicy chili made my mouth water.

"Hi, Riley!" Caroline stood at the stove, her curly shoulder-length hair pulled into a topknot, her feet in fuzzy slippers. Her dark eyes sparkled behind her tortoiseshell glasses. She usually favored muted colors in the more formal attire required by her work at the auction house, but since she'd been dating Jack she'd brightened the palette, and today she wore a coral blouse that highlighted her light brown skin.

"Caroline! How did you know I'd be dying for something to eat?"

"Because *I'm* dying for something to eat. I just got back from Boston a half hour ago and picked up some takeout." Chili bubbled in a large pot on the stove, and four loaves of golden cornbread sat on a plate on the round oak table next to a salad in a plastic takeout container.

"Bless you." I flopped into a seat. "How did that auction go?"

"Really well and then we had meetings afterward, which

is why I had to work so late." She handed me a steaming bowl of chili. "I bet all you've had all day is an ice cream cone."

"You know me so well." I knew Caroline well, too. She'd bought all this food hoping that a certain police chief would stop by. "Will you see Jack this weekend?"

Caroline's wide mouth curled in a grin. "Hope so. He's been tied up with a couple of burglaries lately." Jack was her first serious relationship—actually her only serious relationship—and her happiness was infectious. I'd gotten wrapped up in one of his murder investigations earlier this summer and while I knew he valued my input, I understood my help put him in a precarious position. Most police departments don't welcome amateurs sticking their noses in where they didn't belong. Caroline was so happy with Jack, I didn't want to do anything to mess up their relationship or be a wedge between them.

Just then, Caroline's phone dinged. Her lips turned down as she read the text. BUSY WITH WORK. WILL CALL TOMORROW. JACK

"I'm sorry, Caroline. I know why he's busy." I cut a piece of cornbread and slathered it with butter as I told her about the discovery of Adam's body.

She lowered herself into a chair at the table, her eyes wide. "No wonder Jack hasn't called."

I hesitated. *Bee. Wasp.* I looked at the clock ticking loudly on the wall over the sink. It was almost eleven and I was too exhausted to go into my theories. I'd save them for tomorrow.

I rinsed and washed out empty bowls while Caroline put the leftovers in the refrigerator.

I noticed the gold-rimmed bowl on the floor next to Rocky's bowl of kibble. It was full. "Where's Sprinkles? Is she okay? Looks like she wasn't hungry?" I wiped my hands on a dish towel.

"In the parlor." Caroline sighed.

We walked down the hall to what Buzzy had called the parlor. The small room was crammed with comfortably worn old furniture: a small TV; bookcases overflowing with games, puzzles, and books; and a games table with a checkerboard painted on top, scratched by many years of use.

An impossibly fluffy white Persian cat sprawled on the floor in front of the television, her gold eyes reflecting the glow of *Dancing with the Stars* on the screen. Rocky sat nearby, grooming a paw, keeping watch over his friend.

"Hey, Sprinkles." I crouched down to greet her. She didn't move.

Caroline sighed. "Dr. Pryce said she was fine at her last checkup, but I think she's depressed. I've taped the whole season of this show for her and it usually perks her up." Caroline threw herself into a wooden rocker. "It's my fault she's so down. She's been acting out because she hates being in Boston."

"Don't be ridiculous, Caroline. You baby Sprinkles."

"I thought she'd be happy with me but I think she misses Rocky more than anybody."

I didn't want to say anything, but I did think Sprinkles was happier to see Rocky than anyone else. Generally, she was the one basking in adoration, no, *needing* adoration, generously providing an opportunity for others to worship, but lately she followed Rocky everywhere each time she and Caroline came home. I was afraid she'd try to follow him when he squeezed out the torn screen in my bedroom window at night.

"I don't know if Sprinkles will ever adjust to Boston." She sighed.

"You know she can stay here." As soon as I said it, I knew Caroline couldn't do that. She'd so recently lost her brother and her wonderful mom, Buzzy, who'd adopted both

Caroline and Mike when they were kids. The fact was Caroline needed Sprinkles more than Sprinkles needed Caroline.

I considered how uncomplicated my life was now. Caroline was trying to pursue her career in Boston, care for Sprinkles, and manage a kind of dating life with Jack. I was barely managing not to put on weight running an ice cream shop. My career as a librarian at the CIA (with occasional undercover assignments all over the world) was on hold—if not over—and I had no love life, unless you counted Rocky.

Rocky wove himself around my legs. As I reached down to give him a pat, he darted away to sit by Sprinkles.

"And what should I do about Jack?"

I had to laugh. I'd dated more than Caroline, but no one special. Travel was my first love. To be honest, I had terrible taste in men. The story of my life, especially recently, was that I'd made some big mistakes in the man department. Caroline should probably do the exact opposite of any advice I'd give her. I didn't trust myself. I'd been burned badly by a guy named Paolo on my last assignment in Rome. "Luckily, Jack's no Paolo."

I could tell what Caroline and Jack had was special. Sure, the whole long-distance thing—two hours between Penniman and Boston—was a challenge, it was for any couple. They'd been keeping it light, but I knew Caroline, and I knew she was in love.

Sprinkles tolerated Jack at first. Now the little beast had reverted to the behaviors that had gotten her kicked off the cat-show circuit—biting, scratching, general vandalism, and attention seeking. She was a diva to everyone, but she saved her worst for Jack.

Caroline blushed. "I made an appointment with a cat therapist. He's coming to check on her tomorrow."

"There are cat therapists?" Who was I kidding, of course

there were cat therapists. On the bulletin board at the vet's office there were ads for cat masseurs and cat hypnotists. I'd recently seen a sign for a pet personal trainer.

"I know what you're going to say." Caroline sighed and brushed cat hair from her pants. "I'm nuts. I own it. I just have to get her out of her funk."

"I'm serious, Caroline. Sprinkles can stay. She'd have Rocky." Somehow the adventurous, cool black ninja cat was a calming influence on the bad-tempered queen.

"Thanks, Riley, I mean it, but I want to see what the therapist says. And I don't expect you to be here when Doctor Von Furstenburg comes over tomorrow."

"Dr. Von Furstenburg, the cat psychiatrist." I chuckled, then wished Caroline good night and headed for bed. As I drifted off to sleep, the image of Adam's crumpled body surfaced. A one-in-a-million bad-luck death. I couldn't buy it.

I rolled over, determined to push the image and questions away when new questions rose: How was Vye? Where was Vye?

Chapter 15

An indistinct thud and high-pitched feline yowl woke me from dreams of dungeons and keys and beehives.

Caroline yelled, "You darn cat!"

I ran into the hallway and looked in Caroline's open bedroom door. An oil painting of a field of sunflowers lay on the floor next to the toppled easel, a corner of the canvas torn.

"Sprinkles went psycho on my painting!" Caroline moaned.

I glanced around the room. There was no sign of the vandal. "Do you think it can it be repaired?"

Caroline picked up the shredded canvas and sighed. "It's not worth it. Dr. Von Furstenburg can't get here soon enough."

I headed toward the stairs, my senses alert. Sprinkles had ambushed me more than once by darting out of Buzzy's bedroom as I headed downstairs to breakfast but this morning, she'd limited her acting out to Caroline.

Sprinkles sat in the middle of the yellow linoleum kitchen floor, grooming a paw.

"What is up with you?" I said as I spooned her froufrou cat food into her bowl and poured Rocky's kibble. She ignored me and took a few bites, then pushed away her bowl.

She walked to the powder room and looked at me expectantly, her tail swishing like a whip crack.

"I haven't missed this little chore," I said, but still I obeyed and flushed. Sprinkles went in. Physics be damned, she managed to angle herself on the toilet and drink. "To each his own," I muttered. "If your fans could see you now."

After a quick run, I showered and dressed. Caroline insisted housework calmed her and we couldn't afford a housekeeper, so I left her to her vacuuming and headed back outside to sweep the porch.

A classic black Mercedes sedan oozed to a stop in front of the house. Prentiss jumped from the driver's seat and ran around the car to open Maud's door. He wore a Barbour barn jacket over a plaid shirt and jeans along with a tweed driving cap, every inch the fashionable country gentleman.

"Good morning, Riley." Maud was the picture of casual elegance in designer jeans and a caramel suede jacket with fringe that matched her ankle boots. Today her hair was smoothed back in a chignon. How did she manage to look so pulled together, especially after yesterday's shock?

"How are you?" Suddenly self-conscious, I smoothed the purple Udderly Delicious T-shirt I'd tossed on with my yoga pants.

"Fine. We were pulling up at the farm stand when we saw you come out of the house, and I wanted to ask how you're doing," Maud said. "It's not every day one is on scene when a body's discovered."

Actually, this had happened to me more times than I wanted to admit. "I'm fine, really. Thanks."

"And"—she cleared her throat—"I thought it best to confirm that yes, we are still going ahead with the Art Foundation dinner tonight."

I almost choked. Being present when Adam's body had

been found had driven my promise to make Maud a special Scottish-themed ice cream dessert right out of my head. "Yes, of course. I'll deliver it tonight." I remembered the Scottish dessert called cranachan. I'd have to get started on it right away.

"Some, people thought, ah—" Maud paused delicately.

"That it's disrespectful to have the dinner, what with the police still investigating in the castle." Prentiss leaned against the hood of the car.

"The police are still there?" I said.

"They blocked some areas off." Maud sighed and gave the tiniest shrug of her shoulder. "Of course, no one was planning to go to the—" She hesitated.

"The death scene," Prentiss said.

Maud took a deep breath. "The wing of the castle with the dungeon."

"The police still have tape up," Prentiss said. "They came by this this morning and asked more questions. Something's up. There was a different detective, a big guy with a beard, a mountain-man type."

Jack.

I noticed Maud's long fingers toyed over and over with the bee pendant at her breast. Her feelings must be complicated. After all, she and Adam had once been married.

Still, it was best to tread carefully. "I'm sorry for your loss."

"Adam? Thank you. Yes, I lost a lot with Adam. It's best to forge ahead, always forge ahead. The people on the foundation are busy, with full lives, so it's difficult to reschedule." She smoothed the fringe of her jacket. "Also, we, and the police, haven't been able to find Vye. She's no longer at the castle. Have you seen her?"

I shook my head, a surge of concern flooding through me. "Is her SUV still parked at the castle?"

Prentiss folded his arms. "No. Looks like she packed her stuff and did a runner."

Maud shot Prentiss a look. "Prentiss!"

I could only imagine how shaken Vye had been by Adam's death, and her shock must've been compounded by her tangled feelings for him.

"Where did Vye live? Did she"—I hesitated—"live with Adam? Did she go home?"

"She had a room in Adam's brownstone in Brooklyn," Maud said. "I asked his agent to check. She's not there. The car's not there. His agent's on his way here now."

Prentiss looked away, but didn't bother to hide an expression of distaste.

Maud slid her sunglasses on. "If you see her, please tell her we're concerned."

"Of course."

Prentiss said, "I can't wait to see what you whip up tonight. What's it called again? Give us a preview."

I pronounced it slowly. "Cran-a-kan. It has a lovely combination of flavors: toasted oats, raspberry, whiskey, cream, honey—"

"Honey!" Maud beamed. "Oh, you must use some of mine! I insist. I did my last harvest for the year."

"It's in the she shed," Prentiss said.

It would be easy enough to incorporate Maud's honey into the whipped-cream topping, plus I was dying to see the inside of her fairy-tale cottage. "Yes. I'll come by this afternoon."

"Wonderful. If I'm not there, I'll leave it on the front steps of the"—she threw Prentiss a look—"she shed."

He gave her a brilliant, wide smile.

Rocky emerged from the side of the house and circled Maud. "Oh, what a dear! I adore black cats." She crouched and beckoned him. "Here kitty kitty . . ." Rocky sniffed her hand and let himself be petted for a moment then, bored, strutted away.

A scratching sound made us turn. Sprinkles batted at the screen door, staring out at us.

"Now *there's* a cat!" Prentiss laughed. "Looks a bit grumpy. Did someone get up on the wrong side of the bed?"

Sprinkles' flat face had a limited range of expressions, from baleful and grouchy to haughty and supercilious, but now she looked . . . starstruck.

Maud climbed the porch steps to the door. "Is this your cat?"

"In a manner of speaking," I said. "She lets me live here."

Maud laughed, a low-pitched throaty chuckle that made me think of an evil queen in a fairy tale. "Well, hello, gorgeous."

Caroline ran up and picked up Sprinkles, then brought her outside. "Hi, I'm Caroline Spooner and this is Sprinkles."

Sprinkles stretched her head to face Maud. *Please don't lunge at Maud*, I thought.

Maud beamed. "I'm Maud Monaco."

"Prentiss Love." Prentiss waved. "I'll stay over here. I'm not a pet person. Everything makes me sneeze."

Sprinkles turned her supercilious side-eye on Prentiss and dismissed him. Her haughty face turned again to Maud, and to my surprise, Sprinkles let Maud stroke her and even purred. One queen recognizing another. Still, Caroline kept a death grip on Sprinkles' front paws. You never knew if Sprinkles would snap.

"Good thing I love you, Prentiss. You're the only reason I don't get a pet. Well, off to get some things to decorate the old homestead." Maud floated down the stairs, wafting a faint scent of jasmine. "By the way, Caroline, we didn't get a photo of you for the cookbook. Perhaps when we locate Vye, we could do that?"

Caroline blushed. "Yes, of course."

Prentiss wagged his eyebrows at me. "Make it taste like Scotland."

Maud stopped at the car. "Oh, Riley, you still have your badge?"

"Yes, I do."

"I've seen you jogging around town. Keep the badge to show to security. You're welcome to jog around the gardens any time." Maud turned to Caroline. "Both of you. It makes me happy to share the grounds with neighbors."

Jog through the acres of beautiful gardens and rolling hills? "I'd love that. Thank you."

Maud and Prentiss U-turned back to the farm stand and parked directly in front of a No Parking sign.

"Thank God Sprinkles didn't attack." Caroline's shoulders sagged with relief. "She's been in a mood all morning."

"Did you hear the part about the police still being at the castle? Jack's investigating."

Caroline's lips turned down. "He texted that he was wrapped up in a case. But if it's Adam's death, I thought the death was accidental? He had an allergy?"

My mind started churning, replaying what I'd seen yesterday. I longed to sit and think, but Adam's death had completely driven my agreement to create a dessert for Maud's Scottish dinner out of my head. I had to get started. "I'd better head down to the shop."

Caroline took Sprinkles inside. "I'll come down as soon as I get Her Majesty settled."

As I hurried down the lane into the kitchen of the ice cream shop, a new concern surfaced: Vye. She had to be a person of interest for the police. With a sense of dread, I'd recalled the scene I'd witnessed between her and Adam. Dree and Adam had also had a fraught exchange, but it looked like Dree had spent the night outside the castle. Where?

I took a deep breath. "No time for sleuthing. First things first. Dessert."

The last time I'd been in Scotland I'd toured Edinburgh, and afterward, I'd had dinner at a pocket-sized inn on a cobblestoned lane at the foot of the castle. The friendly cook had made me a delicious dessert, richly flavored with whiskey, toasted oats, and sun-ripened raspberries. I scrolled through posts on my Rhode Food travel blog and found the recipe. I'd made it several times before and it was one of my favorite last-minute desserts, simple and delicious. "Cranachan."

"Excuse me?" Caroline came into the kitchen and put on an apron.

I explained my dessert as I gathered ingredients.

"I'm sure it will be magnificent." Caroline's voice took on a wistful note. "You know, I've never been inside a castle. Edinburgh or Moy Mull."

I checked the daily employee schedule and saw that two of the farmhands were scheduled, as well as Flo, Brandon, and Willow, which meant I'd get Luca for free. Plenty of staff. "Why don't you come with me to the castle? At least you could see the kitchen, which is amazing. Oh, I forgot to tell you, Maud gave us some very sharp uniform jackets. I put one in your closet."

Caroline's eyes glowed. "I'd love to. That is, if Sprinkles doesn't need me."

"She'll be fine." I spread a layer of oats on a baking sheet and put them in the oven to toast. "She has Rocky."

Caroline pressed her lips together and smoothed her apron, her nervous tell.

"When does Dr. von Frankenstein come?"

She laughed and threw a towel at me. "Von Furstenburg. Three o'clock."

"The dinner's at seven. Come with me at five thirty," I said. "We'll have time to check out the grounds before I assemble the dessert."

I called Pru and asked her to send over some late raspberries to layer in the dessert and then set to work.

The parking lot filled and our line of customers grew as I gathered the rest of the ingredients for my ice cream variation of the traditional Scottish treat: sugar, double cream, honey, whisky.

As luck would have it, Buzzy had a closet she called the packy more than amply stocked with liquors she used to make her specialty "boozy" ice cream. A lovely amber bottle of scotch whiskey beckoned, and I set it on the kitchen table.

Using alcohol in an ice cream recipe can be tricky, as alcohol lowers the freezing point. I'd carefully infuse the whiskey flavor into rich cream and milk, then work on the layers of toppings. I'd also have to think about how to serve the dessert. I couldn't present a simple bowl of ice cream to Maud's guests. I called Bitsy and explained what I needed.

"So you want to layer it like a trifle?" Bitsy said. "I have the perfect things you can use—mini parfait glasses that I can set on some darling plaid chargers!"

I sighed with relief. "Great. See you this afternoon."

"Don't forget, bring it to the castle kitchen, that's where the dinner will be, in that amazing dining room with Old Ben Clitheroe looking down on everyone from his portrait. I'm so lucky Barry will be handling the reception after the photography professor's presentation at the Barn Gallery. Then he'll close up shop there and come over to help at the foundation dinner at the castle afterward. His reception's easy, the usual WCF—"

"WCF?"

"Wine cheese fruit. We can do those in our sleep." Bitsy's voice warmed. "That's why the ice cream reception was so much fun. You know, we should talk. The ice cream hors d'oeuvres we did last night are all over social media, and I've already had people asking about them for parties. I'd love to use your ice cream again."

"I'd like that." I'd only been developing my own ice cream flavors for a couple of months, so praise from a successful and talented caterer like Bitsy made me glow with satisfaction.

She sounded so upbeat that I wondered if she'd heard about Adam's death. "Bitsy, you heard about Adam Blasco, right?"

"Yes," she said, "but if Maud wants to carry on, then we carry on."

"Right. See you later."

Maud was carrying on. But wasn't it cold of Maud to continue with this dinner when her ex-husband's body had been discovered only yesterday? Well, Prentiss said they'd divorced years ago. But then why invite him to do a show at her art festival? Maybe it was good business? There was a hard-heartedness about Maud that gave me pause.

I mulled how I'd incorporate Maud's honey into my cranachan. There was no time to get it and mix it into the ice cream base because I needed several hours for it to harden. I'd use Luca's honey for the ice cream itself and I'd make an extra whipped cream with Maud's. A cloud of whipped cream infused with Maud's honey and a bit of the whiskey would be a nice touch and would take only a few moments to make.

After I pulled the toasted oats out of the oven to cool, prepared the whisky ice cream mixture, and put it in the freezer to harden, my thoughts returned to Vye. Where had she gone? Where had she been last night? Did she have anything to do with Adam's death? Even in the short time I'd known her, I liked her. I shook off the last question and joined Caroline behind the counter. We scooped nonstop until three, with only a short break when Pru brought sandwiches for lunch. Caroline looked at her watch. "I've got to get up to the house for Sprinkles' appointment."

Seeing Caroline's worried expression, I gave her arm a reassuring squeeze. "Good luck."

Flo joined me in the shop, tying on an apron that was printed with disco dancing cows and the words "Mooove It." "I heard that you're going to Moy Mull tonight."

I stopped wondering long ago how word got around. "Yep. Bringing some lovely whiskey-infused ice cream for the Scottish dinner." I told her about the cranachan.

"Oh, that sounds good. We must put that on the menu." Flo waited on a customer and topped a pumpkin spice sundae with a generous scoop of caramel, whipped cream, and a heaping spoonful of candied pecans. After she handed it to the customer, she whispered, "I heard that Vye packed up and ran off, and the police are looking for her. I wonder where she is."

"That makes two of us."

Flo frowned. "I mean, she worked for him. Wasn't he her mentor? Why would she run away?"

Later, I turned over Flo's questions as I hurried up the lane to the farmhouse. Maybe stepping in for Adam and giving the presentation gave Vye the confidence and impetus she needed to make a break from him. After all, she'd been doing all the work and he'd been taking all the credit. Maybe she'd had enough. But the timing of her escape couldn't look worse.

I kept going over our discovery of Adam's body, especially the locked door. It was impossible. The longer I thought about it, the more convinced I was that Adam's death hadn't been some lightning-strike rare death.

Wasp. Bee.

It was intentional. It was murder.

I hesitated for a moment, then called the Penniman Police Department. I had to tell Jack what I'd seen.

"Penniman Police Services." A familiar voice answered, rich and throaty with a hint of sit-next-to-me-and-spill-the-tea. I winced. It was Tillie, the police department secretary I'd seen volunteering at Moy Mull—the other reason I hesitated to call the police department. While Tillie had given me some very off-the-books help with my last murder investigation, she was the loosest of cannons, and I didn't want her to know I was sleuthing again.

"Hi, Tillie—"

"Riley Rhodes," she breathed. "You were at Moy Mull! This must be about that dead photographer! I knew it! No wonder Jack went to Farmington! It's murder!"

Say what you will about Tillie, the woman could put two and two together. Farmington was the location of the office of the state's chief medical examiner.

"Has Jack returned?" I asked.

She lowered her voice, adopting a dry, by-the-books tone, a signal that a law enforcement coworker was nearby. "No, would you like to leave a detailed message?"

That was the last thing I wanted to do. "Please tell him I called. Thanks." I hung up, berating myself for tipping my hand to Tillie.

The screened front door burst open and a rotund man in a tan suit with a bow tie stormed out. Caroline ran after him holding out a brown leather case. "Dr. Von Furstenburg, wait, you forgot your briefcase!"

He stopped and yanked it from her hand. As he did, I caught a flash of his knee through a tear in his pants. "Prin-

cess Hortense Ophelia Tater Tot"—uh oh, he was using
Sprinkles' show-cat name—"is completely out of control
because she's spoiled rotten. I'm sending you the bill for my
pants. Good day."

He got into a Mini Cooper with a license plate that read
FELIN FINE, slammed the door, and tore off.

Rocky darted around the corner of the house and followed as I climbed the stairs with Caroline.

Inside, Sprinkles sat at her bowl, scarfing down her food,
unconcerned by the mayhem she'd unleashed.

"What happened?"

Caroline sighed. "It was going pretty well. As long as
we were admiring her and talking about how beautiful she
is, she behaved. Dr. von Furstenburg said that she may have
been missing the adulation from her glory days on the cat-
show circuit."

"Adulation?" Laughter bubbled up inside me but I pressed
my lips together and turned around so I could get control
of myself. True, Sprinkles had been a champion on the cat-
show circuit, but as she aged she'd grown increasingly bad
tempered, biting judges, scratching, peeing, and unleashing
other unhinged diva behavior.

Caroline scooped up her curly hair and twisted it into
a thick bun as she sank into a chair. "When the conversation switched to behavior modification, I swear she understood every word. She turned on Doctor von Furstenburg,
and well"—a blush surged up her cheeks and her voice
got small—"she got her little teeth into his pants and tore
them."

"Yikes." It was awful for Caroline, but then the image of
Dr. von Furstenburg running for the car surfaced. I struggled
to smother my laughter and keep my expression serious.

We watched the little beast, sitting quietly now, wondering at the demon fury lurking under the heavenly fluffy

white cloud of fur. Rocky padded into the kitchen. The two made eye contact and then together they sauntered down the hallway to the parlor.

"That was a bust." Caroline shook her head and her hair fell back down on her shoulders. "An expensive bust."

"We'll figure it out, Caroline. Let's get your mind off Sprinkles for a while. Ready to go to Moy Mull?"

Chapter 16

Caroline's expression had been serious as I told her all I'd seen and learned about Adam's death on the drive to the castle, but she turned to me with a mischievous look as I parked Sadie in the gravel service lot of Moy Mull. "Do you remember that night I had to rescue you after Manuel Lizzaralde dared you to climb up the wall of the castle? And then he couldn't even make it two feet himself?" She doubled over with laughter.

"How could I forget? I spent an hour waiting for him up on that porch roof!"

We hefted our boxes of supplies and walked over to the trellis, where I ran my hand along the craggy stone wall of the castle. Climbing the walls of Moy Mull had been the challenge undertaken by generations of Penniman kids. The rough stones did afford handholds, and the wall to the porch in the front of the castle was the easiest route, with several decorative flourishes to hold onto and a comfortable perch on the porch roof at the end. This side of the castle, with walls uninterrupted until the balconies of the library and Maud's suite, would be much more in the wheelhouse of an experienced rock climber.

"I bet you could still climb it." Caroline nudged me. "Dare ya."

I looked up the irregular wall and laughed. "Oh no. I'm not sixteen anymore!" We headed to the kitchen.

Caroline spun, taking in the castle, the garden, and the long view down the lawn to the Barn Gallery. "Remember how it looked back then, all covered with vines and graffiti, and beer bottles and trash everywhere? Maud worked wonders."

I pressed my badge to the reader by the kitchen door and we headed inside, where we were immediately hit with a wall of sound and energy generated by Bitsy's bustling catering crew.

"Hi, Riley! And you're Caroline Spooner, right?" Bitsy took the box from Caroline's arms and set it on a counter. "I knew your mom, Buzzy."

"Nice to meet you." Caroline's jaw dropped and Bitsy followed her eyes to the almost-ceiling-high fireplace.

Bitsy smiled. "Wait until you see the rest of the place."

I stowed the ice cream in the freezer, cream and raspberries in the refrigerator, and the box with the rest of the ingredients for the topping on the last few feet of free work space on the wooden countertop. "Maud wants me to incorporate some of her honey, so I'm going to get it now. Then we can get to work. It's a pretty simple recipe."

Bitsy showed me the tiny parfait glasses and chargers we'd use for my version of cranachan. The little glasses were rimmed with gold and picked up the gold tones in the plaid chargers. "Got them at an estate sale. What do you think?"

"They're perfect," I said. "Thank you."

"Your dessert's quick, easy, different, and has a story. I like it," Bitsy said as she deftly tugged us out of the path of a guy carrying a crate of vegetables. "The presentation at the gallery's supposed to end at six. Wine and cheese if folks want it there at the barn, then they're free to walk through the gardens. Dinner at seven for the lucky ducks on the Foundation Board." Bitsy may have been a woman wearing a tam-o'-shanter and a fuchsia pink plaid dress with a frilly pink apron, but she organized with military precision. "Maud had to make some changes because of, you know . . ." She waved a spoon in the direction of the stairs to the dungeon. "Originally she'd planned a little tour, but that section of the castle's closed off, of course. The guests will all enter through the front door, past that small bell-desk area that just screams the old hotel, but what can you do?"

Closed off? That meant no one else would be there to see me check out the dungeon. "It's okay if we take a quick look at the dining room and great room? I promise we won't get in your way."

"Okay by me. Maud's in her garden and everyone's at the talk. The president of the Moy Mull Art Foundation manages the talk, and Maud hosts the dinner party. You know"—Bitsy lowered her voice—"Maud did seem distracted, but having someone die in your house would do that to a person. But at the dinner she'll be Maud, the Lady of the Manor. Just wait till you see the dining room, she's gone all Scottish hunting lodge. Tartan. Dozens of candles. Fire in the fireplace." She turned to a guy with shaggy dark hair who was so thin his pink Creative Caterers jacket hung on him. "Travis, is the fire laid?"

He gave her a quick thumbs-up as he left the room.

"That's Barry's son, Travis." Bitsy beamed. "He's taken to the catering business like a dream."

Caroline and I followed Travis's path through the swinging kitchen doors. I showed her the dumbwaiter and we passed by the steps that led down to the dungeon. A velvet rope was set up to prevent access. I started toward it, but Caroline tugged me across the hallway. "Riley, look!"

Maud had gone with a harvest cornucopia theme on the long dining room table set for thirty with glittering crystal wineglasses, gold chargers, and tartan napkins. A tablecloth of rich garnet red was topped with dozens of pumpkins of white, orange, and gold, interspersed with gourds, miniature bundles of wheat, dozens of brass candlesticks, and even bird feathers. Running through the arrangement was a black ribbon dotted with tiny ivory cameos I'd seen before, on the portrait of Oona in the Great Room. One of Bitsy's staff nodded to us as she fussed over a crystal goblet at a place setting.

"The feathers," Caroline said. "Grouse. Has to be grouse. Isn't that a Scottish bird?"

"With Maud's attention to detail, I would bet it is."

Caroline sighed. "You know this room is the time period I love. It's chock-full of amazing pieces. And look"—she pointed—"Ben Clitheroe even had his own coat of arms."

The wooden shield above a massive sideboard was painted with two lavender thistles in the upper-left-hand corner, two entwined crimson hearts in the upper-right-hand corner, all above a large gold lyre at the pointed base.

"Thistles for Scotland," I said, "hearts for Oona, the lyre for his other love, music? I've seen that motif in other parts of the house." *On the dungeon's lock.*

We stepped into the great room. While Caroline gaped at the furniture and artwork, I went into the lobby and marveled at the great carved front door of the castle. The lobby was surprisingly bare. There was a counter with a fresh arrangement of Montauk daisies and dried pink hydrangea, but Bitsy was right, the flowers couldn't mask that this area had been a bell desk from the castle's hotel days. I peeked beyond, to a cloakroom and a hallway with evenly spaced, closed doors. Hotel rooms. The long, empty hallway was the creepiest thing I'd seen at the castle.

One of the doors opened suddenly, making me jump. Dree exited her room, her long hair obscuring her face as she dropped a tray outside her door and went back inside, letting the door slam shut behind her. Two wine bottles on the tray clinked as they toppled over.

A petite but broad-shouldered woman in a housekeeping uniform of black dress and white apron walked briskly down the hall from the other direction. Her hair, tightly pulled back in a bun, spoke to professionalism, but she put her hands on her hips and shook her head before picking up the tray and taking it with her back down the hall.

I'd be exasperated too. What I'd seen of Dree's actions was the embodiment of treating a friend's home as a hotel. Was Dree truly a friend? I cast my thoughts back to the party at the Barn Gallery. I hadn't seen Maud and Dree together once.

I returned to Caroline. She stood at the foot of Oona's painting, completely enthralled. "Oh, Riley, I'm in love. Look at Oona's cute little terrier!" Caroline pushed her curls from her forehead. "I remember one of the ghost stories about the castle, about how her little dog cries for her on the full moon."

"That's Jamie. The dog's included in some of the tales of the castle," Tony said as he descended the stairs. The historian wore Highlands formal, a kilt paired with a dinner jacket that barely contained his broad shoulders and biceps. Caroline's jaw dropped and mine almost did, too, at the accurate and very handsome vision from the castle's past. "A pining dog's an element in stories about the Weeping Lady on both sides of the Atlantic. Hi, Riley."

I pulled myself back to the present. "Hi, Tony. You didn't want to go to the gallery talk?"

He shook his head. "I've had enough of Adam Blasco. Sorry, that didn't come out right." He chuckled. "I should say I much prefer history to modern photography."

"I know what you mean," Caroline said. "His work's not my cup of tea."

"Oh, I'm sorry, Caroline Spooner, this is Tony Ortiz," I said. "He's pulling together an exhibit on Moy Mull's history for the opening of the house tours next year."

"Nice to meet you," Tony said as they shook hands. "You're both from Penniman, right? I'm researching stories from the folks from the town, their viewpoint on the castle. Perhaps you could come back and tell me what you know and I'll show you the rest of the house."

"One of my employees at Udderly is president of the Penniman Historical Society," I said. "Geraldine Hunt. I can have her contact you and I'll see if I can think of anyone else who might be helpful."

"That would be great." He spread his arms. "I didn't put my cards in my kilt, but I do have my cell phone."

We laughed and exchanged numbers.

Reluctantly, I checked my watch. "I have to get the honey from Maud's cottage and start dessert." And, I didn't add out loud, I wanted to get down to the dungeon for a look around.

Tony said, "I'm going to walk down to the reception at the Barn Gallery. Don't tell anyone I skipped the talk." He waved and exited through the front door.

"Come on." I pulled Caroline through the great room and the dining room but pulled up short at the stairs to the dungeon. I could hear voices at the bottom of the stairs as a security guard moved into view. I jerked back. "Darn."

"What are you up to? Forget it, don't tell me," Caroline said.

We hurried back through the controlled chaos of the kitchen, dodging Bitsy's crew as they chopped and sauteed and stirred. As we stepped outside, Caroline nudged me. "Tony was cute and he was wearing a kilt." Caroline knew my weakness for men in kilts.

"Ah, but no accent. Actually, I detected a bit of Midwestern twang," I teased.

She grinned. "You've always been sucker for accents."

"You know me so well." So shoot me, Caroline was right. An accent, especially a Scots accent? My knees go weak.

She gave me a sly look as we crossed the gravel parking lot. "You know, Dr. Pryce asked about you when I took Sprinkles in for her physical last week."

"Really?" I was surprised, and I'll admit, pleased. Dr. Liam Pryce was Penniman's answer to St. Francis, *People*'s Sexiest Man Alive, and any other incredibly handsome man you could name. Plus he had another attraction beyond his love of animals, athlete's build, movie-star looks, single status, and good nature: the remnants of a soft Jamaican accent.

"He was polite enough to ask about me so he also has good manners," I said. "Add that to his list of attributes."

"Big brown eyes. Chiseled jaw," Caroline teased. "He's a runner, too! Flo said he cooks at the homeless shelter sometimes."

"He's too perfect. Did I tell you I actually saw him help a little old lady across the street?"

Caroline punched my arm. "Hey, he knows who you are, and cared enough to ask about you."

"I'll capitalize on that next time I see him," I said. "Though with my luck, he has an insane wife locked up in his attic."

We stopped at the open gate of Maud's garden. "Oh, Riley, this is like a movie set!"

We approached Maud's cottage, marveling at the slate roof, leaded windows hung with lace curtains, and heady fragrance of the late-blooming roses that covered its walls. From the dovecote behind the cottage, I could've sworn I heard a bird call. Several marigold plants in ceramic pots decorated the front steps, but I didn't see a jar of honey.

"Maud say she'd leave a jar on the steps if she wasn't here," I said.

"She's here. I saw her walk past the window," Caroline said.

We climbed the steps, careful not to disturb the pots that sat on each. A brass bell on a leather pull was mounted by the door, and even the pull was embossed with roses and bees. As I reached for it, I noticed a security camera shielded by some climbing ivy. I blinked. I'd been so charmed by the cottage, I didn't expect this intrusion from the modern world. I lifted my hand to the bell pull but froze as I heard Maud's voice, strained, almost a shriek, through an open window. "Prentiss, it was right there in the cabinet. I put it there myself and now it's missing."

Caroline and I exchanged glances and stepped back from the door.

I didn't hear Prentiss reply and realized Maud must be talking on the phone because we could hear only her side of the conversation.

"I don't know what to do, Prentiss." Maud swore. "What if the police find out? I knew, I knew as soon as I saw that drone!" Caroline's eyes widened behind her glasses and she tugged my arm. I put a finger to my lips.

Drone? I looked up at the sky, thinking of high-tech spy drones, then I caught sight of Maud's apiary. Drone, a kind of bee. The bee, not a wasp. Everything shifted into place but also sent a shock through me. *Maud knew Adam's death was not an accident.*

Maud moaned. "I know, Mama said the truth shall set you free. But, Prentiss, what if it doesn't?" Caroline and I shared another shocked look.

After a moment, Maud continued. "Well, I'm not doing it tonight. I'll get through the dinner party first. I'll barely be able to do that."

Caroline jerked her head to the castle and mouthed, *Let's go.* I shook my head. If we moved, Maud might see us through the open window and realize that she'd been overheard. Caroline tugged again and stepped backward, knocking one of the pots off the step with a loud thud. Her shocked eyes met mine and she scrambled to right it.

Chapter 17

M aud muttered, "I have to go."

I lifted my hand to the door pull as Caroline set the plant upright and frantically brushed away soil.

A breath later, Maud opened the door. I pasted a smile on my face and pretended I was just about to pull the cord by the door. "Oh, hello, Maud. We're here for the honey."

Maud was a good actress; a pleasant, welcoming smile curved her lips. "Hello. Yes, of course. Caroline don't worry about that plant. Please come in."

The only signs of Maud's distress were an unnatural brightness of her eyes and the pale knuckles on her hands as they clutched her bee pendant. "Oh, yes, the honey," she repeated. An expression of relief relaxed her features. "This way to the work room. You'll have to forgive me for not giving you a full tour. I must dress for dinner and I'm running late."

"Of course."

Caroline and I followed. I was so rattled that I didn't notice much of the homey living room beyond a massive fireplace, an overstuffed couch, and a rocking chair.

We moved through a whitewashed room with long wood counters over stainless steel cabinets with glass doors, a pristine combination of farmhouse and laboratory. On a broad worktable, I noted a marble mortar and pestle next to a microscope, two scales, and rows of empty glass bottles. An advertising poster with a close up of Maud's lovely face was set on a wooden easel in a corner.

Maud rushed ahead and moved the easel in front of one of the cabinets. Caroline complimented Maud on the poster, in which Maud held an amber pot of a creamy lotion under the words "Bee-U." I tried to angle myself to see what was in the cabinet Maud had just hidden and keep my expression neutral as Maud's words sank in: *a vial was missing.*

Had she just hidden a cabinet full of vials of bee venom?

My mind whirled—bee venom. Who knew Adam was allergic? Maud, his ex-wife certainly did, and so did Prentiss. He'd told me about the wasp nest removed before Adam's arrival. Vye knew—she'd told me at the photo shoot. I couldn't see behind the poster without moving it but I would bet there were syringes there, too, though in any event, it wasn't difficult to get syringes. They were sold in every drugstore and on the internet.

Maud's voice recalled me from my thoughts. "I store my honey right through here." We followed her into a room where the dirty work was done, with roughhewn wooden tables, an old stove, and racks of beekeeping equipment and tools. Several white, full-length bee suits and netted hats hung from pegs by the back door. Maud opened an antique jelly cabinet and handed me a jar of golden amber honey. "I can't wait to taste this in the dessert tonight. Thank you again."

Instead of leading us back through the cottage, she opened the door to the outside. As we thanked her and stepped down stone steps into the growing dusk, I glanced up and saw the gleam of the lens of another security camera on the roofline here, too, though this one was almost completely obscured by ivy. I should tell Maud to trim the ivy, but instead I filed this away. We headed up the garden path, passing the same housekeeper I'd seen earlier. She carried a large garment bag and nodded pleasantly, but there was something about her that made me turn back. She stood on Maud's steps, watching us.

My heart pounded as Caroline and I hurried up the path. "I'm not sure what we heard back there, but . . ." Her voice trailed off. We looked back at the light glowing in the cottage windows, the picture of tranquility. The housekeeper had pulled the door shut firmly behind her. Caroline and I hustled out of the garden and I pulled her into the shadows of its wall.

"What do you think that call was about?" Caroline whispered.

I started to speak, but caught sight of the burning end of a cigarette by the kitchen door and held my finger to my lips. Dree Venditti stepped in a glowing circle cast by security lighting.

A group crossed the lawn from the Barn Gallery. These were the lucky members of the Foundation Board invited to dinner by the Mistress of Moy Mull and they were dressed for the occasion, most wearing evening dress or outfits with touches of plaid. Gallery director Max Truwitt escorted the woman with silvery blond hair I'd seen him with at the exhibit opening. I wondered if she was his wife, and if she'd seen him flirting with Dree. She chatted excitedly with a woman wearing a long plaid skirt.

Dree tossed her cigarette into the gravel and joined the group rounding the castle to the front door. She and Max didn't greet each other.

I checked my watch. "We have time," I whispered. "Let's walk around the lawn. I have a lot to tell you." I filled Caroline in on everything that had been going through my mind since the discovery of Adam's body. "Did you notice when Maud moved the poster in front of that glass cabinet?"

Caroline shook her head. "I thought she was making room for us to pass. Why?"

"I bet she has bee venom in there."

Caroline clutched my arm and whispered, "You think she killed Adam? By injecting him with bee venom?"

Doubt rankled. "I'm not sure. She seemed truly upset on the phone just now. Surprised even."

Caroline and I tossed around theories as we circled the lawn. We passed several twisting paths that led to the small cottages Maud rented to artists, each named with Moy Mull's Scottish heritage in mind: Loch Lomond, Highland Heather, Nessie. Tucked deep in a stand of sprawling old rhododendron by Loch Lomond Cottage was a charming stone wishing well covered by old roses that perfumed the air with a spicy, heady fragrance.

A few attendees from the gallery talk lingered on the steps of the Barn Gallery. Two Creative Catering vans were parked by the rear door, and a security guard watched as a staffer carried a box out of the kitchen.

As we turned back to the castle, I marveled at the scene Maud had set for her guests. Six-foot-high metal torches had been placed along the path to the front porch of the castle, their flames casting orange and yellow light on the rough stone walls. Spoiling the illusion was a blue Buick with New York plates parked at an odd angle in the circular drive.

Maud, setting a scene. Could Maud have been acting when we overheard her earlier? Had she seen us approach the cottage? Was that phone call staged for our benefit? Her shock upon finding Adam's body had seemed genuine, but she'd been a top a model, a woman accustomed to creating illusion.

Chapter 18

I didn't have time for more musing as we rejoined the bustling caterers in the castle kitchen. I pulled heavy cream from the refrigerator and started prepping my dessert. I didn't mind not being a guest at Maud's extravagant dinner party. I couldn't imagine how I'd make small talk with Maud's words in my head.

"Riley, you're a million miles away," Caroline said in a low voice. "I know you, you're plotting how to get back into the cottage."

And the dungeon. I plugged in a mixer and smiled ruefully. "Unfortunately Maud has security cameras on it."

"All you have to do is tell Jack. Let the police handle it." Caroline opened the jar of Maud's honey. Under ordinary circumstances, I'd be able to admire the regal design of the Moy Mull Apiary label, with a gold crown over the Moy Mull heraldic shield, and the gorgeous amber honey inside, but now I had to push away the thought that the woman responsible for it might be a murderer.

I checked my cell. "If only he'd return my phone calls," I muttered, but I wasn't going to complain too loudly of this to Caroline.

"You girls quit gossiping and get to work now. Time to

prep dessert." Bitsy brought us a tray of parfait glasses. "Let's make these look fabulous."

Together we set up an assembly line: Caroline scooped ice cream, I layered in raspberries and toasted oatmeal, and Bitsy topped everything with the cream. She took taste and fanned herself. "This cream's so delicious and light I'm going to faint. I can't believe how simple it is, too. Oh, look." She dug in a box of odds and ends—kitchen tools, spools of tartan ribbon, bottles of spice—and unearthed a small bottle. "When Maud said 'Scotland,' I thought, what's Scottish, right? Kilts, tartan, heather. I got this from my supplier." She turned the bottle so we could see the label.

" 'Culinary-grade heather,' " I read.

Bitsy chortled. "Right? Who knew?" She sprinkled the purple petals on the cream and the charger. "Just enough to make it special."

She signaled to her servers and they took the desserts into the dining room.

"And that's why she gets the big bucks," I said.

We followed and watched from the doorway as the servers entered the room with almost military precision. Bitsy announced the dessert, and even pronounced "cranachan" correctly.

Maud took a taste and nodded approval. "Fabulous."

I threw a longing glance at the stairs beyond the velvet rope, but there were too many people around. We went back into the kitchen to finish cleaning up and gather our things, and I gave the half-empty jar of honey to Bitsy. "That I can use." Her eyes gleamed. "Honey with a pedigree!"

Barry wrapped her in a tired bear hug. "We're all set. Everything from the Barn Gallery reception's packed up."

Bitsy savored the hug for a moment, then looked up at him. "You didn't forget the tables in the lobby? The tablecloths?" Bitsy broke from the hug and gave one last wipe to an already shining countertop.

"Nope. All set."

"You're the best, babe." Bitsy turned to us. "Thank you so much for that delicious dessert. You're going to send me the recipe, right? Now I'm gonna go home and soak my feet."

"I will," I promised.

As Caroline and I went outside, I breathed deep of the moist night air. The sounds of a successful party in progress—music, conversation, laughter—streamed from the front of the castle and we followed. Through a window I saw Prentiss in his white jacket complete with red carnation, suave as James Bond. Well, no one was that suave, but Prentiss wore it surprisingly well. Maud wore a gray dress with the sheen of taffeta, with a long tartan scarf draped around her shoulder and waist, a tartan that matched the one worn by Oona in her portrait. She showed no trace of the intense emotion we'd witnessed at the cottage.

As Caroline and I headed back to Sadie she said, "We have to tell Jack what Maud said."

We got in the car and headed home. "I called him earlier. Hopefully Tillie passed on my message, though . . ." I turned to Caroline. "You're his girlfriend. You can call him any time, right?"

Caroline dipped her head. "He works constantly and never gets enough sleep. I hate to wake him. Riley, I barely know how to be a girlfriend, let alone a cop's girlfriend."

"Has he texted you?"

Caroline checked her phone. The guard at the security shack waved as we drove past.

She shook her head, and I felt her disappointment.

"He's busy, obviously," I said, stressing the last word. "You have to tell him that your crazy friend will talk to him

tomorrow with brilliant insights into the mysterious death at
Moy Mull."

She smiled and tucked away her phone.

"I need to think some more," I said. I didn't know for
sure that bee venom was in that cabinet, but I had a strong
suspicion. Would that be enough for Jack to investigate?

We closed at nine o'clock in the fall, cutting back from
eleven on summer nights, so all was quiet and dark at Udderly. As I parked Sadie at the farmhouse, my headlights
illuminated a silver SUV. Its door opened as I exited the car.

A security light on the side porch was triggered by the
driver's movement, and its bright beam backlit a short figure
in an army jacket and black watch cap.

"Sorry," Vye said. "I don't have anywhere else to go. Can
I please stay here tonight?"

Chapter 19

Sprinkles and Rocky regarded Vye with typical feline nonchalance as she hunched over her second bowl of chili. I served her another slice of cornbread and Caroline poured her a cup of tea.

"Thanks." Vye pulled off her black watch cap and ran her fingers through her matted blue hair. "It's been a long day."

I took the seat next to her at the kitchen table. "Where have you been, Vye? Everyone's been trying to reach you."

"I know, I've had everyone calling me. Prentiss, Maud." Vye sighed. "Nicky Dawson."

To my blank look she explained, "Nicky is Adam's agent, lawyer, go-to guy. I turned off my phone because after I heard about Adam, I lost it. I'd been so angry with him." She waved her hat toward the farm across the road. "He was so interested in Willow. Then when he went missing, I was so worried that something happened to him, or that he was with Willow. Then I had to do that talk and then I hear he's dead. I still can't believe it. A stupid bee sting."

Caroline and I exchanged a careful glance.

"Didn't he have an EpiPen?" Caroline asked.

Vye nodded. "He had a few. One in his studio. One in

the camera bag and he always had his camera bag with him, always. We carried a spare in the car. I know Maud keeps bees"—her voice strained—"so I checked his bag to be sure it was there. Guess it didn't matter in the end."

"How did you hear all this?" I said. "I thought you didn't talk to anyone."

She showed me a chain of texts on her phone. She'd texted Prentiss: HOW DID HE DIE? Prentiss replied: BEE STING. ADAM DIDN'T HAVE EPIPEN WITH HIM.

Caroline sat down, pulled Sprinkles onto her lap, and stroked her cloud of fur. Rocky nudged Vye's leg and Vye picked him up. "What happened to your ear, little guy?"

"Rocky's a rescue." I sipped my tea. "He'd had a rough life and lived off the land until I found him this summer. Or maybe he found me."

"A survivor." Rocky leapt down, and Sprinkles slid off Caroline's lap. Vye's expression relaxed as she watched the two felines retire to their parlor.

"Where have you been, Vye?" I asked.

Vye leaned back in her chair. "I had to get out. I couldn't stay in that castle, not with Adam dead there. I packed my stuff and"—she threw up her hands—"drove. I went up some back road, got lost, slept in the car, drove around some more. But I guess I have to face reality. Adam's dead. I don't know what I'll do now. I can't stay in that creepy castle, though."

"You can stay here," Caroline said. "There's an extra bedroom."

Vye's voice was small. "Thank you."

Later that night I listened to the house settle, squirrels scrabble on the roof, the water in the shower turn off, and Caroline pad to her room. She shut her door firmly, keeping Sprinkles inside. I could just make out the squeaking of the frame of the old brass bed across the hall. Vye was having trouble falling asleep and had tossed and turned for an hour.

Rocky's eyes glowed amber in the bit of starlight that edged the shades. My room had been Caroline's brother's, but when I'd redecorated it—painted the walls, replaced the mattress, brought in a soft emerald green silk duvet I'd bought in a Malaysian boutique, plus the quilt my grandma Riley had made for me—I'd run out of time before I had a chance to select curtains. Running Udderly took up every spare moment.

Maud's words rang in my mind: *"I knew as soon as I saw that drone."* Knew that Adam had been killed, that this was no accidental death, no death by bee sting. So that meant she didn't kill him. But did she have a guilty conscience because she wanted her ex-husband dead? If she hated him enough to kill, then why have his show at her estate, why invite him to take the photos for her cookbooks?

Why couldn't Vye sleep? I, too, tossed uneasily. Was it a guilty conscience? I'd heard Vye threaten Adam, heard him belittle her. Had we let a killer into the house? If she'd killed Adam, she was a good actress, pretending to be saddened and shaken now. My gut told me her emotions were genuine, but the memory of my former boyfriend Paolo surfaced. My gut had failed me then. Was it failing me now?

Paolo. I'd been on an assignment at the US Embassy in Rome, working in an office that was stuffed with antiques and antiquities. I'd been summoned to the HR office by a phone call, and I'd left Paolo waiting for me in my office. When I returned in a panic, after discovering that the HR office had closed two hours earlier, Paolo was gone along with a small figurine of a goddess that had been on display. She'd been worth a lot of money. The only thing that kept me from more than a reprimand in my file was a recording of the theft by a security camera I didn't know was hidden in my office ceiling.

I tossed onto my side. I recalled Paolo's tousled curls, his lush lips, the sparkle in his eyes, his beautifully sculpted hands, the hands of an artist. Hah! Con artist. I stroked Rocky. No, my gut hadn't failed me. No, I had to admit, I'd discounted and dismissed the alarms. He was dangerous and I'd played with fire. That was the worst part of the whole Paolo affair. Caroline's eyes always radiated sadness when the subject of Paolo came up—pity that I'd been fooled. I hadn't been fooled. I'd fooled myself.

What had been Adam's appeal? It wasn't physical charm, unless you liked glowering, short, skinny guys who only wore black and looked at you with eyes that seemed to peel away your skin. His personality was powerful. He'd poured the charm on for Willow, I'd seen it myself. It was the allure of genius that some people found irresistible. Look at Hemingway and Picasso, they'd had scores of relationships. They'd burned every one.

Vye had been burned. I recalled the secret she'd shared with me. Was it even true? Had she taken Adam's later photos? Only an artist would know, or someone who worked with art. Good thing one was sleeping in the bedroom next to mine.

Chapter 20

On a normal Monday, I'd take my usual five-mile run and do errands and banking for the shop. Today I'd fit in a trip to the police station. Jack hadn't called me and I was starting to wonder if Tillie had relayed my message.

Also on a typical Monday, Caroline would head off early to Boston to beat the traffic—she's a nervous driver. But today I'd asked Caroline to go to the Adam Blasco exhibit with me. I didn't tell her, but I wanted to do an experiment to see if there was any difference between Adam's early and later works, the ones Vye said she took. Not that I didn't trust Vye, but I knew it paid to trust and verify.

After my run I headed upstairs. There was no sound when I passed Vye's closed door and knocked on Caroline's bedroom door.

"Come in." Caroline set a stack of clothes in her suitcase and checked her schedule. "I have to be back in Boston at two o'clock, but that gives me time this morning." I knew she was still worried about Sprinkles and bummed she hadn't seen Jack, and that sticking around for a few hours would give her a chance to spend time with both.

"Have you had any word from Jack?" I asked.

"Just a text that he's busy." She sighed.

He'll be busier after I talk to him, I thought. "I'm going to grab a shower."

"I'm going to make omelets for breakfast," Caroline said as she went downstairs.

Caroline had the omelets ready when Vye, bleary eyed, dressed in plaid pajama bottoms and a tattered, oversized T-shirt printed with Andy Warhol's soup cans, came downstairs, accepted a cup of coffee, and sagged onto a chair. "You can tell I'm a city girl, right? Adam and I wouldn't get up till noon some days. Then on other days he'd be wired and work all day and night. Once he worked for thirty-six hours straight."

Caroline served Vye an omelet. "Hope you like spinach and cheddar cheese?"

"Great, thanks." Vye dug in as Caroline started the dishes.

Sprinkles sat at the door to the bathroom, swishing her tail with impatience. "Hang on, Hortense." I went inside and flushed.

Vye chuckled. "I had a cat that liked the toilet water, too. Her name was Des Moines."

I poured myself a cup of coffee and topped up Vye's. "That's an unusual name for a cat."

Vye rubbed her eyes. "I haven't thought of her in years. Des Moines. When I was little, I thought that was the most beautiful name in the world. Des Moines, as if it were one word."

Sprinkles emerged from the bathroom and heaved herself upstairs.

"You're from Iowa?" Caroline asked as she hung up a dish towel.

"Yeah." Vye's phone dinged and she read a text.

"Excuse me, I have to finish packing," Caroline said as she went upstairs.

Vye looked up from her phone. "Maud texted. Nicky Dawson's coming to Moy Mull this afternoon at three o'clock. I'm not sure why but he wants to talk to us. Maybe about Adam's will?" She hesitated, then said in a small voice, "Riley, would you please come with me? I think I may need an ally. Nicky's always treated me like dirt."

An excuse to return to the castle? "Sure," I said.

"Sprinkles!" Caroline shrieked and I rushed upstairs.

Sprinkles had decided to tear through Caroline's suitcase, tossing socks and shirts to the floor, leaving them covered in white hair. While Caroline examined her clothes for any further signs of Sprinkles' mischief and repacked, I headed down to Udderly and checked the schedule. Gerri and Flo had the early shift, so I'd be able to relay Tony the hunky historian's request to Gerri when they arrived.

We opened at eleven and it was only 9:45, so I did a quick check of flavors in the shop's dipping cases. As a flavor ran out, my staff erased its listing from the chalkboard on the wall behind the counter. We were keeping up well, easing off the frenetic pace of summer when the lines went out the door and traffic backed up Fairweather Road. I pulled up short when I saw the faint traces of the erased words "Bloody Mess." We'd sold out of Brandon's new flavor already?

Pumpkin spice was running low. I'd put off errands, I had just enough time to mix some up and get it in the chiller before heading to the Adam Blasco exhibit. I flipped open the thick binder of Buzzy's recipes we referred to as the *Book of Spell*s and got to work, using fresh pumpkin puree Pru had delivered straight from the farm. Soon the heady scent of cinnamon, nutmeg, and ginger suffused the kitchen.

Flo and Gerri bustled into the kitchen at ten on the dot.

"Is that Vye's car at the house?" Flo said. "Is she okay?"

"She seems to be." I hesitated. "But she's worried. She

has to go to Moy Mull today for a meeting with Adam's agent-slash-lawyer."

"For a will reading at the castle?" Flo's eyes glowed. "How very Agatha Christie!"

Gerri waved a dismissive hand then tied on an apron. Her dark eyes were shrewd. "Wills take more time than that. I wonder what this is really about." I remembered that one of Gerri's ex-husbands had been a lawyer.

"Vye did seem confused," I said. That was an understatement.

Flo started the waffle maker. "Do you think he left her all his artwork? Or the rights to it?"

Gerri frowned as she placed hot fudge into the warmer. "It might bring in a pretty penny in certain circles, but I found most of Adam Blasco's work to be well beyond the bounds of good taste and propriety."

"But that portrait of Maud's spectacular, isn't it?" Flo said. "She's a sphinx, isn't she? He captured her completely."

"That's a perfect way to put it." Sphinx. I remembered what Prentiss had told me as I stirred a touch more cinnamon into the pumpkin mixture. "Prentiss said Maud and Adam were once married very early in her career."

Gerri dropped her ladle into the pot of hot fudge. "I didn't see that coming. What an odd couple."

I hadn't considered the ramifications of her words—they were an odd couple. "Prentiss said it was a Vegas wedding and that Maud was so young she had to have a letter of permission from her parents to get married." Now I wondered, in light of Adam's history, had young Maud been one of a line of young women used by a master manipulator?

Gerri and Flo exchanged glances. "A Gretna Green marriage?"

"What's that?" I asked.

"Gretna Green is a town in Scotland, right over the border from England," Gerri said. "Years ago, people too young to marry in England would cross the border and marry in Gretna Green, where the legal age was younger. It was a whole industry."

"Like Vegas for us," Flo said. "Well, Maud's first marriage didn't work but her second marriage was happier."

Gerri snorted. "Of course, she married royalty, Prince Frederic of Terbinia. One of those wealthy little European countries on the Mediterranean."

"I remember seeing it on the news." Flo's eyes misted. "Maud was such a beautiful bride, she looked like a princess from a fairy tale. I never heard about her first marriage or divorce from Adam."

"I imagine it was a point of contention with the royal family of Terbinia," Gerri said. "They were very traditional, and it caused quite a stir for the prince to marry a commoner who was not only American and Black, but also a divorcee."

"Love conquers all," Flo said.

Gerri raised a skeptical eyebrow, and I realized these opinions were based on personal experience. Flo had been married to the same man for decades. Gerri had been married three times, and from what I'd heard, the third really hadn't been the charm.

I remembered Tony's request and relayed it to Gerri along with his phone number. "He's trying to find people with connections to Moy Mull, who had ancestors who worked at the castle in its heyday."

Gerri thought for a moment. "Bridget Flynn, on Merchants Lane just off the green, had a great-grandmother who worked at the castle. I'll ask her. She's very proud of her family connection to Moy Mull."

"Wonderful." I poured the pumpkin spice mixture in the

chiller and wiped my hands. As I put away my ingredients, I noted a half-empty bag of marshmallows, which brought to mind Brandon's terrifying new flavor. "We sold out of Brandon's Bloody Mess fast."

Flo laughed. "Teenagers love it. The grosser the better with some kids."

Gerri shuddered.

"Did you try it?" I asked.

Gerri's pained expression said, *Are you kidding?*

"I liked it," Flo said. "Tastes good, if you close your eyes when you eat it."

Chapter 21

Five minutes later, Caroline and I headed out to the Adam Blasco photography exhibit at the Barn Gallery. She threw an uneasy look back at the farmhouse. "I hope Sprinkles will behave for Vye."

When I'd left, Vye had been sitting on the kitchen floor playing with Rocky and there'd been no sign of Sprinkles. "Fingers crossed."

Several dozen people jostled in line at the entrance of the Barn Gallery as I parked in the lot. Word of Adam's death had hit the news.

Once inside, Caroline and I stopped with several others to admire the photo of Maud. She sighed. "Wouldn't you love to have a portrait like that? She's so beautiful, but mysterious too."

I recalled Flo's assessment. "A sphinx?"

"Yes, a mysterious but contented one," Caroline said.

As we walked through the exhibit, I considered the difference between Maud's photo and the others and realized one emotion radiated from her eyes that was missing from the other models. Trust. That was the difference. The balance of the relationship between Maud and Adam had been equal, or at least more equal. All the other photos revealed a very different and unsettling power dynamic. I was so lost imagining Adam's twisted relationships with his models that I startled when Caroline touched my arm and asked if the exhibit was arranged in chronological order.

"Yes. They sequestered a lot of his earlier work in the Over Eighteen section." I noted all the red stickers discreetly alerting buyers that a work was sold. I watched Max Truwitt put a red sticker on a photo of two women standing at the base of a grain silo, the image streaked with thin raised lines of white paint.

"Good morning, Riley, Caroline." Max looked like a man who couldn't believe his good fortune. "Sad news about Adam, but his work's selling like the proverbial hotcakes." His phone buzzed and he excused himself to take the call.

Caroline said, "Good news for the gallery, they get a nice commission for each work. Now that Adam's dead, there'll be a buying frenzy and the prices will skyrocket. It's simple supply and demand. There won't be any more photos by Adam Blasco."

I was dying to tell Caroline that Vye said she was the actual artist behind Adam's later works, but I bit back the words. Instead I'd continue with the experiment. Would the difference between Adam's work and Vye's be obvious to someone who worked in the art world? Was Vye telling the truth?

We passed the entrance to the sequestered gallery, and Caroline said, "I'll skip this. I've seen his stuff from that period. Hard to believe some people want those photos hanging over their sofas."

"It's odd," I mused. "Maud was Adam's first big work. Then he started doing these." I waved toward the sequestered gallery.

"Sordid? Degrading? Angry works?" Caroline said.

I nodded. "Think about it. He took those photos after

Maud left him for Prince Frederic. Maybe it was Adam's way of getting revenge. He couldn't act out on her so he took it out on these women. They're proxies."

Caroline pushed her glasses up her nose and gave me a surprised look.

"What?" I said.

"That's deep," she said. "I think you're right."

We went into the area with Adam's later work, where Max was stickering another sold label. As we walked slowly to the end of a grouping of landscapes, Caroline came to a stop. She settled slowly on a bench in front of a photograph of two little girls playing hopscotch, their images reflected in a puddle. This work was simply a print, with none of Adam's usual paint or textural additions.

"What are you thinking?" I said, trying to stay cool.

She pursed her lips. "Well, first of all, you know my specialty is nineteenth-century American decorative arts, silver, furniture, so take what I say with a grain of salt. I work with a guy who only does photography, and I'll ask him to come down. I think he planned to anyway. We'll start with the obvious. At the beginning of his career and through the years, Adam shoots portraits, very personal, extremely intimate portraits, and now the work includes landscapes, which are so expansive. Lots of artists switch it up like that, but you also have a few portraits here that feel so different from the earlier work. The closeness doesn't feel intrusive or voyeuristic." She shrugged. "Call me crazy, but it feels like a different person took these pictures."

I leaned close. "Vye told me she did the later work," I said, "and Adam took the credit."

Caroline didn't respond with surprise, she simply took off her glasses and polished them on the hem of her cardigan, shaking her head. "No wonder she seems so mixed up."

I flipped through the pages of the exhibition catalog. "It's funny. Why is a photographer like Adam, who does *this* stuff"—I turned the pages to *Dallas*, the photo I'd seen Adam scrutinizing the night he died—"what is he doing shooting pictures for Maud's cookbook?"

"Maud wanted him to?" Caroline rose and started back through the gallery, brushing some of Sprinkles' white hairs from her slacks. "He likes cookbooks? He needs the money?"

"A simple explanation's usually the right one," I muttered, but it didn't feel right. I flipped to the end of the catalog, where there was a list of Adam's works. The list included Maud's cookbooks. "Listen to this: *A Moy Mull Christmas. Thanksgiving at the Castle. Window onto Villa D'Amore, the Home of Her Serene Highness Maud of Terbinia.* Do those sound like the work of an edgy genius photographer?" Was it simply business? I mused. Did Adam still have a soft spot for the woman he'd been married to so long ago? Did she still have feelings for him? Then why put him in the cottage farthest away from her home?

Caroline shrugged. "I want to see *Dallas*. Most experts consider it his best work. It's where he started adding elements like paint spatter to his photos, which was also a smart career move. Textural elements like that made his works one of a kind."

Caroline and I stopped in front of *Dallas* as she said, "Don't you wonder where she is now? Would you want that photo of you out in the world for everyone to see?" She blinked. "What the heck?"

Even I could see it. Adam's other works were framed and mounted with simple black wood gallery frames and soft white matting. This was a wrinkled duplicate matted in a cheap black metal frame. "That wasn't here the other night!"

Caroline's voice shrilled. "If that's here, where's the original?"

We ran to Max and told him what we'd seen. He bolted for *Dallas* and the poor man almost dropped dead on the spot. He didn't even go to his office, he phoned Maud on his cell. When he hung up, his hands trembled so much we led him to a bench and I offered to get him a glass of water. He shook his head and kept repeating, "There's no way, no way anyone got that out of here."

Within minutes a golf cart pulled up to the front door of the gallery and Maud strode in, followed by Prentiss and Tony. Maud was dressed in a trim gray business jacket and slacks, and she radiated such barely controlled fury I understood Max's shaking hands.

Maud stalked to the fake work in the shoddy frame, hands on her hips. "Get this trash off the wall," she said. She whirled on Max and pulled him into a quiet corner of the lobby. Prentiss, Tony, Caroline, and I hovered nearby pretending not to listen.

Maud was so angry, she didn't appear to notice us. "How could this happen? That's Adam's most valuable work," she seethed. "It was the original. It was not for sale."

Max raised his hands. "Of course—"

Maud cut him off. "What happened?"

"I don't know." Max's face reddened and a vein throbbed at his temple. "I walked through the exhibit last night after the reception. *Dallas* was here then, I swear."

"Who saw you leave?" Maud said. "Were you the last person to leave the building?"

"Of course, well, I came back after the catering crew left, plus—" Max bristled. "Wait a minute, Maud. You know I've been working day and night to make this exhibit succeed. I've even been staying at Loch Lomond Cottage for the past three days so I could be right at hand if anything needed attention." He pointed at the doors. "There was security outside making sure everyone left and the building was clear. They watched the catering crew leave, and believe me they scrutinized them." I recalled Barry complaining that the crew hadn't been allowed to prop the doors. "Security went through, no one was hiding in the building," Max stammered. "I don't know how someone could've gotten it out of the building without being seen."

I wrapped my hand around the badge in my pocket and scanned the ceiling. I didn't see any security cameras.

Tony noted my glance as he zipped a sweatshirt with a logo from Rhode Island Design University on the chest. He said quietly, "Cameras are mounted by the doors outside, but there are no alarms on the artworks themselves."

Caroline nodded. "That kind of security's costly, only the bigger museums and institutions can afford it. Max will have to call the police to get a report for the insurance company."

Prentiss whispered, "That won't take long. The cops are already at the castle. They're searching the dungeon."

Caroline's eyes met mine.

So it was *murder,* I thought.

Chapter 22

"D o you think someone killed Adam to make his art more valuable?" I asked Caroline as I drove us back toward the castle. I was sure Jack, as Penniman's sole police detective, would be on the scene, and I didn't have to ask Caroline if she wanted to try to see him.

"You have the strangest thoughts, Riley," she said.

"It's a coincidence, right? Adam's killed. Maybe someone stole *Dallas* intending to sell it and take advantage of the rise in prices after his death," I said.

"Stolen art's radioactive to a legitimate dealer," Caroline said. "If even a breath of rumor gets out that you buy or sell stolen goods, you're finished."

"But someone would buy it?" I persisted.

She shrugged. "Depends on how hot it is. However, with high-profile art, a famous image like *Dallas*, the thief's usually commissioned."

"You mean someone wanted that particular artwork and hired a thief to steal it?" I asked.

"Yes. Then it disappears, probably to hang over the fireplace of some billionaire hedge fund manager. That's the real crime. The art disappears. The FBI has a database and a system where they send an alert to galleries, dealers, art and antiques shops when something like this is stolen, so it's pretty hard to fence at a place where you might get your money's worth. You can't just walk into any old pawn shop and get anywhere near what museum-quality work is worth. But a collector will pay to make it worth a thief's while to get a work of art they desire."

"Pretty dangerous game for a thief," I said, flashing back to Rome and the little marble goddess Paolo had stolen.

Caroline read my mind. "Yep, I'm sure Paolo probably had a buyer, especially for work from a high-profile, secure place like the embassy. If it's any consolation, he must've been an exceptionally good burglar to get that commission."

"Lucky me," I muttered.

"There's no explaining the passions of art collectors. Any collector really," Caroline said. "Look at the folks who buy classic old books, like your dad sells."

"I can understand that," I said.

"Because you love to read."

"I was a librarian, I can't help it," I said. "But Adam's art's disturbing. I still don't get the appeal."

Caroline's brow wrinkled. "Now that you mention it, I do remember hearing something about *Dallas*. Hang on, I'm going to text my friend in the photography department." She texted as I pulled up to the back of the castle and slowed down by the kitchen door. Two police SUVs and two state police vans were parked by the rear entrance. Penniman, like most small towns in Connecticut, wasn't big enough to have its own crime lab, so it depended on the state for expertise in major crimes like murder.

As I swung into a space and parked, Caroline's phone dinged and she read: "A few years after that photo was published, the subject drowned herself at a beach in San Diego."

"That's awful." I googled "Adam Blasco and Dallas" on my phone and found an article in *Art Monthly*. "So the photo wasn't taken in Dallas. It was the girl's name. Dallas Whitaker."

When I looked up from my phone, I followed Caroline's gaze and saw Jack huddled over a clipboard with another investigator. We got out of the car as a CSI tech beckoned him from the door and he went inside.

I patted Caroline's arm. "Sorry, Caroline."

Maud, Prentiss, and Tony pulled up in the golf cart, and Prentiss and Maud got out. Maud gave us a curt nod, stalking through the gate into her rose garden. Prentiss joined us as Tony waved and drove off in the cart. Prentiss' expression clouded as he watched Maud walk down the path to her cottage.

"Quality time with her bees?" I asked.

"Yes, Maud finds solace with her bees." He shook himself, and a bit of his sparkle returned. "I escape the old-fashioned way. Want to join me inside?"

"Is it legal?" I asked.

"Entirely." Prentiss craned his neck toward the police vehicles. "I wish I knew what was happening with the cops, but I also want to stay out of their way. No need to put myself on their radar."

Caroline threw a longing glance toward the door where Jack had disappeared then checked her watch. "I have a few minutes," she said, and we followed Prentiss into the kitchen. He went to the freezer and pulled out one of the tubs of ice cream I'd brought yesterday.

"You were kind enough to leave leftovers of the whisky ice cream." He opened the lid. "Just enough for three. That'll hit the spot." He gathered bowls and spoons and scooped generous servings as we took seats at the table.

"I thought you were going to say, 'It's five o'clock somewhere,'" I said.

"I was. Right now, I need some old-fashioned comfort.

This day has been a total mess already, and Adam's lawyer hasn't even arrived yet." He savored a bite of ice cream. "If you thought Adam was delightful, you'll love Nicky. He has Adam's papers, as he put it. I guess that means will."

"Do you have any idea what's in it?" I said.

He shrugged extravagantly. "My policy's to always expect the worst, then I'm pleasantly surprised if anything good happens. But Vye—" He shook his head. "Poor kid."

"She's staying with us at the farm," Caroline said.

I don't know if I would've volunteered any information, but it was too late. My gut—now pleasantly full of whiskey ice cream—trusted and liked Prentiss, but he was a man totally devoted to Maud. And Maud was missing a vial of bee venom and a syringe.

Prentiss had been with her since they were both teenagers. Could Prentiss, who was regaling Caroline with a funny story, have killed to protect Maud?

I waited until they finished laughing. "Prentiss . . ."

"You look so serious." Prentiss leaned toward me. "Just like that cop with the beard who's been asking questions about Adam's death. I guess we have to put our alibis on the table. Where were you Friday night between ten and midnight?"

Ten and midnight. I'd seen Adam leave Dree in the tea garden just before ten.

"Driving Willow home from the festival," I said. "Having a late dinner with Caroline."

"Ditto, dinner with Riley," Caroline said.

"Hah!" Prentiss scoffed. "Fishy that you're each other's alibi. I have three alibis. I was playing poker with three friends over in Highland Cottage."

"Pretty iron clad," I said.

"Especially since one of them's an aspiring watercolorist from Hartford whose day job is district attorney," Prentiss said.

I tried to keep my tone casual. "And Maud?"

"Maud was in her cottage," Prentiss said. Caroline and I exchanged glances at this less-than-solid alibi.

Prentiss raised his hands, then rose and gathered our empty bowls and spoons. "She's on the security tape coming in at midnight. She said she didn't see anyone. One of the security guards told me there were two guys talking to Adam on the security tape. He said one of them worked for Creative Catering."

Caroline and I exchanged shocked glances. One of Bitsy's employees? "He didn't say who?"

Prentiss shook his head.

Chapter 23

*C*aroline and I drove back to Udderly, Caroline insisting she had a few minutes to help in the shop before she left. Two emotions drove my best friend: guilt because she felt she should be helping in her mother's shop and hope that by staying close to home there'd be a chance she'd see Jack.

A familiar red VW Beetle drove down Farm Lane. I watched it turn into the parking area in front of Udderly and pass several open spots. I walked to the big picture windows in front of the shop, and Caroline joined me as we watched the driver park in the spot farthest from the road, angled beyond the blacktop onto the grass by the dumpster. Tillie got out, adjusted her sunglasses—a very autumnal orange today—and scanned the lot.

"Good luck," Caroline said.

To my surprise Tillie didn't head for the front door like a customer, but instead walked around the building to the kitchen door. She threw a glance across the road to the crowded farm stand, then waved through the screen.

"Hi, Tillie." I greeted her with trepidation and opened the door.

She entered, taking in the kitchen's black-and-white-checkerboard floor, gleaming farmhouse sink, and back wall covered with black chalkboard paint and Willow's artwork. "So this is where the magic happens."

"Well, hello, Teresa O'Malley," Flo said as she emerged from the shop's office.

"Hi, Mrs. Fairweather," Tillie said.

"Tillie was one of my students." Flo beamed. "How have you been, dear?"

"Great. How nice to see you." Tillie angled so she could see out the door, as if checking to see if she'd been followed. She was here for an information exchange, not ice cream.

Tillie was ten years older than me, so I hadn't known her growing up, but everyone in Penniman knew she was the daughter of the beloved retired chief of police. However, Tillie'd washed out of the police academy before taking the secretary job at the station. She and I were bound by some not-quite-legal activity from a case a few months earlier. What we'd done had led to the apprehension of a killer, but it had put me squarely on Jack's watch list.

"What's up, Tillie?" I asked.

Tillie must've decided Flo could be trusted because she blurted out, "Jack watched the security footage from last night at the castle. He wants to talk to the kid from Italy, Luca."

Flo's eyes went wide as my heart rate ticked up. "Why?" I asked.

Luca hadn't come home until midnight. What had he done between ten and twelve?

Tillie bit her lip and threw a guilty look out the door.

"Tillie, why?" Flo repeated.

Tillie took a deep breath. She couldn't refuse Flo. "Jack reviewed the Moy Mull security footage from the castle hallway outside the death scene. At ten thirty Friday night, Luca argued with Adam."

And I'd seen him fight with Adam in the garden. My heart fell. I'd forgotten to mention that when Officer Ruiz took my statement.

Tillie turned back to the door. "They reviewed the footage from the hallway outside the security office. It films everyone coming inside the castle by the back door. Not the whole hallway, unfortunately, but it showed the security office door, the door to the conference room, and the exit door."

Conference room. The dungeon.

So many questions swirled through my mind. Why had Luca continued his fight with Adam? Did he purposely look for him? How did he get in the castle? I remembered him and Willow wearing red badges, but red badges didn't unlock doors, they simply identified the wearer as a volunteer.

I wondered how Tillie had learned this information, but pushed the thought aside and recalled what Prentiss had told me earlier. "There was someone else there too, right?"

Tillie continued, "Yes, there was another guy with him. Barry Esposito from Creative Catering. Barry was questioned and he said Adam chewed the kid out."

"What was Barry doing there?" I asked.

A black Penniman police SUV pulled up to the farm stand and Tillie angled away from the door. Jack got out.

Tillie said, "Barry said his son, Travis, told him he thought he dropped his cell phone in the dining room. He had a couple of minutes and decided to get it instead of coming back the next day. He had a yellow entry badge so he could get in. He said seeing Adam fight with Luca was embarrassing and he left."

Worry tightened my chest. "Did anyone check out his story? About the phone?"

Tillie shrugged and said in a sly tone, "Don't know."

"So why do they want to talk to Luca? Are they accusing

Luca of . . ." My voice trailed off. Murder. *Hot-headed Luca . . . what had he done?*

"Why indeed?"

Tillie's sly tone was driving me crazy. "Tillie, spill."

She held up a finger and Flo and I joined her by the screen door, watching as the crowd of weekend shoppers parted before Jack as he approached the farm stand where Luca and Willow worked. His broad shoulders curled forward slightly, as if he carried a weight, and his expression was troubled as he spoke with Luca. My heart twisted as Willow's smile faded and was replaced by a panicked look as Jack led Luca to the farmhouse. Willow's dad, Darwin Brightwood, stopped unloading a wagon of pumpkins and jogged after them. After a quick word with Jack, all four went into the house, Darwin with his hand on Luca's shoulder.

"Well, he's not taking Luca to the police station. That's good." Flo's brow wrinkled. "Right?"

Tillie's eyes slid to mine. "That's right, Mrs. Fairweather."

I tried not to show it, but there were times I truly regretted that I'd asked Tillie for help earlier that summer. She was a snoop extraordinaire, a frustrated detective, but also a fountain of information about things that should be kept confidential.

She also seemed compelled to answer her former kindergarten teacher's questions.

I stood behind Flo and said in a low voice, "Did the police find any actual evidence that Luca's involved in Adam's death?"

Flo turned to me. "Oh, he couldn't be!"

"I didn't catch that?" Tillie said.

Flo replied, "Did the police find any actual evidence that Luca was involved in Adam's death?"

Tillie's eyes gleamed. "They found Adam's EpiPen in Luca's backpack."

"No!" Flo breathed.

So that was the news Tillie'd been dying to share. "Wait a minute," I said, "how did they know it was Adam's?"

"It's prescription," Tillie stated in a tone that told me how dumb I was. "Adam's name's on it. They're checking prints."

I could see through to the shop where Caroline kept vigil at the window.

Tillie lowered her voice. "I heard you were there when the body was found. Want to get lunch tomorrow and compare notes?"

Compare notes meant find out what I know—the quid pro quo. "I have to check the schedule."

"They're supposed to get autopsy results tomorrow morning," Tillie said.

I'd definitely make it. I flipped the pages of the schedule. "I can do lunch at noon. Lily's?"

"Lily's at noon it is," Tillie said.

I'd made a deal with the devil again but it was the only way to find out what was going on with the investigation. The thought of Luca involved in Adam's murder made my stomach churn. He was in the US on a visa. There were strict rules, but being deported would be the least of his worries if he was charged with murder. Willow's heart would break. My heart would break.

I was going to find out what happened to Adam in the dungeon.

"See you tomorrow, Tillie."

After accepting a pumpkin spice cone on the house from Flo, Tillie got back in her car and took off. A few minutes later, Jack emerged from the Brightwood farmhouse, deep in conversation with Pru and Darwin. He bid them goodbye, then walked up the lane toward our farmhouse.

"That's your cue," I called to Caroline. "You'd better run."

"I'll call you." Caroline dashed out the door.

She called out and I saw Jack stop for her by the pen behind the shop, where we'd sometimes have llamas or baby goats for kids to pet. Together they walked up the hill.

Flo watched them, then turned to me with a sparkle in her eyes. "Wedding bells for those two, mark my words."

I smiled. "Next summer?"

"I like Christmas weddings." Flo held open the kitchen door and made a shooing motion. "Well, what are you waiting for? You're not on the schedule. Go over and see what happened with Luca."

Chapter 24

Luca sat at the long farm table in the Brightwood kitchen, his shoulders hunched, staring into a cup of fragrant black coffee. Willow was next to him with her cheek resting on his shoulder. Generally, anyone in Pru's kitchen would be drinking her herbal teas, but Luca had bought an espresso machine for the Brightwoods, and the aroma of freshly brewed coffee filled the room.

I took a seat across from him. "Luca, are you okay?"

"Signorina Riley, I'm okay. I think." He shrugged. "I'm not sure."

Willow's usually carefree expression was troubled. "Did you hear the police found an EpiPen in Luca's backpack?"

I nodded. "Do you have any idea how it could have gotten in there, Luca?"

He pushed his thick dark hair away from his brow and leaned on his elbows. "No. I shouldn't have forgotten my backpack." He swallowed. "I shouldn't have done many things."

"What happened Friday night, Luca?" I said quietly.

"I will start from . . . my . . . explosion." He turned to Willow, his voice thick with regret. "I saw Adam taking your photo, Willow, and I'm sure it will be very beautiful, but I felt he was a wolf."

Willow looked down, then away.

Luca's words came in a rush. "So when I lost my temper, you ran off. I ran off, too, looking for you, but I couldn't find you. I ran into the woods behind the gallery and got lost, but by then I cooled off. I found my way back, the party had ended, so I decided to walk to the castle to get my backpack and go home. I left it in the cloakroom like all the other volunteers.

"I tried to open the back door near the cloakroom but the red badges didn't unlock the doors. Another man came, Barry from the catering company. His badge opened the door. We went inside together. Well, we barely got inside when we saw Adam."

Luca threw back the rest of his espresso. "Adam"—he said the word as if it tasted foul—"was in the hallway, I think he must've come from the cloakroom. He saw us as soon as we walked in and he, how do you say, blew up. Swearing. Saying many bad names and pointing. I was so embarrassed. He said, 'What are you doing here? Are you crazy? Stay away from me! Get out!'

"Barry and I ran out. Barry said, 'He's nuts' and I said, 'He's angry with me.' We walked outside and I headed down the driveway. I think Barry went across the lawn, toward the Barn Gallery, some of the caterers were still there. I walked home. I think the security guard saw me, the one at the Fairweather Road gate."

"So you're Barry's alibi and he's yours," I mused. Sort of. Barry also had his coworkers for an alibi. "What time was this?"

He shrugged. "Ten thirty? Eleven? I didn't check my phone."

"Someone must've planted that EpiPen in Luca's backpack." Willow spoke with such certainty that Luca smiled.

I agreed. Someone wanted it to look like Luca had played a part in Adam's death. I reached across the table and squeezed Luca's hand. "Everything will be all right." I tried to put some of Willow's certainty into the words.

As I headed out, my phone buzzed. "Hi, Caroline."

"I'm on my way back to Boston," she said. "I hope Sprinkles will behave for you."

"I'm sure she will. Rocky'll keep her in line."

"I hope so." Her voice brightened. "I talked to Jack."

"And . . ."

Caroline's voice was light. "He wasn't surprised about what you said, about the bee. I mean, he can't say anything, but he did say, 'Is that so?' and then he told me that his granny used to raise bees. So I think he's thinking along the same lines you're thinking."

I headed up the hill. "That someone injected Adam with bee venom and wanted it to look like an allergic reaction."

"Not in so many words. You know how professional he is." She said "how professional" the way other people would say "he's so handsome" or "he's so hot." "But he had this look, he was pleased but trying to hide it."

Pleased. Ha!

"Did he talk to Vye?" I asked.

"He didn't have time to stay," Caroline said. "He's going to interview her later."

"Thanks for letting me know, Caroline. Drive safe."

Chapter 25

I entered the house, watching for furry, white tripping hazards. Vye's voice led me to the parlor, where Sprinkles sat on the couch and Vye had set up a camera and tripod. I paused at the door. Vye looked more relaxed than I'd seen her since she and Adam had rolled up on Friday. So much had happened to change her world in such a short time. But now as she focused her camera and cooed at Sprinkles, she looked younger, open, and relaxed.

"Come on baby, that's it! Beautiful! Sprinkles, you're a star!" Vye cooed.

Sprinkles, fascinated by the camera, raised her chin, as if to say, *This is my good side.*

Who was I kidding? Sprinkles thought every side was her good side.

Rocky watched from a distance, his head ping-ponging from Vye to Sprinkles. Rocky and Vye turned to me as I entered the room, but Sprinkles' attention remained focused on the camera.

"How are you, Vye?"

Vye grinned. "Having fun with Sprinkles. She's a natural! I've never seen a cat sit so long and be so cooperative."

"Cooperative?" I laughed. "Are we talking about Sprinkles?"

Vye sighed. "She loves the camera and the camera loves her."

Sprinkles blinked and swished her tail lazily, as if accepting the compliment.

"Did Caroline leave for Boston?" Vye asked.

"Yes."

Vye stretched out a hand to stroke Sprinkles. I held my breath, but Sprinkles allowed it.

"Did you have lunch?" I asked. "Would you like some tea?"

"I had some of the chili. Tea would be nice," Vye said.

I made tea and realized I was starving. I sliced the last loaf of cornbread, put the remains of the takeout salad in a bowl, and carried it all to the parlor. Vye took a mug of tea and thanked me. Vye, Sprinkles, and Rocky all sprawled on the floor. Everyone looked so relaxed, I hated to spoil the mood but I had to ask.

"Vye, what did you do Friday after you and Adam left here?" I searched my memory. "I didn't see you at the opening of the exhibit."

Vye shrugged. "Well, I guess I better get my story straight before I talk to the cops." She wrapped her arms around her knees and gnawed on a fingernail. I noticed several black titanium rings on the fingers of her left hand, and a tarnished gold signet ring on her right. She wore a long-sleeved plaid shirt over gray leggings and a tank top. The leggings rode up as she moved, revealing an ankle tattoo of vining pink flowers with a yellow center. She saw me notice it and smiled. "Prairie roses."

"Pretty." I offered the plate of cornbread to Vye.

She shook her head. "I'm fine, thanks." She blew on the tea, leaned against the couch, and sighed. "Friday. The day started well with the shoot here, but Adam and I had a big fight when we got back to Moy Mull."

I kept my face composed and took a bite of salad; I didn't want her to ever know I'd witnessed their fight.

"That"—her brow furrowed—"was the last time I talked to him. I hung out at the castle, walked in Maud's garden, and later went to the reception for about five minutes, but I've done a million of those. I ate some delicious ice cream"—she raised the mug in a toast—"and then I went to my room in the castle, read, sketched, played some games on my phone. Had a snack with Tony, that was later, say elevenish? Oh, I saw that flake, Dree Venditti, drift through."

"Dree Venditti?" I said. "In the castle? What time was this?"

Vye shrugged. "I don't wear a watch. After Tony and I ate. Eleven thirty? Midnight?"

I remembered the scene she'd had with Adam. "Did you talk?"

"I tried to avoid her, but she caught me by surprise. Tony and I were heading upstairs and had stopped in the great room to look at the portrait of Oona, and she was going through."

I remembered she'd told Prentiss she moved to a down-stairs room from Oona's suite. "Where was she going?"

Vye shrugged. "Looked like she was heading toward the kitchen."

"Did Dree say anything?"

Vye rolled her eyes. "Unfortunately. She wanted to talk about the same thing she always wanted to talk about. She wanted me to convince Adam to do her crazy book. You should've heard him complain about her."

"Dree was writing a book?" She didn't seem the book-ish type.

"She needed permission to use the photos he took of her and she wanted him to write a foreword." Vye snorted. "Like that was ever going to happen. She'd already posted some of his photos on her website and Adam was going to sue her for unauthorized use."

I blew on my tea, absorbing this new information. "What did Adam tell her?"

"That she was a talentless hack and, well, he used some words I won't say around Sprinkles and Rocky. Dree was one of his models years ago, before Maud even. I think they lived together for a while. About two years ago, she started taking her own photos. Here—" Vye scrolled on her phone and turned the screen to me.

I read aloud the text superimposed over a sunset of vibrant colors. "I'm Dree. Moving from the front of the camera to behind the lens, I share my heart and artistry with the world." I scrolled through her pics and commented, "Beautiful photos of sunsets."

Vye rolled her eyes. "It's hard to take a bad picture of a Hawaiian sunset."

I stopped short at a photo of a much-younger Dree and Adam, both holding wineglasses in a gallery. The next photos were obviously taken by Adam. Dree sat with her back to the camera on a beach, her naked shoulder blades sharp as knives. In the next she crouched at the water's edge, her dress sodden, her lovely hair matted with sand. Her lips pouted but her eyes were blank. I shuddered. There was something feral about her pose and her expression; Adam had stripped her of her humanity. This photo was how she wanted to represent herself?

I scrolled further and read the next page. "I learned about photography at the feet of the master, ADAM BLASCO, and can't wait to share my vision with the world. Watch this space for news of my new book, *Model: My Affair with a*

Genius." I set the tablet on the couch. "Whew. That's laying it on thick."

Vye leaned forward, took a piece of cornbread, and said in an exasperated tone, "Adam told her he'd get a restraining order on her, but he didn't."

We chewed in silence. Rocky sniffed my salad, judged it unworthy of his attention, and trotted to the kitchen. Sprinkles looked from Vye to Rocky, then followed Rocky out of the room.

Vye shrugged. "Anyway, getting back to your original question, when I saw Dree that night, I told her to get lost. I didn't see anyone else after Dree."

"Back up. You said you and Tony had a snack around elevenish?"

Vye nodded. "That's right. He knocked on my door, said he saw my light on and asked if I wanted to get a snack. Someone, the caterers I guess, left a beautiful brioche on the table with a tag that said Eat Me. Tony and I ate it with some terrific jam and honey we found on the counter." Her expression softened. "Tony had been working in the attic. He had a cobweb in his hair and I brushed it away. He told me working in dusty old attics was an occupational hazard of historians. There were some beers in the fridge, and we had one or two. Then we went back upstairs together, well, not that kind of together." She blushed and waved her hands. "I went to my room and he went to that big storage room at the end of the hall. Maud calls it the attic. That's where Tony goes through the old Moy Mull stuff."

Her expression clouded as she put down her mug. "So if Adam died from a bee sting like Prentiss told me, why are the police asking questions? I mean, do they think someone unleashed bees near Adam? There were plenty of people who knew about his allergy. I knew, and so did Prentiss and Maud. I heard Maud mention it when she and Tony were talking about how she had a wasp nest removed from the castle."

"If Dree lived with Adam, she'd know of the allergy," I said.

"Everyone who spent five minutes with him knew," Vye said. "He was always going on about it."

I sipped my tea and considered. Everyone who stayed in the castle the night of Adam's murder knew about his allergy. Maud, Prentiss, Vye, Tony, Dree. Had anyone else stayed there? I remembered the housekeeper. I'd ask Prentiss if she lived onsite.

"You said Tony went upstairs," I said. "He lives there?"

Vye nodded. "There are some old hotel rooms on the fourth floor, near the big storage area. That was a perk Maud gave him."

"You didn't hear him leave the attic after you went back to your room that night?"

"You'd think I would've, since that floor creaks like crazy and I couldn't sleep. I have insomnia and I guess Tony does too. He said he works late a lot." She shrugged. "The way that floor creaks, I would've heard him go back downstairs."

Vye looked at her phone. "I guess it's time to see Nicky. Ugh." She put her camera and tablet in her bag, while I gathered the plates and mugs and put them in the sink.

Sprinkles came into the kitchen, sat at the bathroom door, and leveled a look at Vye. Without hesitation, Vye flushed the toilet then ran upstairs, calling, "I'm going to freshen up. Back in a sec."

Sprinkles went into the powder room with a satisfied swish of her tail. How quickly she'd trained Vye.

Chapter 26

Since Maud had invited me to jog around the grounds of Moy Mull, I figured I'd take a run while I waited for Vye to finish her meeting. Well, that's what I told Vye. What I really hoped to do was get inside the castle and look at the lock on the dungeon door.

An angular white Maserati was parked in the circular drive at the front of Moy Mull, next to the battered old Buick I'd seen earlier. As I drove around the castle to park, Vye sneered, "That Maserati's only one of Nicky's collection. He's loaded. He reps all the big names in the art world, plus some pro athletes and music stars."

"He's doing well," I said as I parked Sadie in one of the service spots. I'd gone reflexively to the service entrance by the kitchen. Visiting the castle was getting to be a habit.

A CSI van was parked by the rose trellis at the back entrance. I'd give anything to see what they were doing in the dungeon. I watched a tech go into the castle, then I realized Vye hadn't said anything, so I turned to her.

Her eyes were closed and her lips moved soundlessly.

"Vye, are you okay?"

She nodded. "My gran told me to always say my prayers when I'm stressed, plus I'm saying my mantra. 'Be brave.'"

"Sounds good," I said.

Vye took a deep breath, held it, then blew it out in a long exhalation, but her chin dipped to her chest and she said in a small voice, "Did you ever have a secret, Riley? One you've had for so long that you've almost forgotten why it was secret in the first place?" She opened her warm brown eyes and patted my arm. "Sorry, I'm just nervous." She smiled. "I can't imagine you with a secret. You're so open and honest. You even look honest."

My CIA handlers had done a good job. I did look like an open and honest person.

As we got out of the car, I donned the badge with the yellow lanyard. "I'm going to do a few miles, then maybe hang out in Maud's garden. Text me when you're done."

Vye squared her shoulders. "Right. Wish me luck."

I gave her what I hoped was a reassuring smile. "Good luck."

"Hello, Vye, Riley," Maud called from the garden.

Any sign of Maud's earlier anger at the theft of *Dallas* was gone and she cast a look of approval at my running outfit. "Riley, I'm glad you're taking me up on the offer to jog here. If you get thirsty, please feel free to use your card to get some water in the kitchen."

"Thank you, Maud." An invitation from the lady of the castle. Perfect.

Maud flicked a careful glance at Vye, one that hinted at a complicated history. Still, Maud said, "Let's go, Vye. We're meeting in the study," and made a graceful gesture toward the kitchen door, where she pressed her card to the reader and opened the door.

As soon as the door closed behind them, I jogged past the entrance where the CSI van was parked. The door was propped open—what would Maud think?—and I saw a tech kneeling in front of the door to the dungeon, intently examining its lock. A security guard stood at the door chatting with the tech. "And that's why the Pats are gonna win," he said.

I jogged toward him, holding up my yellow badge, but he waved me off. "Sorry, you'll have to go in the kitchen entrance."

I wanted to see what was happening with that lock. I realized that running by one more time would capture the attention of any security personnel who happened to be watching, so I jogged back the way I came, thinking I'd give Maud and Vye time to get to their meeting, and then take advantage of Maud's invitation. I ran down a gravel drive into the woods past Maud's cottage, past an overgrown pond and a dilapidated building that had once been a garage. There were two bays in a stone front wall, but the roof had collapsed and filled the structure with years of debris and leaf litter. Metal No Trespassing signs affixed to the building were so weathered they were barely legible. A quarter mile past, the drive was blocked by a fallen tree, so I retraced my steps to the castle.

As the castle loomed into sight, I remembered that the balconies—Maud's and the library's—overlooked the area where the CSI van was parked. If I could get to one, there was a chance I might overhear some of the investigators' chatter. I remembered Tony's request for help with Penniman residents who might have a history with Moy Mull. I could tell him that I'd reached out to Gerri and she'd found someone. A slim excuse, but it would have to do.

Swiping my forehead for effect, hoping I looked thirsty, I jogged to the kitchen door and let myself in. No one was there, but I drank a glass of water, rinsed it, and left it in the sink. Vye's mantra passed through my mind and I repeated it: Be Brave. I walked to the velvet rope, casting a casual glance down the stairs, and heard the investigators continue to banter about football. I kept walking, aware that there could be cameras anywhere in the castle and remembering to act cool. The key to looking like I belonged was to act like I belonged. I passed through the great room, hesitating slightly at the sound of muffled voices from behind double doors at the far end of the room. The study? I hurried up the staircase.

Just as I topped the stairs to the third floor, I saw Tony disappear up the stairs to the fourth, carrying a stack of boxes as easily as I'd carry a pint of ice cream. I dashed past the suits of armor through the open door of the library to the balcony, the twin to Maud's.

My heart was pounding so hard I barely registered the million-dollar view over the rose garden, Maud's cottage, the pond, and the hills beyond. A small, weathered, marble bench made a lovely catbird seat, and the old rose vines shielded me from view of anyone on Maud's balcony.

Moments later, Jack pulled up in his SUV. I jumped up and crouched in the back corner of the balcony, squeezing myself farther into the shadow of the vine, tilting my head and contorting my body to see through the stone columns of the railing. The CSI tech exited the castle and greeted Jack. I couldn't make out their conversation and Jack's low rumble of a voice made it difficult to hear what he was saying, but he rubbed his hand over his beard, a gesture I'd seen before. He was faced with a puzzle, one that was not easy to solve.

The tech laughed and his voice carried up to me. "I'm not kidding. A locked-room mystery!"

I knew it.

Jack thanked the tech and went inside.

I'd been so busy focusing on the bee venom that I hadn't focused on the lock. I searched my memory and replayed the discovery of Adam's body. How Prentiss ran to the office and took the key from a wooden box on the wall. He'd said there was only one key.

I mulled this as I walked between the bookcases in the center of the room, stopping by the shelf labeled Moy Mull

House. If there was only one key, and the door had been locked, the murderer had to have returned the key to the office. There was a camera outside the security office. He or she must be on the security tapes. I had to see the tapes, but how?

A face materialized. Tillie.

The loosest lips in Penniman and I had an understanding, but everything was a quid pro quo with her. I'd see her at lunch tomorrow. What would she expect in return for information? And what would happen if Jack discovered I was using his secretary for back-channel intel? I didn't want to jeopardize his relationship with Caroline.

Footsteps and voices made me freeze.

Jack's deep baritone rumbled from the stairs, "Thanks, Mr. Ortiz. I have a few questions."

"Call me Tony. Come into the library. How can I help?"

My stomach dropped. If I didn't announce my presence at once, it would be extremely awkward to be discovered. On the other hand, it was already awkward, plus if I left I wouldn't know what Jack was asking. I melted between the two rows of bookcases in the center of the room, hunkered down in a little needlepoint chair, and prayed he wouldn't need anything from this row . . . like the books about the castle.

"I'm looking for information on the castle." Jack cleared his throat. "Specifically the lock downstairs. It's unique. Ms. Monaco told me that you've found some information about the construction of the house and I'm hoping you have something about the lock."

Tony said, "As a matter of fact, I've moved some materials about the house upstairs. There are letters Ben Clitheroe, the original owner, wrote to suppliers when he had the house built. Let me get that for you."

"Blueprints?" Jack asked. "Floor plans?"

Tony said, "I've moved quite a few of those materials upstairs too. I'll get them and then you can examine them here."

"I'll come with you if that's all right," Jack said.

"Yes, sure."

As their voices and footsteps receded from the room, I exhaled and jumped to my feet. I'd go out to the landing and lie in wait for Jack, taking advantage of some alcoves I'd seen earlier, then pretend I'd just arrived. I stepped into the hall, taking in many oil paintings of the Scottish Highlands and castles. I paused before a small watercolor of a terrier sleeping in a basket. A brass plate underneath read Jamie. What a sweet little guy.

I thought of Oona, Jamie's owner, and what it must've been like to move across the ocean so far from family and friends. To a castle, but still. She must've grown unhappy with Ben, since she'd run off with the chauffeur. My steps took me past a small hallway painted the lightest pink, and I caught sight of a brass plaque next to a set of double doors. Oona's Suite.

The gleaming oak doors had fancy brass knobs. I cast a glance back down the hall and prayed that the doors weren't locked. They weren't.

I stepped into a spacious room filled with light from two tall windows framed by pale pink velvet curtains. A four-poster bed with a cream silk duvet dominated the space, but matching blush and cream pillows and sheer white curtains updated it.

Instead of the massive fireplace I'd seen in Maud's suite and the library office, Oona's was only chest high with pretty white marble carved into delicate roses and ribbons. Two armoires flanked the door to the updated bath. I peeked in the armoires: one contained a television and the other a well-stocked mini bar. Maybe that's why Maud put Dree in here. Mentally I chided myself. Dree must be a good friend of Maud's to rate this room. It was sophisticated, bright, and well appointed, probably second in comfort only to Maud's suite. Well, I hadn't seen Prentiss's room. I wondered where he stayed.

Two armchairs with a low table made a cozy seating area in front of the fireplace. On the table was a small booklet: "The Story of the Weeping Lady" by S. W. Randall. I picked it up and flipped through. "Commissioned by the Penniman Hotel 1959." The real story of the Weeping Lady?

I skimmed, listening for any sign of Jack's return. The outlines of the story matched those Flo had shared, and were linked to a real-life place in Scotland called Fyvie Castle.

A tower, a dungeon, stained glass, a portcullis, even a ghost story—in building his castle, Old Ben Clitheroe had thought of everything.

Chapter 27

The sound of footsteps descending the stairs, then Tony's voice, called me out of my reverie. I set the booklet back on the table, closed the doors softly behind me, and headed back to the hallway, where I ducked into an alcove behind a tall aspidistra.

Tony was saying, "You can spread out on this worktable."

"Thanks," Jack replied. "Would it be all right if I take photos? With your permission?"

"Of course. I'll be upstairs if you need anything further."

Jack thanked Tony and I heard Tony go back upstairs. I waited two beats then walked into the library, where Jack bent over sheets of newsprint on a long worktable.

"Hello, Jack."

Jack sprang back, clutching his chest, not his sidearm, thank goodness. "You spooked me. I should've known you'd be in the library. What are you doing here?"

I bent the truth a bit. "Vye asked me to bring her here and Maud knows I like libraries."

"Ah." Jack parsed this and I felt my face heat, certain he knew I was an interloper.

"Old papers are fascinating," I said, joining him at the worktable.

He rubbed his beard, the scratching sound oddly comforting and pleasing. He didn't know what to do with me. I was a problem to be solved. The paper in front of him was a schematic for a fancy lock with the curvy handles you see on French patio doors, with two complicated mechanisms in between. I don't have a ton of talents, but one of the ones I do have is the ability to read text in any direction, sideways or upside down. The heading on this advertisement read "Genuine Ingenuity! Doors Locked from Within and Without!"

I decided a frontal attack was only fair.

"There's only one key to that lock," I said.

He looked at me with an unnerving lack of expression, saying nothing, so I filled the silence.

I cleared my throat and pointed to the old advertisement. "Since we're talking about the lock. When we were trying to get into the dungeon, ah, conference room, it was locked. Prentiss had to get the key from the office. He said there's only one key."

Come on Jack, say something. He didn't so I said, "I'm going to go. See you later. Stop by for an ice cream."

"Thank you, I might do that."

Stonewall Voelker.

As I left Jack in the library, I remembered something else Prentiss had said. *Nobody will hear you, the walls are three feet thick.* The killer had chosen well, chosen a place no one would hear Adam struggle. I shook off the unsettling image. Prentiss had an excellent alibi, but still I considered that here was a man with motive to kill Adam. He'd stuck with Maud for decades, even while she was married to another man, no, to two other men. Prentiss was definitely in the friend zone . . . had he been happy there? Or had he tired of Adam's sway over the woman he loved?

Chapter 28

I had questions for Tony, so I ran up to the fourth floor.

The stairs led to a long, carpeted hallway, but the wooden floors underneath were so uneven I had the sensation of walking on a sailboat in a gale, and a noisy sailboat at that. The wood complained and squeaked with every step. I recalled Vye's comment that if Tony had left his room she would've heard him. Her story checked out. There were eight doors on each side of the hall, closely spaced, but only every other one was numbered. One door was open to a hotel-style room with maple furniture, an oval rag rug, and brass lamps. I stepped inside. Two smaller rooms had been knocked together, the other room an en suite bathroom with white tile and a claw-foot tub. Servants quarters reconfigured into hotel rooms.

At the end of the hall, an open door revealed a large and airy space. Contrary to the mental picture conjured by the word "attic"—a dusty cobwebbed space lit by a single naked bulb—this room was spotless. Long shelves ran the whole length, and though piles of bric-a-brac and furniture crowded the corners, every wood surface gleamed with polish and the air smelled fresh. Light and air flowed in from broad, open windows, and a long oak table in the center of the space was covered with trays of papers and photographs.

Tony stacked document boxes on shelving along the back wall.

"Knock knock," I said.

Tony turned. "Hi, Riley."

"Hi, Tony." The view out the set of windows drew me. From this height, Maud's cottage and garden looked like a child's playthings, the furniture on the balconies below like doll's furniture. "What a view."

"Great, isn't it?" Tony grinned as he stacked another box.

I turned back to the room. "This isn't how I pictured an attic in a castle."

"Maud sends her cleaning team up here every week," Tony said. "I have to keep reminding them not to throw something away because it looks old."

"It's been crazy around here, hasn't it?" I said. "First the business with Adam and now the stolen portrait. I was talking with Jack Voelker downstairs." Didn't hurt to name drop.

Tony pulled a stack of books from a shelf. "It's been a lot for Maud, that's for sure. Adam was her first husband." There was sadness in his voice and I wondered if Tony was in love with Maud, too, like everyone else in her orbit.

A stack of old photos drew my attention back to the table. "Do you think with everything going on she'll cancel the castle exhibit?"

"Maud quit?" Tony shook his head. "No. She's put so much into it already and she loves this place. It may take a while for Maud to regain her equilibrium, but she will, and we've unearthed some terrific artifacts for the exhibit."

An old steamer trunk in the corner behind him caught my eye. "Was that Ben's?"

Tony's face brightened. "Check this out." He lifted the heavy domed lid of the trunk, revealing woolen sweaters, piles of rope, sturdy leather boots, and a climbing axe. "Some of Ben's climbing equipment. He made headlines for climbing the highest peak in Scotland when he went over to marry Oona. Can you believe they climbed with this stuff? Rope, metal, and sheer guts."

"Incredible," I breathed.

He handed me a photo from a stack on the table. A man with a curvy moustache in a dark suit and bowler-style hat stood with his foot on the running board of a vintage car. Several other men stood at attention behind the vehicle. "That's Ben?"

"With his favorite car," Tony said. "He had several, which shows you how wealthy he was. All those men were his mechanics. It took a team to keep that baby on the road." His voice took on a conspiratorial note as he pointed out a clean-shaven young man in a chauffeur's uniform in the crowd of men behind the car. "And there's the chauffeur, the one who ran off with Oona in that very car. It was Ben's favorite, a nineteen-twenty Anderson roadster convertible. What a scandal that was!"

Tony's voice warmed as he handed me a photo of a sweet-looking young woman. "And this is Oona. I guess still waters ran deep."

The Oona in the photo had gorgeous auburn hair, wide blue eyes, and the rosebud complexion of a Scotswoman. "Wait. They had color photos back then?"

Tony nodded. "The process was primitive, yes, but processes for color photography were used starting in the eighteen nineties." The old photo showed a side to Oona different than the fur-drenched lady of the manor in the great room portrait. This younger Oona had the round, open face of a girl who loved the outdoors. Wearing sturdy boots and carrying a walking stick, she gazed at her tiny terrier with the indulgent expression of a besotted parent. Her leather boots were creased and well worn.

"An outdoorsy type," I said. "She was a reverse buccaneer, right?"

Tony nodded. "While American heiresses went to Europe to marry titled lords with no money, she married an American industrialist who had a thing for castles and old Scottish clans."

"Was she royalty?" I set the photo down.

Tony shrugged. "I haven't dug very far into her genealogy."

He showed me a picture of a group in ball dress, posed before the magnificent fireplace beneath Ben's portrait. "Their circle was made up of movers and shakers, plus singers. Ben and Oona loved music." I recalled the lyre on Ben's coat of arms.

Tony warmed to his subject. "Lots of musicians and theater folk from Boston and New York stopped here. Guests would stay for weeks, even months at a time, in all the cottages on the property.

"Both of Ben's wives sang. He called Oona the Highland Songbird, and the second wife, Alma de Luce, actually was on the stage as the Songbird of Sevilla." He showed me an old playbill with a dark-haired singer in a mantilla. "I found a diary entry that said Alma and her mother stayed in Maud's cottage for a couple of weeks the summer before Oona took off with the chauffeur. But after Ben and Alma married, they didn't stay at Moy Mull long. They sold the place and moved to New York City. Even with the parties, Penniman was too quiet for Alma." He handed me a photograph.

Alma had the dark eyes, cupid's bow lips, and heavily plucked half-moon eyebrows of a flapper. Her hair was cropped in a fashionable bob, sleek and sexy, and her sharp little teeth were bared in an expression that wasn't exactly a smile. She was so different from the demure Oona, with her masses of coppery hair, her wide blue eyes, her open expression.

"Alma was quite the vamp," I said.

"I guess Alma helped him get over the shame of losing his wife to the chauffeur." Tony pushed back his tumble of hair and I felt the force of his Clark Kent appeal. Behind his glasses, Tony had chiseled good looks. "The guy took Ben's woman and his ride. Talk about getting a guy where he lived."

He held up a finger. "You'll appreciate this." From a shelf he took a small, rectangular, wooden box with four pull-out drawers. "Oona was a big reader and made her own card catalog for the library. Ben had books like any man of his position, but Oona set up the library and organized it. I'm grateful the other owners, especially the hotel, had the sense to leave that room alone."

I took the box from his hands and opened a drawer, flipping the doll-sized vellum cards covered with careful script. "So personal, to see her handwriting."

"She made up her own categories, as you can see. Cookery. Flowers. Moy Mull. Animals. Literature. Poetry. You were a librarian, right? I saw your eyes light up when I said card catalog. Most people, their eyes glaze over."

I laughed. "True. I miss it sometimes."

"You can come over any time." He placed Oona's card catalog back on the shelf. "I may drag you into helping with the exhibit, though. I could use someone organized. Prentiss is enthusiastic but he can't seem to put anything back in the right place. Without an inventory, it's hard to know if something's missing, moved, or stolen."

Helping Tony would be a pleasure. "What about Maud? Does she like history?"

He tipped his head. "Yes, well, she loves the fashions. You know how successful that exhibit on the clothes of *Downton Abbey* was."

"That reminds me," I said. "You asked me if I knew anyone with connections to Moy Mull. Gerri Hunt. Did she call you?"

"Yes, she's going to introduce me to a lady named Mrs. Flynn. Her great-grandmother worked here when Ben and Oona were alive."

I remembered why I'd come here in the first place. "You mentioned blueprints and floor plans when we were at the gallery opening. Do you have a floor plan of the castle I can look at?"

Tony gave me a rueful smile. "Sorry. I gave everything to the police officer."

Rats. Now it was evidence. "What do you think the police are looking for?"

Tony shrugged. "He asked specifically about the lock on the dungeon door." Tony leaned a hip onto the corner of the long worktable. "The craftsmanship of the lock's amazing when you consider it was made without computer aids. The lock was constructed so you could lock it from the inside and the outside, with the key, of course."

"And there's only one key?" I already knew the answer, but playing dumb never hurt when trying to gather information.

Tony pulled a document from a box and handed it to me. "An invoice. I'll have to get this to Detective Voelker."

It was dated February 1910 and said, "Keys ordered: 4." *Four?* "So where are the other keys?"

Tony stifled a yawn. "It's been over a hundred years. People lose things. I guess that's why Maud never locked that door."

I'd taken up enough of Tony's time and still had to verify Vye's alibi. "Vye said you were up here the night Adam died."

"Working, yes." Tony restacked the photos. "I left the opening after, well, you remember how odd Adam was acting, He must've been drunk. I've been to plenty of art openings and honestly, this is more interesting. Nice change from artists. They can be a little high strung and pushy."

Wait till you meet Gerri, I thought.

"So you and Vye hung out in the kitchen?" I asked.

He put the invoice back in its box. "Yes, we hung out, had a snack and a couple of beers. Afterward, Vye went to her room and I came back here to go through the trunk. I did get up and stretch around midnight, and that's when I looked out the window and saw Maud coming into the castle."

"If Vye left her room, would you have seen her?"

"More likely I would've heard her. That floor creaks. But I do get into my work." He shrugged.

"And Vye said you ran into Dree Venditti?"

"Dree?" His eyebrows knit. "Oh, yeah, Maud's friend. I didn't talk to her but I think Vye did."

"Thanks, I'll let you get back to work."

Tony smiled. "Any time."

Back on the third floor, I peeked into the library. Seeing that the room was empty, I hurried to the balcony and checked the parking area. Jack's SUV and the CSI van were gone.

One thought kept running through my mind.

The key.

I remembered Prentiss running to the office to retrieve the key, the CSI tech and Jack commenting on a locked-room mystery. It dawned on me. Jack's comment meant they hadn't found another key. They'd looked at security footage. There must be no video of someone locking the door to the dungeon after Adam went inside.

But there was only one key and it was outside of the room.

Maybe the killer wasn't recorded locking the door because the security tape was tampered with, the pertinent time frame erased. Who could've done that? Who had the expertise and the nerve to sneak into the office to do it?

Perhaps the killer locked the door and returned the key to the office at a later time. The hallway between the dungeon and the security office must've been packed with people on the morning of the festival. Brazen, but not impossible.

A thought gave me pause. How long did it take Adam to die? The door had to be locked when Adam was in the throes of anaphylaxis. He was right across from the security office; he might've gotten help and survived. More likely, the killer must've watched Adam die. If you're going to take the chance to kill someone, you'd stay to make sure the deed was done.

Why bother to lock the door and return the key the following morning and risk discovery?

The simplest solution was usually the right one. There had to be another key. Where was it? Who had it?

Don't be silly, Riley. The killer.

Chapter 29

*O*nce downstairs, I jogged through the great room. No sound came from the closed door of the study. I returned to the velvet rope and listened carefully. With both Jack and the CSI techs gone, this was the time to get into the dungeon. I just had to make sure I wasn't seen by any security guards.

My heart pounded as I crept down the stairs and scanned the ceiling of the hallway. There was a camera angled over the door of the security office, pointing toward the exit. I knew I'd be picked up going into the dungeon. I prayed no one was monitoring the feed or bothering to check the footage now.

Yellow crime scene tape crossed the open doorway to the dungeon. It was official—Adam was murdered. The sticky gray powder on the lock announced that it had been dusted for prints. I held my breath. I didn't sense anyone in the security office across the hall. Before I could second-guess myself, I ducked under the tape, careful not to brush against the door or lock.

At the threshold I quieted my breathing and my racing thoughts. The room was as I remembered it, except the whiteboard had been wheeled away from the fireplace.

Did the police think the killer had hidden in the fireplace? It was tall, tall enough that I could stand inside, and broad enough that a very small person could hunker—barely—into a corner to escape detection. Did the killer hide there until after Adam's body had been discovered and then run off? We'd all been too shocked to search the fireplace. It wouldn't have been impossible, but . . . I shook my head. I'd scanned the room before we'd left—even crouching in the fireplace, someone would be visible. The security guard had herded me, Maud, and Prentiss from the room. The room had been unattended for maybe sixty seconds. Could the killer have eluded detection and then made an escape during that short interlude? Impossible. I was grasping at straws.

The castles that inspired Moy Mull often had a hiding place called a priest's hole where Catholic priests were hidden by the devout during the Reformation. The price of discovery was their life, so the places were usually impossibly small, cramped, and craftily hidden. Of course, the hunters were also crafty, and many a priest became a martyr in those times.

Had Ben added a priest's hole in the design of his dream castle? If I were designing a dream castle, I would. Money had been no object for Ben, the thread bobbin king.

The lintel, just over head height, was carved with the thistle, heart, and lyre motifs I'd seen so many places in the castle. The large floral arrangement of faded autumn colors had been set to the side. I turned on my cell-phone flashlight and ran the beam along the interior of the fireplace. The stone lining was blackened by the soot of more than a hundred years, but the floor had been swept clean. Maud's housekeeping staff was top notch.

I didn't see anything that looked like a door or a hiding place. I ran my hands along the fireplace walls but didn't feel anything like a handle or a knob. There were tiles inlaid from the floor to just over my head, and my shoulders cramped as my fingers traced their smooth surface. Suddenly, I detected a different texture, and my fingers traced shapes carved into the tile. I crouched deeper inside the fireplace, training the beam on the wall. There were rows of tiles debossed with the same lyres, thistles, and hearts as the front of the fireplace. Who had enough money to decorate the inside of a fireplace? Ben Clitheroe. I ran my fingers over the shapes, pressed on them, but nothing moved. I ducked my head and repeated the process with the tiles the other side. My frustration mounted. Nothing. Moved.

Had someone rappelled down the chimney? I thought of Ben's climbing rope. I angled my flashlight beam up. The flue was in place. Surely some debris would've been disturbed by someone climbing down a chimney, and the clean floor disproved that theory.

I stepped out of the fireplace, stretching my cramped limbs, dusting my hands. I heard heavy footsteps and the squawk of a radio.

The security guard. I inched to the doorway and peered out, just in time to see the officer enter the security office.

I dipped under the tape and hurried down the hall, up the stairs, and into the kitchen.

Prentiss was at the counter looking out the window, holding a cup of coffee. At my entrance, he startled and his eyebrows flew above the heavy black frames of his glasses. "You've been caught gray-handed?"

I looked down at my hands, and my cheeks flared. "Um, I was . . . in the attic with Tony. Dusty papers, you know?" I soaped my hands at the sink. "Is the meeting over?"

Prentiss poured me a cup of coffee and set it on the table. I sat, but he remained standing and paced across the slate floor. "For some of us." His words dripped sarcasm. "As expected, Adam was as charming, generous, and thoughtful in death as he was in life."

"What did the lawyer say?" The warmth of the mug soothed my jangling nerves.

"Mr. Maserati?" Prentiss shrugged. "He's still saying it, to Vye, anyway."

I remembered the other car parked in the front drive. "Prentiss, who owns the Buick out front?"

He rolled his eyes. "Dree."

I sipped my coffee, willing myself to relax and gather my thoughts. "Did Adam have any family?"

"His parents died years ago. He was an only child." Prentiss drained his cup and leaned against the sink, his voice tinged with anger. "After all Maud did for him. What does he do? Leaves her an envelope to be read upon his passing, and when she opened it"—he swallowed, and I sensed the depth of feeling beneath his banter—"I could see the shock on her face. She stuffed the papers back in the envelope and asked to be excused."

I said quietly, "She didn't tell you what the papers were?"

He shook his head. "Said she wanted to be alone." He looked out the window. "With her bees."

Not with him. Poor Prentiss.

I sipped the coffee. My mind went back to the day of the ice cream social, how I'd dropped Luca and Willow at the back door of the castle.

"Did you ever meet Luca Principato?"

Prentiss put his cup in the sink. "The kid who keeps bees? A few times. Kid knows his stuff, though he and Maud didn't agree on everything."

Didn't agree? "You mean ways to keep bees?"

Prentiss sat heavily, worry deepening the lines around his mouth. "Maud uses bee venom in some of her products. She sourced some from labs in California and Europe, but she also used her own technique to extract venom from bees. Luca didn't like it."

At the word "venom" my mouth went dry. "What technique?"

"An electrified plate," Prentiss said. "A charge stimulates the bees to sting the plate. Then the plate dries and the venom's scraped off. It's a painstaking process. That's why her stuff is so expensive."

No wonder Luca was upset. "Wouldn't the bees die? When they sting? Don't they lose their stingers?"

"Not with this process." Prentiss shook his head. "Well, Luca said it was torture. They had a big fight about it a couple of weeks ago but then they kissed and made up. Literally. He's Italian."

Vye joined us. "Prentiss, Nicky wants to talk to you."

"Duty calls," he said.

I remembered I had another question for Prentiss. "Before you go, was the housekeeping staff here the night Adam died?"

Prentiss gave a short laugh. "You should join the police, Riley; you asked the same questions that big cop did. Nope, they'd all left." He gave us a wave and left the kitchen.

Vye dropped into the chair Prentiss had vacated and let out a sigh.

"Are you okay? You talked to Nicky for a long time."

"Nicky likes the sound of his own voice." Vye smoothed her hair. "I still don't understand everything that happened. I blanked out a lot. I think Nicky wants me to hire him as my agent, so that's good. He kept hammering that Adam's work would be more valuable now. Especially whatever Adam was working on before he died. He took photos at the farm for the cookbook. Of Willow . . ." Her voice trailed off.

Our eyes met. "Adam was in the darkroom the night he died," I said. "Let's check it out."

Chapter 30

Was the darkroom a crime scene, too? I pushed the thought away as I quickly rinsed my cup and put it in the sink. I hadn't seen any crime scene tape on that door.

Once again, I hoped the guard would be gone on rounds. Vye and I went downstairs, and I relaxed a bit knowing the security camera didn't cover this end of the hallway. We stopped in front of a closed door labeled Darkroom. Vye took a steadying breath as her hand hovered over the knob, her downturned mouth betraying strong emotion. "Let's do this," she muttered. There were two light switches outside, a regular one and one with a red bulb over it. Vye saw my puzzlement. "If someone's developing pictures inside, they turn on the red light. That way people outside know not to enter."

The darkroom was a cramped, close space, little larger than a walk-in closet, ringed with workbenches and a long shallow sink on one wall. I noted a paper cutter, an enlarger, and a thin wire running around the room at head height. Small clips like clothespins were attached to it at evenly spaced intervals. I remembered that Adam had left his bag in here, but it was gone now. The police must've taken it as evidence.

Vye seemed calmer in her element. "Adam shot old school

sometimes. He liked to play with effects that he could get during the development process." She ran her fingers along the wire.

"I don't know much about the process of photography, but don't the photos get hung up to dry?"

She adjusted one of the clips. "And negatives. Maybe he'd printed some photos. I imagine the cops took all that for evidence. I hope they have his cameras; they were expensive."

A scrap of trash under one of the workbenches caught my eye. I picked up a small strip of photo negative and held it to the light, then handed it to Vye. It was Luca and Willow walking to the barn at Fairweather Farm.

"So he did print some photos." She pushed the scrap into her pocket. "I'll call the police and ask for them."

As we turned to go, I noticed a yellowed 2001 calendar with a photo of the castle tacked up next to a wall-mounted telephone of similar vintage. A list of extensions hung next to it:

OFFICE 41

FRONT DESK 42

CONFERENCE ROOM 43

"I'm sure they'll return everything to you." I remembered that the last photos Adam had shot were of Willow in the tea garden. I wondered how Vye would feel when the police returned them.

The Maserati was gone as Vye and I pulled out of Moy Mull.

"Quick trip for Nicky, " I said.

"He's staying at the inn on the green. The castle has a dozen guest rooms and cottages, but Maud doesn't want him here." Vye toyed with a business card, then slid it into her pocket.

I was dying to know more about what happened with the lawyer, but Vye leaned her head against Sadie's passenger window and stared blankly, seemingly blind to the stone walls and rolling hills as we passed. "It was so hard to concentrate," she murmured. "Maud was so upset."

I thought of Prentiss's words. "She got an envelope."

"Yeah, a sealed envelope for Maud's eyes only. Nicky said he hadn't seen what was in it; it was from Adam's previous lawyer. She opened it and she freaked out and left and Prentiss ran after her. I was surprised to see him in the kitchen with you and not with Maud."

I pushed down a pang of sympathy for Prentiss. "So it was only you, Maud, and Prentiss?" I asked.

"That's because—" Vye turned from the window, her face drained of color.

"Vye, are you—"

"Uh, Riley, would you mind pulling over?"

I swerved into a narrow dirt road that led into the orchards behind Fairweather Farm. "Are you okay?"

With a primal scream, she leapt out of the car and leaning on the door, bent double.

Fearing she was ill, I scrambled out of the car. Was she having some kind of breakdown? "Vye, what is it?"

To my astonishment, she straightened and spun in a circle, laughing. Then she climbed onto Sadie's hood, bent her head, and patted the spot next to her. Her shoulders heaved and I couldn't tell if she was laughing or crying. I cautiously sat next to her.

Vye's head dropped back and she wiped her eyes with the heels of her hands. "Remember what I said to you earlier today about secrets?"

"Yes," I said slowly.

"I have one. I've never told anyone because I promised Adam I wouldn't. It would've ruined his image." She held up her left hand, and pointed to the row of black titanium rings.

She raised her eyebrows and wiggled her fingers. "Adam and I were married."

My first reaction was shock, then disbelief. Vye was a good twenty-five years younger than Adam, and their relationship . . . I managed to say, "When?"

"When I was eighteen, six years ago." Vye turned the black band on her ring finger as her words came in a rush. "First, he wanted me to be his apprentice. I saw history repeating itself with Willow. Adam offering to help her get into art school, Adam offering to be her mentor, Adam taking her photo, Adam telling her it'll be her turn one day, telling her we're together but we're not ordinary people, we're artists. We live differently. The rules don't apply to us." She took a long, gasping breath. "He didn't want to get married, but my grandmother . . ." She wiped away a sudden gush of tears. "I couldn't disappoint her like that. So I told him we had to be married, and we did it at the courthouse in Vegas, where some friend of his worked. It wasn't a church wedding, but at least I did that for my gran. Not that Adam cared. It was just a piece of paper to him. We had an open marriage, well, Adam did. I was too busy working."

Vye lurched at me and grabbed my hands, her eyes intense. "Swear, Riley, you're not going to tell anyone about me and Adam. I don't want to go through the rest of my life known as Adam's wife."

I was too startled to do anything other than nod. I didn't know what to say. I simply listened to Vye's catharsis, as one word after another poured out.

"Adam would get ideas, like let's go shoot in Thailand, or let's rent a car and drive down Route Sixty-Six and shoot everything neon. And we always traveled first class, always five-star hotels. So he'd spend everything, and I mean everything. But then he'd sell some work and we were okay again. When he needed money, he'd call Maud and she'd hire him.

He did that once a year or so, and she always paid well, really well.

"Now Nicky says I'll be rich." Vye snorted. "Guess what? Adam decided to insure some of his work last summer. Timing's everything, right?"

A glimmer of an idea kindled in my mind. Insurance money. "Did that include *Dallas*?"

She nodded.

Chapter 31

Monday nights, I usually had dinner with my dad and stepmom, Paulette. I invited Vye, but she begged off, asking if she could hang out with the cats. "I can order myself a pizza if I get hungry, or get some ice cream," she said.

I recalled the motto on one of Flo's T-shirts: "Ice cream is always a good idea."

The cats were in the parlor, enjoying a patch of warm, late-afternoon sun. Vye joined them and I went upstairs to shower and change.

I passed the wide-open door of Buzzy's bedroom, where Vye had emptied the contents of her duffel onto the bed. White cat hairs—Sprinkles' calling card—covered the mound of dark tops and jeans. From the corner of my eye, I noticed a driver's license on the dressing table. I stepped inside and leaned close, careful not to touch it. Iowa. Violet Yvonne Eddy. VYE.

I showered and changed. Remembering the cat hair on Vye's clothes, I pulled my bedroom door shut behind me as I left my room. I noticed Caroline's bedroom door was ajar. Vye's laughter rose from downstairs as I pushed the door open, filled with foreboding.

Every lamp, book, picture frame, and knickknack had been knocked from the dresser, bookcase, and nightstand. A trail of white hairs told the tale.

Sprinkles!

I hurriedly put things back, shut the door, then made sure to shut the other bedroom doors on my way downstairs. So much for Doctor von Furstenburg. I was living with a psycho.

Vye wasn't bothered a bit by Sprinkles' treatment of her wardrobe. I wished them good night and drove into Penniman, my mind so occupied by the events of the day that I hardly saw the cheerful covered bridge, the trees tinged with autumn hues, and the serpentine gray stone walls that lined the road into town.

Before I knew it, I was pulling into the driveway of my dad's house a block off the town green. The house I grew up in was one of the most charming houses in a town full of them, a Victorian Gothic painted sunshine yellow with black shutters. White gingerbread accented the peaked roofline, and the porch was broad and welcoming. There was a porch swing with striped green cushions where I'd spent hours reading as a child. Two urns spilled over with orange mums and ivy.

Dad had a great commute to work. The back door of his Penniless Reader used bookshop was right across the street from the house.

It was only five minutes until the shop closed at six, but I loved spending time there, so I jogged across the road and in the back door. The sweet must of used books surrounded me as I edged through the cramped storage room and into the main part of the store.

I breathed deep. I could forget Moy Mull for a while.

"Riley!" Paulette, my Stepford stepmom, balanced an arm full of books and gave me an air kiss near my cheek.

"Been dying to talk to you. You discovered the body of that famous photographer, right?"

So much for forgetting Moy Mull. Paulette, a trim retired nurse with champagne blond hair, intelligent blue eyes, and wardrobe by Talbots loved being plugged into Penniman's gossip network.

Dad finished ringing up a customer and wished her a good night. He locked the door, then pulled me into a bear hug against his soft plaid woolen shirt. "Right on time. I'm starving." He raised his shaggy eyebrows. "Guess what? Did you hear I got hit on the head with a book? I have only my shelf to blame."

Have I mentioned that Dad loves bad puns? The more groan worthy the better. Paulette laughed and I helped them close up.

As we entered the house—redecorated when Dad and Paulette married three years ago to suit Paulette's taste for muted colors, modern furniture, and clutter-free surfaces—a delicious aroma filled the air. "Oh, that smells good."

Paulette waved off the compliment. "Chicken marsala. Just some stuff I threw in the crock pot this morning. I'll whip up a salad. Pour the wine, please, Nate."

I had to give Paulette credit, the woman could cook. There was a price to her hospitality, though, and she peppered me with questions about Adam's death as we ate.

"I heard there was a theft at the gallery, too," Dad said. "When it rains it pours."

"One of Adam's most famous portraits, *Dallas*, was taken." I remembered what Caroline had said. "Dad, is it true that the police send out alerts for stolen artworks?"

He nodded. "I get the alerts, mostly to keep an eye out for stolen books or old maps. There's a hot market for them."

"Has anyone tried to sell you anything suspicious lately?" I sipped my wine.

"Had a kid come in with a book, an old guest book, yesterday. Had autographs of some famous historical figures. A few presidents. Inventors. Opera singers. Novelists. Movie stars of the past. Lot of folks cut them up and sell the autographs separately to collectors."

Something Tony had said tickled the back of my mind. *Without an inventory, it's hard to tell if something's missing, moved, or stolen.*

"That guy trying to sell it was shifty." Paulette sniffed. "I knew he was up to no good as soon as I saw him."

"What did he look like?" I asked.

Paulette pulled her cell phone from her pocket and turned the screen so I could see it. "Skinny guy in his twenties. Slight, thin, long nose, cleanshaven. Glasses."

Dad shook his head, but I could tell he got a kick out of Paulette's intrepid photography. I squinted at the blurry photo of the guy's back. It didn't help that the suspect had a black cap pulled over his ears and large sunglasses. Not anyone from Moy Mull, but still I had a feeling I'd seen him before. "What did you do, Dad?"

Dad shrugged. "I didn't buy it. He wanted a small fortune. Tried to find out where the young man had gotten it and he didn't even have a good story about finding it at a yard sale or in granny's attic. He said it was a friend's. I told Jack Voelker about it, but I could tell it's not high on the police priority list."

Paulette pointed to the photo. "He had a tiny mole on his neck. Left side. Below his jawline." She had an eye for detail, especially about appearance and fashion.

"I don't suppose he gave his name?"

Paulette scoffed at the same time Dad said, "No."

"On a lighter note," Dad said, "We had a visit from Maud and Prentiss."

"Yes, we're hosting a signing of her new cookbook when it comes out. What a coup!" Paulette crowed.

Dad beamed at her. "We'll be completely booked for the cookbook signing."

Sigh. Dad and his puns.

Chapter 32

Back at the farmhouse, I found Vye on the couch flanked by the cats, scrolling through photos on an iPad. Her earlier emotional outburst had done her good. Now she looked content and relaxed, though I still felt a bit battered by her emotional revelations.

"Have they behaved?" I nodded toward the cats.

Vye looked up. "Couldn't be better."

Unbelievable. "You're a cat whisperer." How had Vye succeeded where a cat expert had failed so spectacularly? One of the mysteries of the universe. "Would you like a glass of wine or some tea?"

"Wine would be great."

I poured two glasses of pinot noir and joined her, kicking off my shoes, which Rocky immediately pounced on.

I caught sight of a photo of the shop kitchen on Vye's iPad as I sat across from her on the softly worn rag rug. She saw me look and turned the tablet toward me so I could see better. "Maud asked me to finish the cookbook."

I raised my glass in a toast. "That's great."

"Good to have a job." Vye put the iPad aside with a sigh. "How are you doing?" I asked.

Vye gulped her wine and groaned. "I don't know. Adam and me, it was so complicated. I'm sorry I dumped so much on you, Riley."

"It's okay." I meant it.

Vye sighed. "He taught me so much but I did a lot for him too."

As I sipped my wine, I thought how she'd changed her name, and wondered if that had been at Adam's behest. "Vye, you're very talented."

She scoffed, but a blush surged up her chest to her neck. "If I don't pursue photography, I could always be a cat trainer."

Sprinkles opened one eye and looked at me, then snuggled closer to Vye. Usually cat behavior and psychology were mysteries I couldn't plumb, but this message was clear: I was supposed to be jealous that Sprinkles preferred Vye to me. Cats.

"You can stay here while you work on the book, until you're settled," I said.

"Thanks. Riley, the police want to talk to me." She threw me a shy glance. "Will you stay with me when they come?"

"Of course. When will they be here?"

Vye stroked Sprinkles. "The cop said tomorrow afternoon."

"Just tell me when. I'll figure something out."

"And I could help in the shop," Vye said. "I'd really like to. I mean, you've been so sweet to put me up. It would be a way to pay you back."

Too much help was never a problem. "Sure. Come down tomorrow morning."

I said good night and left Vye on the couch with Sprinkles. Rocky tagged along with me. At least someone loved me. I took a long, hot shower and sank into bed, but sleep eluded me.

I thought of Maud in her marvelous she shed and wondered what was inside that envelope from Nicky Dawson that had upset her so much.

What did I know about Maud Monaco, the sphinx of Moy Mull? I reached for my phone and googled, finding dozens of photos of Maud on magazine covers and at fashion shows and exclusive parties. I looked at the webpage of her cosmetics company, Bee-U; it was glossy, sophisticated, and expensive, like Maud herself.

Her marriage. What was her husband's name? Prince Freddie? Frederic? I searched but didn't find as much information or detail as I would have liked. The royal house of Terbinia didn't have the notoriety or cachet of the House of Windsor. I found a few articles from a magazine called *World of Royalty.*

Experience had taught me that not everything could be found on the internet. I checked Penniman Library's databases for *World of Royalty* magazine, but they didn't carry it. Where could I get old copies of this magazine?

Lily's. The owners, Zara and Coleman Hennessey had emigrated from England and were fans of all things royal. Maybe they'd also been intrigued by this fairy tale of the American model and the Terbinian prince. I'd ask Zara if she knew anything about Maud's royal years.

As I set aside my phone and closed my eyes, I thought of Maud and Adam. I hadn't found any photos of Maud's first wedding, the Vegas wedding that was assuredly a very different affair than the royal wedding that had followed just a short time later.

Maud had divorced Adam quickly. The marriage must've been, well, if not a disaster, one that quickly revealed the fault lines in their relationship. Seeing Adam, I couldn't believe the divorce would've been amicable. Then why did

Maud invite Adam to work on her projects? What kind of hold did he still have over her?

A soft snoring came from Vye's room as I headed downstairs early the next morning. I put out the cats' food, but there was no sign of Sprinkles or Rocky, so I checked their usual hangout in the parlor. They sat on the back of the couch, and their heads turned guiltily as I went into the room.

"Fine, don't tell me what you're up to. I don't want to know."

A cool, gauzy fog that promised rain lay over the farm and the rolling hills in the distance. I took a quick run, showered, and scrambled some eggs. As I ate, I read a few chapters of *Death on the Nile*, but Vye remained upstairs.

The snoring told me she was alive. Her appointment with the police wasn't until the afternoon. The soft drizzle turned into a steady patter of rain as I grabbed a raincoat and dashed down to Udderly.

At the shop, I did inventory and organized the bank deposit. I'd been shocked by Buzzy's not-very-secure method of storing cash in a metal box in the bottom drawer of the old rolltop desk in the shop office, but here I was with my Library of Congress tote bag stuffed with over a thousand dollars of wrinkled bills because I hadn't had a chance to get to the bank. I vowed to find a better way when I had time.

Pru was at the stove stirring a custard base for our cherry vanilla ice cream. The rich, spicy scent of vanilla that perfumed the kitchen made me stop in my tracks and close my eyes to savor the fragrance. Pru laughed. "I've made this a hundred times, and it still makes my mouth water."

She playfully swatted my arm as I took one of the candied Bordeaux cherries and popped it into my mouth. "Quality control," I said as I checked the daily schedule. "Vye's offered to work in the shop while she stays here."

"Willow told me how Vye helped with the photo shoot," Pru said. "She sounds like an interesting young woman."

The photo shoot felt like ancient history. "How's Luca?" I asked.

She sighed. "Cat on a hot tin roof. The slightest thing makes him jump. He's up at the apiary. That seems to calm him."

Just like Maud, I thought.

"Working near bees would make me the opposite of calm," I said.

Pru nodded. "Me too."

Pru and I settled into the rhythm of people who work well together. Vye came in and I gave her a quick tutorial on working the ice cream counter. The rain and cooler temperature would keep the crowds small, a perfect time for a new employee to start. Vye clicked with Pru's warmhearted vibe, and her friendliness made her a natural with customers. Willow and Luca and some interns were scheduled for the afternoon and the evening, so I felt confident leaving Vye in Pru's capable hands when I left to make the bank deposit and meet my informant for lunch.

Chapter 33

I wasn't proud about meeting up with Tillie. I scanned the area for anyone familiar as I parked Sadie next to the green by Lily's Tea Room, a renovated Victorian painted lady and my favorite spot for quiet conversation. The pink and teal gingerbread fantasy was almost diagonally across the green from Dad's bookshop.

Zara waved to me from the hostess stand. Regal as the portrait of Queen Elizabeth II on the wall behind her, Zara's customary yellow shirtdress and white apron set off her smooth chignon, her rich brown complexion, and classic red lipstick. "Riley, my dear, it's been too long! I have a cozy table for you."

I hung my raincoat on the coatrack and followed Zara to the front parlor, where a fire glowed in the fireplace. My table was covered by a cloth in a blue floral, and the overstuffed chairs were upholstered in a pale pink gingham. Somehow all the colors and patterns blended harmoniously with the William Morris Strawberry Thief wallpaper, the Stafford-shire dogs on the mantle, and the potted ivy in the corner. An oil painting of a snow white terrier, the pampered pooch the place was named for, kept watch from above the mantle. The basket by the fireplace—where the real Lily usually dozed—was empty.

"Where's Lily?" I asked.

Zara smiled as she handed me a menu. "At playgroup."

Maybe Sprinkles needed a playgroup.

Tillie joined me soon after, stowing her Penniman Library tote bag under the table and glowing at the warm greeting from the Hennesseys. Coleman and Zara were longtime friends of Dad's, and they'd embraced Tillie as one of my friends. If they only knew what we were up to.

We both ordered the full tea, and Zara brought us a steaming pot of Earl Grey and a three-tiered tea tray with scones, miniature sandwiches, tiny jewel-like desserts, strawberry jam, and clotted cream. Lulled by the gracious atmosphere, I decided not to dive into the gritty details of the murder immediately. "Tillie, have the police been to Moy Mull much in the past?"

Tillie sipped her tea with lowered eyes, treating me to the sea green frosted eyeshadow that complimented her ensemble of green and silver silk tunic, leggings, and matching headscarf. "Nope. After the hotel closed, some guy bought it and started renovations that never got finished for years. Kids would go up and party like in the old days, get into mischief and vandalism. It's been quiet in the last couple of years or so since Maud bought the place. Just a couple of emergency calls."

"What kind of emergencies?" I selected two sandwiches, a coronation chicken on brioche and salmon with cream cheese and dill on pumpernickel.

Tillie filled her plate and rubbed her hands. "Trespassing mostly. She brought in her own security team and partying kids had to go somewhere else. Aside from what happened this weekend? There was one EMS"—she

paused—"last year. A guy got stung by a bee. Bad reaction."
She gave me a sly look. "Same guy, wasn't it?"

"If his name was Adam Blasco, it was." I brushed away
some crumbs from the truly excellent sandwiches. Time to
get down to business. "You said the results of the autopsy
report were due today?"

She patted her lips with a dainty pink napkin. "Yep.
Anaphylaxis brought on by bee"—she leaned forward and
said the word with relish—"venom."

I sipped my tea. "Injected?"

My correct guess made Tillie's smile fade for a moment,
but it returned as her report gained momentum. "Jack's so
smart. He asked the ME—that's medical examiner—to look
at the site of the supposed sting. The sting of a bee isn't as
deep as a needle puncture. They might not have looked if it
hadn't been for Jack telling them what to look for."

"He knew the bee was a drone." *How did he know that?
Smart guy, sharp.* I searched my feelings. *Was that pride
I felt?*

Admiration shone from Tillie's eyes. "He saw the injection
site, didn't find a stinger, and realized there was no stinger. I
heard him telling the ME. The ME was impressed."

I stifled a laugh, picturing Tillie listening in on her boss'
phone line. How did this woman keep her job? I appreciated
my pipeline of information, but my throat went dry when
I realized that what I was doing was just as unethical and
illegal as what Tillie was doing. I sipped my tea. *Eye on
the prize*, I thought. I didn't want Luca being blamed for
this death. Even being the subject of an investigation could
endanger his status and get him deported. That would break
Willow's heart.

Tillie's voice brought me back. "You were in the castle
when the body was found, right?"

I nodded and took another sandwich, a miniature lobster roll with a buttery sauce. "Something bothers me. Well, a couple of things. First, why did Adam even go into the dungeon? There's nothing there. He was working in the dark room. I think he was summoned—"

"To his death," Tillie breathed. "That sounds like a title for a book: *Summoned to His Death.* I'd read that."

Was the summons to the dungeon for dramatic effect? The dramatic effect would be dampened by the office furniture and dusty floral arrangements. "The walls are three feet thick," I said. *Who told me that? Was it Prentiss? Wouldn't all the walls in the castle be the same thickness?*

"The murderer didn't want anyone hearing Adam struggle," Tillie said. "Just like ancient rulers didn't want to hear their prisoners screaming for help, so they made their dungeons soundproof—or as soundproof as you could get back then."

I poured myself another cup of fragrant tea and topped up Tillie's cup. "Did the killer call Adam's cell phone?"

"We looked at his phone record." Tillie spread jam and clotted cream on a scone. "No calls after six p.m. Friday. He got dozens of calls Saturday morning when people were trying to find him."

"Cell phones don't work well in that building because the walls are so thick. So the meeting was arranged in person, arranged earlier, or—" I remembered the old-fashioned house phones in the darkroom and the TV parlor. I leaned forward. "Did they check about calls coming from within the castle to the darkroom? Could calls from one extension to another be traced?"

She shrugged. "Don't know."

"There are old-fashioned phones that can call different rooms within the castle. Anyone inside the castle could've called him to set up a meeting." Panic rose in me. What if the call had come from the TV parlor, where I'd sat with Maud and Prentiss while the police were dealing with Adam's body? My prints would be on that phone.

She pointed at me with a sea-green-polish-tipped finger. "So who's in the castle with Adam, summoning him to his death? The ME put the time of death between ten p.m. and two a.m."

"You saw the security tape, right?" I said.

"Yep, but . . ." Tillie bit into a miniature chocolate éclair and shrugged.

"But what?" I replenished our teacups.

"They're wondering if the tape could've been altered because no one besides Adam was seen going into that dungeon—or leaving it—anywhere near the time of death," Tillie said. "An expert's coming to look."

"How could the tape be altered with the security guys coming and going in that office all the time?" I said.

"Maud's security force only patrols outside, and the property's huge," Tillie said. "They go to the office for breaks or meetings. There was plenty of time when the team was out of the office." She leaned back and leveled a look at me. "Okay, my turn. You were on the inside. Give me the scoop on who's staying in the castle."

Quid pro quo. "As far as I know, Maud Monaco. Prentiss Love. Tony Ortiz has a room there, he's working on the history of Moy Mull for an exhibit Maud's opening next year." I swallowed. "And Vye."

Tillie grimaced. "Oh yeah, she's one of those people who goes by only one name. Do you know her last name?"

I figured Tillie could find out on her own. "Just Vye." I'd sworn I wouldn't divulge Vye's secret. Well, marriage was public record. The cops would discover it soon enough along with her surname. I cleared my throat. "There's housekeeping staff and another guest named Dree Venditti." The memory of Dree waving at me from the kitchen door on Saturday afternoon made me wonder. Both Vye and Tony had seen her at Moy Mull the night of the murder. The next day I saw her doing the walk of shame, going home wearing the same clothes she'd worn the night before. She'd been loud and obnoxious to the security guard. Why did she wave to me?

She wanted to be noticed. My mind followed this intriguing lead until Tillie's voice broke in.

"Earth to Riley. You just"—she waved her teacup—"went off into space."

"Has Dree Venditti been questioned yet?" I said. "Former model. Tall, very tan, long blond hair parted in the middle?"

Tillie shook her head. "Not yet, but I think her name's on Jack's list."

"If you learn anything about Dree, would you let me know?"

Tillie gave me a shrewd look, but nodded. "I know Maud required security badges, but I was thinking maybe the killer got in during the day and hid? You could hide anywhere in that place, it's huge. What if the murderer tailgated behind a group and hid?"

"Tailgated?" I asked. "You mean like people do in buildings where you have to be buzzed in? Blend in with a group? It could work. You'd have to check the security footage for the whole day."

Tillie burped softly. "They're looking at that now."

I took another scone and spread it with cream and jam. *How many people wanted to kill Adam? Plenty. Maybe even more than I knew of.*

"They'll look at all the security tapes, but not every door was filmed. Just general shots of each side of the house." Tillie leaned her chin on her hand, her expression disappointed.

I shared her disappointment. "So not enough detail to ID someone." I took a bite of my scone and chewed thoughtfully. "What's the word on the street? Who do you think killed Adam?"

She took one of the romance novels from her bag and looked at the cover. I caught the title on the spine: *Love's Fateful Mistake*. "Local gossip says it's Prentiss. Hasn't he loved her from afar for years? Pined for her? But always stuck in the friend zone, right? She marries someone else, a famous photographer, and then a prince. He can't compete. Then the prince dies and he can make his move, but Adam comes back into Maud's life. Weren't they married at one time? What if Prentiss knew Maud and Adam were going to rekindle a flame?"

Adam's guest house, Ivy Cottage, was all the way across the estate from the castle. If any flame were to be rekindled, that would have to be one very long flame. I shrugged, noncommittal. Prentiss was devoted to Maud, that was clear. He knew about Maud's laboratory and bee venom. He was at Moy Mull when Adam was stung. He knew about Adam's bee allergy. He'd know if Adam had mistreated Maud, if—

I thought again of Maud hiring Adam over and over. What if Adam was blackmailing her? What if Prentiss wanted to free Maud? Whether from blackmail or simply to free Maud from a toxic relationship? I pushed the thought away. I liked Prentiss. Prentiss made me laugh. I shifted uneasily, knocking a poufy chair cushion to the floor. I didn't want Prentiss to be a killer. Shakespeare's line from *Hamlet* came to me: "one may smile, and smile, and be a villain." It was so inconvenient being a librarian.

"Have the police said anything about Tony?" As I retrieved the chair cushion I remembered his soft expression when talking about Maud.

"He's clean, has an alibi," Tillie said.

"Maud?"

Tillie snorted. "She came in at midnight when no one else was around. According to the tape, the last people to see Adam alive were Barry the caterer and Luca, the kid from the farm. Barry buzzed in and Luca tailgated him because he didn't have the right kind of badge."

Tillie glanced at her watch and startled. "Oops, gotta jet. Today's usually my day off, but I was asked to come in. There was a theft at a retirement party in one of the fancy houses on Penniman Lake, the senator's house, so it's all hands on deck."

"Have fun," I said.

"And Riley"—she lowered her voice as she gathered her bags—"you'll let me know if you learn anything, right?"

Deal with the devil. I nodded. "Of course."

Chapter 34

I finished my tea, thinking about what I'd learned. I thought the tape was good news for Luca. Despite Adam railing at him, when Luca left, Adam was still alive. *Unless he tampered with the tape . . .* I pushed the thought away. Impossible.

Zara cleared Tillie's plate and gave me a brilliant smile. "We loved the Lady Grey tea ice cream you made for us this summer, Riley."

"I'm so glad," I said.

"You know, Coleman's making a ginger tea cake for all the leaf peepers this fall and he'd love to serve ice cream with it. Do you know what would go perfectly with that?" She raised her eyebrows.

Inwardly I groaned. *Let me guess.* "Pumpkin spice ice cream?"

She beamed. "What do you think? Could you make some for us?"

"My pleasure." *Pumpkin spice—resistance was futile.* "Zara, could I ask you something?"

"Of course."

"Do you have any old copies of a magazine called *World*

of Royalty? I'm specifically looking for any issues about"—I lowered my voice—"Maud Monaco."

Zara's eyes went dreamy. "Oh, yes indeed! That was a fairy-tale wedding, though his family"—she clucked—" the Royal House of Terbinia, made life hard for her. But it was a love match." She set the plates down. "I'll run up and get them."

Zara returned a few minutes later and handed me a small stack of glossy magazines.

"I promise I'll bring them back. Thank you, Zara." I placed them in my bag and gave her a hug. On the way out, I grabbed my coat and glanced into the bustling enclosed front porch. Every table by the long wall of windows was occupied. A Black man with chiseled features and warm brown eyes behind tortoise shell glasses looked up from his tea and waved. "Riley!"

Dr. Liam Pryce, Penniman's most popular—and handsome—veterinarian. "Doctor Pryce!" I made my way to his table.

"Do you have a minute?" He jumped up and indicated the seat across from him.

For you, an hour, I thought. "Of course."

"And please call me Liam."

I slid into the seat across from him and saw a half-eaten scone on the plate in front of me. He noticed my glance. "My new assistant got up to take a call. I've been showing her the best places in Penniman. We'll be heading to Udderly tomorrow." As he grinned, a small scar puckered the skin above his left eyebrow and that tiny imperfection, in a face so classically handsome, made me like him even more.

"Please do, I'd love to meet her. How have you been?" Had I already asked him how he was? I wasn't used to talk-

ing to him outside of the vet clinic. This felt like a date. My
hands began to sweat, and I wiped them on my pants.

"Great. I heard you were up at Moy Mull for that crazy
business with the photographer. Are you okay? That must
have been very stressful. I've been following it in the news."

I realized that few people had asked me if I was okay,
and I warmed to him. "Yes, I am. Thank you."

Liam leaned forward. "I wanted to ask you . . ."

I was losing myself in his dark eyes. "Anything . . ."

"How's Sprinkles?" Liam said. "Caroline brought her for
her physical, and mentioned her adjustment issues. I wondered if things had improved."

Sprinkles. I blinked, and inside I laughed at myself.
"She's—" How did I put this? I still thought psychopathy
lurked under Sprinkles' fluffy, baleful exterior, but I'd never
say that to him. He truly loved animals, even the less-lovable
ones, maybe especially the unlovable ones. "We think she's
happiest with Rocky, so Sprinkles is staying home at the
farmhouse. She's going to have to adjust to Caroline's absence, I think. But she made a new friend." I told him about
Vye and how she and Sprinkles seemed to have bonded. "Vye
took hundreds of photos of Sprinkles."

"Maybe," he mused, cradling his delicate teacup in his
strong hands, "Vye rekindles good feelings for Sprinkles,
memories of her glory days. The adulation of the show circuit." His warm eyes sparkled with humor.

I didn't know anything about the memory capacity of
cats, or if he was joking. "Maybe?"

A petite woman in a fashionable jumpsuit stopped next
to me, and I realized I was in her seat.

Liam stood. "Riley, this is my new assistant, Imelda Cross.
Imelda, this is Riley Rhodes. She runs the Udderly Delicious
Ice Cream Shop."

Imelda had glossy black hair worn in an angular bob,

pale skin, vivid red lips, and a look in her striking onyx eyes that made me feel like I'd overstepped. "Oh, sorry." I jumped up.

"I love ice cream!" She smiled, but something about the way she settled into her seat made me think of claiming territory. "I'll have to stop by."

"Please do. I have to run. Nice to talk to you, doctor— Liam."

I grabbed my raincoat from the rack and stepped outside. A burst of wind took the storm door from my hands and blew it open, dashing cold rain in my face. I wrestled the door shut and pulled up my hood. I could see Dr. Pryce and Imelda through the window, warm and comfortable in Lily's pretty tea room. "Cozy," I groused and wiped a spatter of raindrops from my face. Feeling sorry for myself, I considered walking over to the library and checking out a tote bag's worth of romance novels, then remembered the Agatha Christie I'd left on the kitchen table. I didn't have time to read the books I owned.

"Riley!" A booming voice shook me from my moment of self-pity. Gerri shut the door of her Lincoln Continental, opened a golf umbrella that coordinated with her turquoise trench coat, and strode over to me.

"Blustery today," she said as she held the umbrella over us. "I'm on my way to see Bridget Flynn. Would you like to come?"

Chapter 35

ridget Flynn?" I blanked for a moment. "Oh, her grand-mother worked at the castle."

"Great-grandmother," Gerri corrected. "She has artifacts for the historian at Moy Mull. Her house is right around the corner. I parked here so I can shop later."

I pulled out my phone. "Let me call Pru to make sure everything's okay at the shop."

Gerri kept the umbrella over us as I called. I couldn't deny the pull of the mysterious castle and the chance to hear about its earliest inhabitants.

Pru assured me that the cold rain was keeping customers away, so I accompanied Gerri a block over from the green to Merchants Lane, a narrow street lined with old oaks and maples, to a white Victorian cottage with green shutters and wraparound porch.

The paint on the shutters was faded, but bright flowerpots hung from the gingerbread trim of the porch. A mobility scooter was parked by the front door and the porch had been reconfigured with a ramp.

A tall woman with snow white hair highlighted by a fuch-sia streak waited at the door. "Come in, come in. I'm Bridget and this beast is Harold." Bridget Flynn leaned on a walker and a friendly mutt padded behind her, wagging his tail. I gave him a pat as Gerri shook her umbrella and propped it by the door.

"This is Riley Rhodes," Gerri said. "You know her father, Nate, at the bookshop."

"Of course!" Bridget squeezed my arm. "Hello, my dear. I remember you working there when you were a wee girl! And you're quite the world traveler, aren't you? I followed your travel and food blog. Hang your coats on the rack and come into the dining room."

Gerri and I hung our coats on a tall oak rack by the door, one that held a spectacular floor-length black fur coat. Gerri and I exchanged glances and she mouthed, *Wow.*

"What was the name of your blog again?" Bridget said.

"Rhode Food." It had been great cover for my occasional CIA assignments.

"You got me hooked on Korean BBQ." Bridget laughed and wagged a finger. "Can I get you a drink?"

Gerri and I demurred, and Bridget led us to the dining room table, where the lacy tablecloth was covered with photos and cardboard storage boxes.

"I've been diving into my granny's boxes. But first things first. Gerri, I have news." Bridget clasped her hands. "I was chatting with that nice young man putting together the exhibit at Moy Mull. Tony Ortiz. He's asked me to do some presentations when the exhibit opens. Life downstairs, all about my great-grandmother, Fiona! I'll even dress up in period clothing."

"That's wonderful!" I said.

"I'm so happy for you." Gerri smiled warmly.

"Very *Downton Abbey*." Bridget's eyes gleamed. "Well, it's a magnificent building with such magnificent history. I'll be glad to be part of it." She gestured at the boxes. "Such treasures! Every time I open one, I learn something new. Did I ever tell you, Granny Fiona said Old Ben even brought stonemasons from Scotland to build the fancy fireplaces? Well, Granny told so many stories of her time at Moy Mull, I recall thinking of them as, well, stories, you know, fairy tales, like Little Red Riding Hood or Hansel and Gretel. I wasn't interested when I was young. But it was all real." She took a seat and pointed to chairs around the table. "Sit, sit."

Gerri and I took seats and Bridget continued. "Now, you were asking me about Oona the other day, right, Gerri?"

Gerri settled her scarf and nodded.

"After Oona ran off with the chauffeur, Ben had the staff make a bonfire and burn all her things. Well, they did what they were told, of course, but being thrifty Yankees..." Bridget pointed to the coatrack. "They made sure a few things were saved from the flames. That winter Oona ran off was so cold, Granny couldn't bear to throw away a perfectly good fur coat, but it was so striking and expensive she couldn't wear it, you see; people would think she stole it, which I guess she did, so she packed it away and forgot about it. So we'll use that in the exhibit. And this—" She indicted a lace tablecloth embroidered with thistles on a side table covered with a dozen family photos in silver frames. "Gran loved to display this lovely tablecloth that Oona gave her. Oona was quite the embroiderer."

Bridget's dog sniffed around Gerri, and when Gerri didn't give him a pat, he came to me. I gave the friendly mutt a scratch. "I heard Oona had a dog, Jamie."

"Ah, yes, the little thing cried for a week after Oona left. Ben couldn't take it. He wanted to give Jamie away, so Granny took him." Bridget pointed to Harold. "He's Jamie's great-, I don't know how many times great-, grandson.

"Well, after Oona left, Ben"—Bridget shook her head—"I guess he fell into a depression, and fired most of the staff, except for the cook and Granny. Cook told Granny late one night she heard moaning and a scream. When she brought Ben his breakfast and told him what she heard, well, he dropped his cup of coffee and turned white as a sheet. That's when the stories about the haunting of the castle started. He left for Boston and hired a detective to look for Oona, but she and her boyfriend had disappeared clean off the face of the earth. Ben called one of his judge friends and got a divorce, and next spring there was a wedding for him and the second wife, Alma."

"Wait," I said. "Oona ran off in the winter and he remarried the next spring?"

"That was quick," Gerri said.

I asked, "Did your great-grandmother work for Alma?"

"Oh no." Bridget waved the thought away. "Alma brought her own retinue—is that the word?—from Boston. She wasn't using a bunch of country bumpkins!"

"Did your great-grandmother ever say anything about the chauffeur?" I asked.

She shrugged. "He was a young man Ben brought down from Boston. Granny didn't say much about him, only how she couldn't believe a shy thing like Oona would go off with a fellow like that. She said Oona was a good girl, but the chauffeur was young and handsome."

I remembered the photograph of Ben's motorcar, the chauffeur's tailored uniform and gleaming buttons accenting a broad chest and trim waist.

Bridget warmed to her tale. "When Oona left with the chauffeur, Granny couldn't believe it. She told the story so many times. 'I cleared out her room but she left her coat. And her pup! She'd never have left Jamie,' she said. Granny was very forceful about that. She thought Oona came to a bad end, but it was better to think of her off with a handsome boy."

"So what did she think happened?" Gerri asked.

Bridget stroked her dog. "She said she talked to anyone who would listen, defending Oona, but the gossip was too juicy. Eventually Granny took a job with the mill-manager's wife, helping her run her house, and then she married my great-grandfather and raised her own family."

My large lunch with Tillie, the cozy room, and Bridget's storytelling had lulled me into a very relaxed state. Reluctantly, I thanked Bridget for the visit and said I had to get back to the shop.

"You know," Bridget said, "I'm leaving for Florida tomorrow to see my daughter. Flo and Gerri offered to bring these boxes over to Moy Mull. Maybe you could help. Three o'clock tomorrow?" Gerri and Bridget shared a glance. "You know, the historical society could use a librarian."

Uh-oh.

"I'd be happy to help deliver the boxes," I said. "And how interesting, a librarian. Well, I'll think about it. See you tomorrow."

I dashed back to my car, chuckling. That glance Bridget and Gerri had shared. Had I been maneuvered into this visit like a chess piece by Gerri? Most certainly. Why had she parked outside Lily's instead of driving straight to Bridget's house on such a rainy day? Everyone at the shop knew I went to Lily's for lunch on my day off. *Gerri, you sly thing.*

Chapter 36

R ain pelted the window of the ice cream shop. For the first time since I'd been managing Udderly, business was slow, and for the first time, I welcomed it. I was too busy mulling what I'd learned as I cooked down pumpkins to make puree for Zara's pumpkin spice ice cream. Willow and Vye chatted amiably as Willow chalked a new flavors board and Vye wiped down tables. Any awkwardness between the young women had vanished.

After setting the puree to cool, I took Zara's royalty magazines out of my bag and flipped through the pages. Pru joined me and together we sighed over the photos of Maud's wedding.

Flo arrived, shaking raindrops off her bright yellow slicker. She hung up her coat, looped an apron over her head, and peered over my shoulder. "Oh, Maud and the prince. Fascinating wedding, fascinating." She put extra emphasis on the second "fascinating."

I turned to her. "What do you mean, Flo?"

Flo gathered her thoughts. "When Maud hired you and everyone started talking about Maud and her marriage, well, it brought out the genealogist in me, so I did some digging."

I remembered what she and Gerri had said. "Gretna Green?"

Pru wrinkled her brow, so Flo explained again. "That was her first marriage. Unhappy, I'd bet from its short duration, but it didn't matter. Soon after that she had the prince sweep her off her feet, right, and they had a good marriage, a love match."

I paged through the magazine to a photo of Frederic and Maud, splendid in royal finery, the train of Maud's wedding gown as long as the aisle of the chapel.

We sighed in unison.

Flo turned the magazine's pages. "There was something else. His family, well, they weren't happy about the marriage. She was an American, she was Black, she was a divorcee . . . they made her sign a big prenup. Kept it quiet, of course, because the prenup was draconian. If Freddie died, she got nothing, nada, and on top of that would have to give back all the royal goodies. But Freddie loved her and wanted to take care of her as best he could." Flo flipped the page to a photo of a lakefront villa so lovely it looked like a movie set. I'd visited the area, which boasted some of the most spectacular and expensive real estate in the world.

Pru read the caption. "Villa D'Amore, Lake Como, Italy."

Flo cleaned her glasses on the hem of her apron. "It was a morganatic marriage arrangement."

"Morganatic?" I said. "Flo, where do you get these things?"

"Genealogy's full of surprises." She put her glasses back on. "Marriage has long been, well, more about business and politics than love. Very rarely, a royal would fall in love with a commoner. Most would do their duty, marry the person they were supposed to, join their countries, and keep their"—Flo waggled her eyebrows—"honeys on the side. But some really did want their marriage to be about true love. Of course, the courtiers and politicians had a cow. If the royal son died, they didn't want some commoner getting the castle or royal jewels or, God forbid, power."

"So they had prenups?" Pru asked.

Flo tilted her head. "Kind of. Royal families would allow marriage to a commoner as long as none of the power and money went to the bride. But, she had to have something, some security. So, there were morganatic marriages."

To our puzzled looks Flo said, "Morgen means *morning*. The groom gave the commoner bride a 'morning gift' the day after the wedding that would be hers to keep no matter what. Prince Frederic gave Maud some doozies."

Flo flipped the magazine's pages to photos of the villa in Italy, an apartment in New York, and a spectacular Highlands hunting lodge. "When Freddie died, the royal Terbinians booted Maud out of all the official royal residences, took back the jewels, the royal yacht, the royal jet, the servants. But Freddie's morning gift was real estate they couldn't take back."

"Italy, New York, and Scotland. Not bad, Freddie," I said.

Willow and Vye joined us.

"I had so much fun. Can I come back again?" Vye hung up her apron.

"Of course," Flo and Pru chimed.

"Yes." Willow smiled.

Vye ducked her head and pulled me aside. "I have to meet the cop. You'll come to the house with me, Riley?"

I nodded and turned to the others. "We'll come back to give you all a dinner break."

Pru said, "I'll make sandwiches and bring them over."

Flo flipped the magazine closed and raised her eyebrows as she handed it to me. She wanted to tell me something else when we were alone.

"I'll talk to you later?" I tucked it in my bag.

She nodded.

What did Flo want to say that couldn't be said here?

Vye and I walked up the lane as a black Penniman Police SUV drew to a stop in front of the house. Jack got out and waited for us by the front door, his broad-shouldered frame filling the porch. Vye's footsteps slowed and I squeezed her shoulder. "It's fine. Jack's a nice guy."

"Riley, if I'm honest, I'm not sorry Adam's dead. Sometimes I hated him. I'm not sorry one bit." Vye crossed her arms, hugging herself. "But that doesn't mean I killed him."

Chapter 37

J ack was polite enough not to roll his eyes or say "you again" when I climbed the steps onto the porch with Vye. "Would you like some coffee or tea?" I'd keep it polite too.

"No, thanks." Jack didn't smile as we entered the house.

Vye got the message.

"Riley, I guess I'll be okay." She took a deep breath and sat at the kitchen table.

"Okay." I hung up my raincoat and shouldered my bag. "I'll check on the cats and head upstairs."

"Good," Jack said. "Then I'd like to talk with you too."

Of course. I'd been at the castle when the body was found. "Right."

I went into the parlor but saw no sign of Sprinkles or Rocky. I found them at the top of the stairs looking down into the hall. Sprinkles started down but I scooped her up. "Come here, Sprinkles." She'd had some bad moments with Jack. I hated taking her into my room, because then everything would be covered in her hair. Instead I took her to Caroline's room, but as I'd feared, the scent of her missing mistress triggered a round of zooming, and within moments

Rocky joined in. I sat on the bed cross-legged and wondered how I'd ended up here and what I'd done to deserve this.

Trying to ignore the cats racing around the room, I took another issue of *World of Royalty* out of my bag and flipped through its glossy pages. What a life. While Maud still lived in a castle, the photos made it clear that during her marriage she'd lived like a real royal, the one percent of the one percent, with servants, parties with movie stars, and meetings with politicians and other royals. The headlines told the tale. "Tongues Wag as Prince Dates Las Vegas Model." "Royal Family Greets American Beauty." "Wedding Bells for the Playboy Prince."

I paged through the most recent magazine, published five years earlier, just before Frederic's death, to a photo of him and Maud hosting a party on their yacht. I recognized Newport Harbor, and a face in the background . . . Tony Ortiz. I recalled he'd told me they'd met there when he was working in a gallery.

Did Tony have a reason to want Adam dead? I recalled the uncomfortable exchange they'd had the night of the exhibit opening. Adam had recognized Tony, but Tony denied knowing him. What was that about?

Vye had seen Tony the night of the murder, spent time with him in the kitchen, then they'd both retired to their rooms on the third floor. She said he'd been working in the attic and that she would've heard him if he'd left.

I went back to the photo. The camera had also captured a younger, slimmer Prentiss gazing toward Maud. Did he love her? He must, they'd stayed connected for thirty years. Or was she simply a lovely paycheck, and he was a bon vivant in love with her jet-set lifestyle?

There was a sudden silence. I checked the cats—they were both exhausted, sprawled on cushions by the window. I went to my room to retrieve my travel notebook, a place I'd jotted memories and notes about places and people I met on my trips. It wasn't getting much of a workout, but list making calmed me, helped me gather my thoughts. I returned to Caroline's room, made sure the cats hadn't moved, and carefully shut the door behind me.

Across the top of a page I wrote "Who Killed Adam Blasco?" The question was too big. I'd break it down, try to organize my thoughts, and list the questions that puzzled me.

Who was in the castle the night of the murder during the ten-to-two time frame?

Vye. Maud. Prentiss. Tony. Dree. Luca and Barry, but, I noted, they were captured by security cameras leaving the castle.

Was it possible for someone to hide in the castle? The badge system would track people coming. What about going? We didn't have to scan the badges on the way out. A killer could've entered with another person without scanning their badge, like Luca did with Barry. Tailgating, as Tillie'd said. I sighed. So it was possible to have X, an unknown person.

Random questions swirled as I lay back and closed my eyes.

Who watched from the shadows as Adam photographed Willow? It could've been anyone who wanted to see the master photographer at work. But still . . . why hide at all? Wouldn't a fan want to meet their idol?

Why did Barry walk past the kitchen door and go in the back door?

What was in the envelope that Nicky Dawson gave Maud? Why did it upset her so much?

Why kill Adam in the dungeon? Why not kill Adam in

the darkroom, where he'd been working? The darkroom was closer to the rest of the house, perhaps there'd be more of a chance of someone seeing the killer. Plus, Maud said it was the first place she'd looked for Adam. No, the killer had chosen the dungeon. Why?

The key . . . why was the door locked? To keep people out until Adam could die. Cold, but there it was. How did the killer lock the door and get the key back into the security office without being seen? And how did the EpiPen get into Luca's backpack? That must be on the security tape. I had to see it. I sighed. I'd have to call Tillie. I couldn't believe I was planning to meet her with the chief of police downstairs.

I recalled the look Flo gave me as she handed me the stack of *World of Royalty.* What was up with Flo? Flo with a secret? She was the most open, honest person I knew. Flo being worried unsettled me more than Adam's murder.

A crash pulled me out of my reverie. Sprinkles was on Caroline's dresser, her paw on the lamp. Caroline's jewelry box lay on the floor, its contents scattered. Sprinkles looked me in the eye and pushed.

"No!"

Thud.

I gathered the jewelry and put the box in Caroline's closet. Sprinkles moved on to scratching at Caroline's closet door. "Stop, you infernal beast!"

Rocky watched, impassive, grooming a paw.

"Can't you stop your friend?" I asked.

The gleam in Rocky's eye said, *Silly human, why would I want to stop her?*

A knock, and Vye looked in. "Your turn with the cop." Her eyes widened. "What happened here?"

"Hurricane Sprinkles," I said. "Are you okay?"

She shrugged. "I guess. He said to ask you to go down and talk to him. I'll take care of the princess." She swooped up Sprinkles and nuzzled the furry, white fiend.

"At least she didn't pee on anything." That was next, I was sure.

Chapter 38

Talk about awkward. For months since the last murder investigation, Jack and Caroline had spent more and more time together. I tried to stay as far out of the picture as possible, not wanting my amateur sleuthing to be a buzzkill to their burgeoning romance. I hoped my conversation with Jack would go smoothly. I was pretty sure no one had seen me talking with Tillie at Lily's.

Jack was thumbing through the copy of *Death on the Nile* I'd left on the table as I entered the kitchen.

I'd play it cool. "Hi, Jack, how have you been?"

He'd decided on the same strategy. "Good. You?"

"Good." Rocky followed me into the kitchen, nudged Jack's leg, and Jack obliged him with a scratch behind the ears. The silence in the kitchen grew until I could hear the hum of the refrigerator motor.

"You were at Moy Mull when the body was discovered," Jack said.

Jump right in, Jack. I took my seat. "Yes." Safe. Next question. Rocky, sensing my nervousness, came over and let me drape him across my lap.

Jack asked me several questions and with each I parsed

what I shouldn't know based on what Tillie had told me. After five minutes, he flipped his notebook closed.

"That's it?"

A quirk of his lips showed a glimmer of humor. "For now."

I realized I'd have to throw caution to the wind. I wanted to know more about how he'd figured out that Adam's bee "sting" was really an injection of bee venom. "The bee," I said as he stood to go. "How did you know?"

"My grandmother kept bees. That bee was a drone. No stinger. So now the question is"—the dark eyebrows over his gray blue eyes quirked—"how did *you* know?"

I gulped. I wouldn't mention Tillie. Instead I nodded toward the apiary up the hill. "Willow and Luca have told me a lot about bees." I hoped he'd buy that explanation. "And I didn't realize it, not right away. But I think Maud did."

"Of course," he said. "She's been keeping bees for years."

"Did she tell you she knew?" I said.

Jack resumed his seat.

"Do you want that coffee now?" I said.

"Sure." Rocky went back to Jack for another scratch as I put on the coffee. He nodded toward my book. "I see you're reading Agatha Christie."

"Trying to," I said, "No time to read lately."

"My granny read them too."

Great, I was like his granny.

I poured two cups and handed him one. "Thanks. Too bad we don't have Agatha Christie here. This one's a real-life locked-room mystery."

I froze. Was Jack opening the door to conversation about the case? Don't mind if I do. "Did Tony have some documents about the lock?"

Jack dipped his head. "The documents weren't as helpful as I had hoped."

Time for a dumb question to get him talking. "Have you watched the security tape?" Of course he had.

Jack ran his hand over his beard and took a sip of coffee. "Over and over. After Adam went into the dungeon at ten forty, no one else appeared in the hallway until Maud came through the door at midnight and went straight up to her room." I knew this corroborated Tony Ortiz's statement that he'd seen her return. "One security guard on rounds came in around two a.m. and stayed in the office until four."

Past the time of death window the ME had estimated, I thought.

"If we were purely speculating, like in a novel," I said, "perhaps the killer locked it from inside."

"Or the victim did and somehow hid the key inside the room before he died." Jack gave a wry laugh. "We searched. No key."

"Then there's only one answer." I met his eye. "A secret passage."

Jack chuckled but I raised a hand. "Ben built himself a castle and he put all the castle touches in it—suits of armor, a tower, stained-glass windows, balconies, a dungeon with chains . . ."

Jack smiled. "No secret passages that we could find. Tony gave me the Realtor's floor plan and there I was knocking on the walls. . . ." He shook his head. "So, if we stay in the realm of the real world—" He leveled a glance at me.

"Someone doctored the tape." That was possible. But who had the expertise to do it? Another possibility occurred to me. "What if Adam was injected before he went into the room?"

"The medical examiner says that was unlikely. Adam would've felt the effects right away, and at any rate, remember he argued with two people before he went in to the dungeon.

He would've been begging them for help. Actually, with the dose of venom he'd received, he probably would've been unable to speak. On the contrary, we know Adam spoke very clearly with no slurring of his words. Plus, the footage shows neither Barry nor Luca got close enough to administer a shot."

"What about the next day? Was anyone seen replacing the key in the security office?"

He took another sip of coffee, avoiding my eyes. "Festival day, dozens of people went past or into that office."

If there was only one key as Prentiss said, it would take just a moment to replace it.

"The security officers don't staff that room twenty-four hours a day." We'd slipped well out of the realm of conjecture and I hoped he wouldn't notice.

He shook his head. "They're in and out. But the recording equipment's in that office."

"What about the EpiPen?" I asked.

He sat back, the old wooden kitchen chair creaking under his weight. "Tons of people in and out of the cloakroom where Luca left his backpack."

"But why Luca?" As soon as the words were out of my mouth, I wanted to recall them. *The argument. The killer must've known that Luca and Adam fought. Who knew?* "Barry."

"Barry went home after the incident with Adam. His coworkers saw him leave, and he went home with his girlfriend." Jack finished his coffee and set the mug on the table. "Luca told me about Adam and Willow's photo session, how he blew his top. Kid seems truthful."

"He's a good kid." I explained how I'd walked into that scene in the tea garden during the fantasy ice cream social. "But there was someone watching, in the trees. I'm sure of it."

"Man? Woman?"

"I couldn't tell. But I'm sure someone was there."

He tapped the Agatha Christie novel. "A shadowy figure."

Jack's radio squawked with that language intelligible only to police and our comfortable spell was broken. He thanked me for the coffee and took off.

I washed the cups, then got a text from Pru. SAND-WICHES AT THE SHOP IF YOU'RE HUNGRY.

Pru was an angel.

"Vye, are you hungry?" I called. "Pru brought sand-wiches to the shop."

"Starving!"

We hurried down the lane and stepped into the bright-ness and warmth of Udderly's kitchen. The rain had kept customers home and closed the farm stand, and there was a party atmosphere as farmhands and my staff crowded around the table.

Luca carried French bistro chairs with curly iron backs from the front of the shop and set them in the kitchen. Wil-low spread a cloth on the worktable.

"I did some nice roasted veggie sandwiches on toasted ciabatta." Pru reached into a large brown basket. "And there's roast beef with cheddar on honey whole wheat if you prefer."

I preferred both, happy that Pru always sliced sand-wiches into halves so we could have both kinds. "Made with honey from the apiary?" I asked.

"Yes," Willow said.

Luca beamed. "There's a loaf on the counter for you to take home."

Vye sampled a slice of the hearty bread and sighed with pleasure. "I could eat a whole loaf of this bread. Who baked it?"

Pru raised her hand with a smile. "But it's the honey that gives it such nice flavor. That's all Luca's doing."

Vye turned to him. "You're into raising bees? Maybe have your own apiary some day?"

Luca said, "My heart wants to raise bees, but my father, he wants me to continue my education, so I'll return to school."

Willow frowned, and he said, "But not right away." She threw her arms around him.

I smiled. "What are you going to study?"

"I'm halfway through a computer-science program," he said, "but I took a break to work here."

Happy chatter filled the room, but I almost choked. Computer science. Did he know enough to doctor security tapes? Did Jack know what Luca studied?

Of course he did. He'd be back.

A surprising number of hardy customers braved the cold rain, and many bought pints of ice cream to take home. New Englanders eat ice cream all year and the cold snap was a warning to stock up. Pumpkin spice was flying out of the shop.

"I'll bring more pumpkins tomorrow," Pru said.

Later that night as I was about to turn off my light and go to sleep, my phone buzzed with a text from Tillie. BLUE BUICK REGISTERED TO ANDREA VENDITTI, MAMARONECK, NY. Andrea had reinvented herself as Dree.

The phone buzzed again. SHOPLIFTING AND DRUG CHARGES, DROPPED IN CA THIRTY YEARS AGO. MARRIED TWICE. WORKED IN REAL ESTATE. ANYTHING NEW?

Lots new, I thought. *Just nothing I can share.* I texted: NOTHING NEW. THANK YOU.

I scrolled through the photos on Dree's website, but nothing new jumped out at me. My eyes fell on the art book I'd borrowed from Moy Mull, the one marred by the wine stains Dree had left behind. I pulled the heavy oversized book onto my lap: *Elegant Despair: The Women of Adam Blasco*. Even the title was pretentious.

I flipped through page after page of portraits of Adam's women. The book didn't start with Maud's magnificent portrait, as I expected. It was chronological and included a biographical section with some casual shots of Adam and his circle, and a few portraits he'd shot that showed technical mastery and hints of the emotion of his later works. The first portrait, the first "Woman of Adam Blasco" had been Dree.

I flipped through a few more pages, and a word in a photo caption caught my eye. *Iowa.*

The model, barefoot in an oversized T-shirt and cutoff jeans, stook on railroad tracks. She was young with coltish legs and hair to her waist, but that open freckled face was Vye's. She had a camera hanging over one shoulder and her hand hovered over it like a gunslinger ready to fire. Her other hand was clenched in a fist. Unlike Adam's other models, Vye's pose radiated confidence and power.

I flipped back to the biographical section. There were some photos from a party, including one I'd seen before— the photo of Adam and Dree from her website. Photographs from the same party showed two young women with their arms around each other, surprised, unposed, but still beautiful. Maud and Dree. Well, they'd been friends, right? There was a photo of Adam and Dree, Dree on his lap, and Maud sitting close to another guy.

I wondered. It looked like Adam and Dree had been a couple. Then Maud had arrived. He'd married Maud, not Dree.

I turned a few more pages. Such beautiful people but most seemed somehow tarnished by Adam's camera. I closed the book with a shudder and set it on the floor against the nightstand.

Chapter 39

The next morning, I rose before the sun. I couldn't sleep anyway, as images from the past few days tumbled through my mind: Maud in her wedding gown, *Dallas*, Luca and Adam fighting. I dreamed that I went to a tea party at Maud's cottage and a figure approached dressed in a white bee suit, the face covered with netting. The figure was tall and regal like Maud, but when I pulled aside the veil, Vye's face was revealed.

Since I was up so early, I decided to take a longer run. Remembering Maud's invitation to jog at Moy Mull, I looped the security badge around my neck and headed out.

The sound of a tractor engine echoed from the hills as the sky brightened. Darwin and the hands were in the orchards, picking apples and pumpkins. At the Brightwood farmhouse, Pru was parking her station wagon by her lush kitchen garden. She wound a blue woolen shawl around her shoulders, and I noted she was still dressed in the same clothes she'd worn last night.

"Did someone have a baby or are you getting home from a really good date?" I called.

Dark circles ringed her eyes, but she smiled. "A little girl for the Goffmans."

I flashed her a smile and a thumbs-up as I jogged west onto Fairweather Road. My pace slowed as I went up the slight hill leading to Moy Mull, and I vowed to run more often and lay off the ice cream, the same vow I made at least once a week. I approached the guard shack and he scanned my badge and waved me through, more concerned with his coffee than me. I guess I didn't look dangerous? A small smile curved my lips. If he only knew. My unassuming exterior had fooled a lot of people in my days of undercover assignments.

One of the questions I'd written in my notebook surfaced in my mind.

Who had stood in the shadows watching Adam photograph Willow?

The castle loomed above the trees as my footsteps pounded the gravel drive to the tea garden. I slowed as I stepped into the elegantly landscaped space surrounding the pagoda tea house, enjoying the mazelike path bordered by walls of boxwood. At the back of the garden, I stopped where Adam had taken the photos of Willow and then stepped off the path into the trees where I'd seen the shadow. I scanned the still-damp ground and kicked aside a few orange and gold leaves that had fallen from the oaks. The rain of the past few days had eradicated any traces of the watcher.

From this angle, Willow would've been hidden behind a boxwood hedgerow, but the spot where Adam worked on the path was clearly visible. So the shadow was watching Adam, not Willow.

I took off, heading past the Barn Gallery, closed now, and jogged west to the castle, its tower visible above the trees. So many people dream of living in a castle, but most castles were dank, cold, unhealthy places that were the setting for the darkest deeds humans could conjure—including murder. I recalled the tale of the Weeping Lady. Had the very stones of Moy Mull been cursed? Lights glowed warm in Maud's she shed. I wondered if she wouldn't stay in the castle, fearing Adam's ghost.

I cut down the unused, overgrown road to the pond where I'd jogged earlier in the week. From here, I could look down into Maud's walled garden. Stacked wooden bee boxes faced southeast in a horseshoe configuration. A tall, graceful figure that had to be Maud moved slowly, deliberately, away from the hives toward the cottage. I raised a hand, not sure if she could see me, but she removed her bee hat and netting and made a beckoning motion.

I jogged through the garden gate to join her at the front door of the cottage. She'd removed her bee suit and was wearing a simple navy sweater and jeans.

"Good morning," she said. "I'm glad you took me up on my invitation. It makes me happy when the castle grounds are used."

"It's a beautiful place to run," I said.

"Oh, my manners," Maud said. "Can I get you a drink of water?"

I wasn't thirsty, but I wasn't passing up a chance to talk to Maud. "Yes, please."

We went into the cottage and I took the opportunity to look around as she took a pitcher from her refrigerator. The room was dominated by an oversized fireplace, a twin of the one in the dungeon, right down to the carved roses, hearts, and lyres on the lintel. Maud had hung an oil painting above it, an oil of the Casa D'Amore, the Italian villa Freddie had gifted her. The rest of the room was a dream image of a Cotswold cottage: a wooden farm table piled with fall produce, overstuffed furniture deep with pillows in softly faded pastel florals, and lace curtains at the windows.

"Our well water's very good," Maud said as she handed me a glass.

"Thank you." She indicated a chair, but I waved her off. "I'm too sweaty."

"So Vye's staying with you?" Maud said as she sat at the table. "I noticed you drove her over to meet with Nicky."

I sipped slowly to stall for time. If Maud was the killer, would she have reason to harm Vye? *Don't be ridiculous, Riley.* "Yes, she is."

Maud dipped her head and looked up at me from under her lashes. "I feel like everyone's avoiding me lately."

Did she mean Vye? Prentiss? Dree? Tony? I thought of all the fairy tales. The princess in the tower must be lonely.

Maud looked out the window toward the castle. "I guess she had her reasons."

Did she mean Vye had reasons for deciding to stay away from the castle or for killing Adam? I remembered that Maud had once been a young woman like Vye, caught in Adam's web of charisma and control.

"Do you know Vye well?" I said, delicately.

She stiffened, her glance darting to an envelope on the table next to a vase full of bronze and yellow mums. "Vye's special. She has talent. I'd really like to talk to her. She answers texts but won't pick up when I call. I'd like to have a real conversation with her." Maud walked to the door and opened it. "Would you please tell her to give me a call?"

Audience over, I was dismissed. I thanked her for the water and set off, wondering if the Mistress of Moy Mull had any idea that Adam and Vye were married. At any rate, if I'd thought she'd let down her wall of royal reserve for a good chat, I'd been mistaken.

Disappointment rankled, and I decided to burn off energy by doing a loop around the lawn. As I emerged from Maud's garden, I caught sight of Dree Venditti exiting the castle's kitchen door dressed in expensive matching jogging tights and wind jacket. I slowed my steps, but it wasn't her outfit that gave me pause. She was hiding something under her jacket, something with hard edges, something shaped like a folder or large envelope.

I leaned into some lunges and stretches, giving her time to get ahead of me, then I loped after her in an easy jog. Dree jogged with excruciatingly slow, short baby steps, so I again stopped to stretch, this time behind some laurel bushes.

She reached the charming rose-covered wishing well tucked in a stand of huge rhododendron bushes in front of Loch Lomond Cottage, took a manila file folder from under her jacket, and put it in the bucket. Then she scurried back to the lawn and continued her run.

A term from my days at the CIA surfaced: "dead drop," a way to pass information by leaving messages in a prearranged "dead letter drop." This was clearly a dead drop, the prettiest one I'd ever seen.

Chapter 40

I was dying to know what was in that file and who would pick it up. Who was I kidding? It had to be Max, judging from their behavior all weekend. I was torn. I could run up, take a quick peek, and pray that no one saw me, but the wishing well was directly in front of Loch Lomond Cottage and I remembered Max telling Maud he'd been staying there.

I jogged in place, then decided to go for it. I darted past the well and approached it from behind, bushwhacking through the cover of the rhododendron. I scrambled onto the ledge of the well, keeping my back to the cottage, and pulled the folder from the bucket. When I opened it, I saw Willow's face, and shock almost made me drop it.

Inside the folder was a stack of photos. I quickly thumbed through. Images of Willow by the barn, Willow in the garden. I blinked. The police hadn't taken the photos from the darkroom. Dree had.

I heard a screen door squeak open and shut softly.

I dropped the folder back in the bucket, jumped away from the well, and dashed back into the bushes, running as fast as I could to put distance between me and the dead drop.

I made it back onto the path and tried to slow my breathing and look like any other jogger. I kept my eyes focused straight ahead, using peripheral vision to watch Max leave the cottage.

He did an exaggerated sweep of the area, his head swiveling back and forth several times, either somehow missing me or deciding that I wasn't important enough to notice. It dawned on me: he didn't mind being seen, he just didn't want to be seen with Dree.

He jogged to the well and snatched up the file so quickly he set the bucket swinging. Then he did the same obvious checking-to-make-sure-the-coast-was-clear move and dashed back into the cottage.

I took off again, replaying the weekend. Dree and Max had been together at the exhibit opening, I'd seen them flirting. But when I'd seen Max later, he was with the woman with the silver blond hair. She had to be his wife. He'd escorted her, not Dree, to the foundation dinner.

I stopped and threw myself into a few jumping jacks. In the distance, Dree slowed near the Barn Gallery, gasping for breath and holding her hand to a stitch in her side.

Three things were clear: Dree had stolen the photos Adam had developed in the darkroom, Dree and Max were in cahoots, and Dree was not a regular jogger. I turned around and ran home.

After I got home, I poured kibble for Rocky and spooned Sprinkles' froufrou diet food into her gold-rimmed bowl, then jogged upstairs and tripped over the fluffy beast herself, who looked as surprised as I was. She'd set up her usual ambush for me coming from my bedroom, not from the stairs, and I'd been so preoccupied, it worked. "Darn cat." She hid her surprise and preened on her way downstairs.

I showered, dressed, then searched on my phone. I found many photos of Max and his silver-haired wife, Kim, at charity events, equestrian events, and gallery openings. They lived on a horse farm a few miles from Moy Mull. Their racehorse, Baxter's Biscuit, had lost his last two races.

Vye groaned awake across the hall and emerged from her bedroom, leaned on the doorframe, and mumbled, "Good morning."

"Good morning," I said. Sprinkles came back upstairs and Vye scooped her up with an exclamation of delight. "How are you, my ray of sunshine?"

Sunshine? Sprinkles?

"I saw Maud this morning," I said.

Vye stiffened. "Was she here?"

"No, she was at Moy Mull. She'd like you to call her."

She held Sprinkles closer. "Did she say what she wanted? Was it about the cookbook?"

"She didn't say anything about the cookbook." Vye looked so spooked, I said softly, "She complimented you. She just wants to talk. Come downstairs and have some breakfast." I scrambled eggs and made some toast while she played with Sprinkles and regained her composure.

I set the food in front of her, brewed her a strong cup of coffee, and waited while she gulped it down. She'd had such an emotional twenty-four hours I didn't know where to start. "Are you okay, Vye? Did Maud do something to upset you?"

"No, that's not it." Tears sprang to her eyes. "It's the way she looks at me. I always had to come to Moy Mull when Adam did jobs for Maud, because I did most of the work. She pities me. I can't stand the way she looks at me."

I squeezed her hand. "Then why did you agree to shoot the cookbook?"

"Because it's money, and, besides, now all I have to shoot

is the food. Adam already did the lady-of-the-castle stuff where Maud pretends to cook."

I sat back. "She pretends?"

Vye wiped her eyes and huffed a laugh. "It's all make-believe, Riley. I'm going to shoot at Bitsy's tomorrow. Want to come and see how it's done?"

Chapter 41

I'd arranged to go to Moy Mull at three o'clock with Gerri and Flo, another deal with the devil. I was being roped in to joining the historical society and could feel the noose tighten.

I left Vye to clean up breakfast and gather herself, her ever-present shadow Sprinkles hovering at her feet. Rocky was nowhere to be seen; he'd probably slipped out through the tear in the screen in my bedroom window and was off hunting.

As I stepped onto the front porch, Flo was power walking down the lane, swinging small hand weights. She called, "Good morning!"

I'd forgotten I meant to talk with her. "Hi, Flo, I meant to call you." I ran down the steps and said, "What did you want to tell me when we were in the shop talking about Maud Monaco?"

Flo looked around and whispered, "I didn't want anyone to hear this, because it could be nothing." Her worried expression belied her words. "Well, you know how I like genealogy, and when Maud first moved to Penniman, I got interested, like I said, in Maud's marriage."

Flo's worry was so uncharacteristic, I knew what followed wouldn't be good news. "To the prince."

"Well, no." She shook her white curls. "Her first marriage, to Adam Blasco. Now it may be nothing. Mistakes happen. Papers get misfiled."

"Mistakes?"

Flo threw a look at the house and tugged me along. She lowered her voice. "I have a genealogist friend who's a whiz at computers. Maud's marriage to Adam is recorded in Las Vegas, well, Carson County, Nevada. All legal, nice and tidy. But"—Flo's forehead wrinkled—"my friend said there's no divorce decree on file. Now, Adam and Maud could've moved and filed elsewhere, but my friend's been searching everywhere for a long time and . . ."

Flo's words hit me. "Wait. Maud and Adam weren't divorced?"

"Sometimes papers get lost, but . . ." Flo's eyes were troubled. "I wouldn't say anything, of course, not even to Gerri. Let sleeping dogs lie, right? Could be a mistake, because if they weren't divorced . . ."

The magazine said Maud had met the prince in Vegas. Had she stayed there after the divorce? Flo's words faded as I thought about the ramifications if this bombshell were true. If Maud hadn't been divorced from Adam at the time of her marriage to Prince Frederic . . . "That would mean her marriage to the prince was—"

Flo whispered, "Invalid."

I looked up at the house where Vye was probably playing peacefully with Sprinkles. Flo didn't know the half of it. If Adam and Maud were still married, that meant Vye's marriage was invalid too.

Adam was a bigamist. Was Maud a—I realized I had no idea if there was a term for a woman married to two spouses.

We'd reached the shop. "I'm with you, Flo. This is . . ."

Flo's skinny shoulders slumped. "Some things you don't want to know. No one has to know. Don't worry, my friend's very discreet." She patted my arm and walked away, swinging her weights.

I went into Udderly's kitchen, numb, wondering if Adam had been blackmailing Maud all these years, taunting her with the fact that her marriage to Freddie, the love of her life, had been invalid.

I went through prep on autopilot.

I checked the schedule. Pru would be in while I went to Moy Mull with Gerri and Flo at three o'clock. Two farmhands came in to work and handled the customers while I mixed up more pumpkin spice, my mind churning like the cream. How could that happen? How could the divorce not exist?

One of the hands called back, "When will be have more Bloody Mess?"

It took me a second to switch mental gears. "Brandon's flavor? He said he'd come in tonight to make some for the weekend."

Bloody Mess and pumpkin spice. My most popular flavors. I'd be mixing pumpkin spice for at least another month and had to make sure to make extra for Coleman and Zara to serve at Lily's. During breaks, I sat in the office and did research on the shop laptop.

My searches for Maud got plenty of hits, photo after photo, but there wasn't much about her early life, or that early marriage to Adam. Maybe that was how Maud wanted it—forgotten. If it was true that Maud's marriage to Freddie was invalid, how could Maud have ended up in such a predicament? I thought of Adam's agent/lawyer. Was Nicky Vickers Maud's lawyer too?

I texted Vye. QUICK QUESTION. HOW LONG DID NICKY WORK AS ADAM'S LAWYER?

She texted back. THREE YEARS. HIS OTHER LAWYER WAS AN OLD FRIEND WHO DIED BEFORE NICKY CAME ON-BOARD.

An old friend might've helped Adam hide his old sins.

My thoughts turned to Vye. I searched for her online but found very little. I glanced toward the door to be sure I was alone and plugged in the name I'd seen on her license. Violet Yvonne Eddy. There were a few hits, scholarship announcements to art school and work at an art camp for gifted teens. I was relieved that there was no public engagement or wedding announcement.

Idly, I searched Prentiss Love. I was grasping at internet straws, looking for a motive for murder.

Prentiss Love turned up in dozens of articles and photos. He'd represented many musicians and models, and in every photo he was smiling, always in the orbit of a beautiful woman. In the most recent photo, he and Maud mugged in chef's hats at the release of her latest cookbook. Prentiss's smile was infectious even on a computer screen. I couldn't believe he'd murder anyone. But would he help Maud do it?

I moved on.

Adam Blasco had a website, just as glossy and pretentious and annoying as he'd been in life. His bio read, "Life is life. I live to live. I see to see." *How ridiculous.* Adam glowered from the screen. He wasn't a handsome man, but I had to admit the photo was compelling. I wondered if it was a self-portrait or if Vye had taken it for him.

I'd already seen Dree's ridiculous website, but I did another search on her name. Lots of information, and page after page of photos for charity events tied to her real-estate business popped up. I leaned closer. Most of the events were tied to her ex-husbands' real-estate businesses. Did she need money? Selling Adam's final work would net her a pretty penny.

Who else was in the castle the night Adam was murdered? I typed in "Tony Ortiz."

Tony Ortiz had no social media accounts, nothing except a newspaper article about an exhibit of historical photography he'd organized in Newport. But I'd seen his sweatshirt from RIDU. Maybe there was alumni information somewhere. Before I could dig deeper, the sound of voices outside the workroom door distracted me from my search and I stepped outside.

A crowd gathered around the pen where we'd usually show Willow's baby goats or llamas from a nearby farm. I moved to the side of a small crowd to see what was happening. Vye had pulled a picnic table in front of the pen and set Sprinkles on it. Sprinkles' carrier was behind her, the plush pink leather embroidered with a swirling S and a silver crown.

My jaw dropped. Besides trips to the groomer and vet, Sprinkles hadn't been outside farther than the porch in years, never mind in the open air. Yet here she was, surrounded by a crowd, not just unfazed, but preening, turning her head side to side so her subjects could get a better look.

Vye waved to me. "Sprinkles followed me out the door and I thought she'd like a change of scenery. I wanted to get a shot of her by the shop, you know, Sprinkles and ice cream."

Sprinkles' emergence from the house was like the sighting of a creature long considered extinct. "As long as she's happy," I said. "Vye, I have to warn you. Her good mood may not last."

"No worries." Vye beamed at Sprinkles as she basked in the adoration of the crowd. "I won't let her to get overexcited."

"Good luck," I said.

An hour later, Vye came in, washed her hands, and started making waffle cones as if she'd been doing it for years.

I didn't see any scratches or torn clothing. "Everything okay?" I asked.

"Sprinkles is home, napping," Vye's eyes sparkled. "She's wiped out, but she loved having her picture taken. I've never seen such a ham, human or animal."

Gerri's Lincoln Continental slid to a stop in front of the shop and I hung up my apron. "Vye, I have to step out for a while. " She was in such a good mood, I didn't mention I was going to Moy Mull. "Pru will be here in ten minutes. Give me a call if you need anything."

Vye waved me off. "I've got this."

I ran out to the car and Flo gave me a significant glance from the front seat as I climbed into the back. I knew what she was thinking and I gave her a subtle nod. I wouldn't say a word about our discussion of Maud's marriage.

"Time to storm the castle." Gerri whipped her scarf over her shoulder and stomped the accelerator.

Chapter 42

We swung into town to pick up Bridget's boxes and parked at the back door of the castle at three o'clock on the dot. Tony was at the door waiting, casual in jeans and a red polo that showed off his biceps.

I introduced Flo and Gerri as Tony held the door wide.

"Nice to meet you." Tony smiled. "And how nice that you can join us, Riley."

I returned Tony's smile, but all I could think was that I was mere feet from the dungeon and I was itching to search it one more time.

Tony stacked the two large boxes, hefting them easily, and led us up the stairs past the darkroom. He loaded the boxes into the dumbwaiter and sent them upstairs as Gerri peppered him with questions. The delicious aroma of soup stock and Prentiss' voice singing a Motown tune wafted from the kitchen.

"I have to speak to Prentiss then I'll catch up," I said. I did have a question for Prentiss, but I hoped to detour to the dungeon after I spoke with him.

Standing at the counter next to the stove, Prentiss chopped vegetables with professional speed.

"You look very Top Chef," I said.

He struck a pose, then went back to his vegetables. "Did I hear the delegation from the Penniman Historical Society? Are you part of it?"

"In a manner of speaking," I said. "Prentiss, when we found Adam, you said the walls are three feet thick. Was that a figure of speech?"

Prentiss shook his head. "It's on the blueprints. This place isn't just a castle, it's a fortress. That's why cell phones don't work well and you have to hang out the freaking window to get a signal." He stopped, his knife in midair. "Does that have something to do with Adam?"

I took a breath. Did I trust this man? Did I want to admit my ridiculous theory? I said slowly, "Did you ever hear about a secret room or staircase here?"

"So that's why the cops asked Tony about blueprints!" Prentiss set down his knife. "I saw that big cop poking around downstairs in the TV parlor, knocking on walls. He even looked in my room. They searched the place top to bottom but didn't find anything." He shrugged. "Well, they didn't tell me if they did."

"Too bad." If there wasn't a secret way into the dungeon, then the tape must've been altered. Could the security staff be in on Adam's murder? Was there a cover-up? "Prentiss, how well do you know the security guys?"

Prentiss added the vegetables to the stock, then stirred it with a wooden spoon. "The security guys are great. I play cards with them sometimes, why? Oh . . . you want to know what's on the tapes." He waggled the wooden spoon at me, took off his apron, and turned down the heat on the pot. "Well, so do I. Sleuthing's more fun than chopping veggies. Come on, let's visit the security office."

The security guard on duty, Zach, a poker buddy of Prentiss, obliged us and fast-forwarded the security tape.

We watched the confrontation with Adam, Barry, and Luca several times, but I gained no new insights.

"So there's no way the file was doctored?" I asked.

Zach shook his head. "All digital. In the cloud. They'd have to have CIA-level stuff to get in there."

Having worked for the CIA, I thought he exaggerated a bit. "You don't remember anything unusual happening the day of the murder?"

"Nothing out of the ordinary," Zach said. "Prentiss came in for the security brief of the day."

Really? "That sounds official."

"I am the major domo," Prentiss huffed.

"Plus, he usually brings us coffee cake or donuts," Zach said. "Good stuff, homemade."

Prentiss bowed.

I remembered that Adam's EpiPen had been planted in Luca's backpack in the cloakroom. "Can you play Saturday morning?" I didn't mention that I wanted to check the tape to see if anyone who knew Adam, including Prentiss, went into the cloak room.

Zach fast-forwarded the tape and we watched as the hallway filled with festival volunteers. "Wait, stop the tape. That's Tony."

Zach scratched his head. "Oh yeah, he was checking in volunteers and had to get the box of volunteer badges." He started the tape again and we watched Tony step out of the office and go into the cloakroom.

Prentiss said, "Why would he go into the cloakroom? He lives here."

Zach laughed. "Long trip back upstairs to his room for the bathroom."

"Let's watch one more time," I said, my thoughts tumbling.

Tony was only going into the bathroom, Riley. Or planting

Adam's EpiPen in Luca's backpack. Had he been the figure in the trees watching Adam shoot Willow's picture? If so, he'd know Luca had fought with Adam.

Zach's voice called me back. "The morning of the festival was nuts; it was so busy." An understatement, I realized, as I watched with growing frustration as dozens of people streamed in and out of the security office, the cloakroom, and up and down the hallway. So many familiar faces—Maud, Vye, Tony, Barry, Luca, Willow, and Prentiss—all appeared on the tape.

One person I didn't see: Dree Venditti. I'm certain I would've noticed the statuesque former model.

Prentiss pointed at himself on screen. "There I am!"

"I don't see you, Zach," I said.

"Security staff were deployed to the parking lot and one of us was always at the gallery too," Zach said.

"Stretched thin," I said.

"We were hardly ever here in the castle," Zach pointed to the screen, "until the body was discovered."

We replayed the scene twice, and I felt frustration mix with the surreal feeling I get when watching myself on tape. Too many people had access to the security office.

Prentiss and Zach chatted as the tape played on, but I felt a headache build. I rubbed my forehead, and my eyes wandered from the screen to the rolltop desk in the adjacent room. Old ledgers crowded its shelves and it was flanked by two sets of battered filing cabinets.

Librarians have a saying about preserving books and knowledge: Lots of copies in lots of places. If the books in one library are destroyed, with good planning there are copies of those books safe in another. I remembered that Tony had given the castle blueprints and floor plans to Jack. I wondered if there was another set here in the former castle office. "Has Tony looked at the files in there?" I asked.

Zach shook his head. "No, he has enough to do in the attic and library."

"Riley's with the Penniman Historical Society," Prentiss teased. "She adores dusty old papers."

"Well, if Prentiss says it's okay for you to look through that old stuff, be my guest," Zach said.

I thanked Zach, and told him I'd return later.

"Fine," Zach said as he sat at his desk, "Now if you'll excuse me, I've got paperwork." Unfortunately for me, Zach's desk looked directly out on the door of the dungeon. My plan to slip in and search would have to wait.

Prentiss and I headed down the hallway. "I guess it's official," I said. "I'm a member of the Penniman Historical Society." I left him in the kitchen and took the stairs to the attic.

Gerri, Flo, and Tony chatted excitedly as I joined them. "Sorry, Prentiss needed some help in the kitchen," I said. "What did I miss?"

"Prentiss kept you too long. Look at these marvelous old photos of Ben."

Gerri handed me a stack of photos, but I didn't see a single one as I flipped through them. My mind kept turning to the old rolltop desk and filing cabinets downstairs. Lots of copies in lots of places. Tony had given floor plans to the police. Jack had searched for a secret passage without success, but maybe he'd missed something on the plans. I was used to dealing with documents—maybe I could spot something Jack had missed. I could ask Tillie to give me access to the plans, but I wanted to avoid relying on the loosest lips in Penniman any more than I had to. Besides, I suspected there might be another set of floor plans stashed in the old files downstairs.

An hour later, Tony looked at his watch. "I'm so sorry, ladies, I wish I didn't have to leave but I have an appointment at the gym with my personal trainer. I could use help organizing these photos and newspaper clippings. Can you come back another time?"

"Of course, Tony." Gerri dipped her chin and looked at Tony through her lashes. Was she flirting?

"Great," Tony said. "Maybe tomorrow afternoon, at say three?"

"Certainly," Gerri said. "My pleasure."

Certainly? She didn't even ask if she could have the afternoon off! But it was all right. I'd come back too.

"Thank you," Tony gestured toward the stairs. "Let me see you out."

Crud. I needed to stop in the office and search for floor plans, and here Tony was escorting us out of the building. As we passed the cloakroom, inspiration hit. "I'm going to stop at the restroom. See you later, Tony," I said.

Tony strode to the door and waved. "Have a nice evening."

As soon as the door closed behind him, I rushed into the office with Flo and Gerri trailing. Zach had gone.

Gerri frowned. "Riley, I thought—"

"Ladies, I need your help. I'm looking for floor plans of the castle and I think, I hope, they're in here." I gestured to the battered metal file cabinets and old desk.

Flo rubbed her hands together and pulled open a file-cabinet drawer. "I feel like I'm in an episode of *Mission Impossible*!"

Chapter 43

"A re you sure we should be in here?" The skepticism in Gerri's tone made her opinion clear.

"Prentiss and the security guard okayed it." I tried to sound confident. Did Prentiss have the right to okay searching the castle's property? *Of course he did, Riley. He's the major domo.*

Flo dug in a drawer and held up an old postcard like a trophy. "Gerri, look at this antique postcard of the town green! Isn't it delightful?"

Gerri took the fragile card from Flo's hand and flipped it over. Her eyes widened. "Signed by Ben Clitheroe himself."

"And here are some old letters, postmarked from the thirties." Flo passed one to Gerri.

I tried not to laugh as Gerri's resolve was swept away by her own desire to poke through old records.

But after these finds, we discovered that most of the stuff in the file cabinets was from the hotel years. Flo gamely paged through dusty plumbing invoices. Gerri took one side of the rolltop and I the other, and we methodically worked through the drawers.

Gerri unearthed another cache of vintage postcards and breathed, "Score!"

I figured the object of my search was oversized and rarely referred to, and would be forgotten behind the hanging files in the bottom drawer. Beneath boxes of number two pencils and carbon paper, I found a folded piece of heavy, yellowing parchment labeled Plan of Moy Mull Castle. "Bingo."

"You found the floor plans? Good. But do we have to leave? This is fun," Flo said.

"We can come back"—I checked my watch—"but I have to get to Udderly."

We rode back in the Lincoln and Gerri even gave the horn a cheerful toot as they sped home after dropping me off at the shop.

I tucked the floor plan carefully in my bag, where it would be safe from any spills. I could barely keep my mind on ice cream as I worked.

I rushed home at closing, opening the door to find Vye sprawled on the kitchen floor rolling a ball with Sprinkles and Rocky. "Hi, Riley. I ordered pizza again and there's plenty left over if you like. I'm going to Bitsy's tomorrow morning, eight o'clock, before the shop opens, if you want to watch the shoot."

I grabbed a piece of pizza on my way upstairs. "Sure, I'd love to."

Remembering with great fondness the ancient castles and stately homes I'd visited on my travels to Scotland, I sat on the floor of my room and pored over the plan of Moy Mull castle. How I loved the romance of hidden passages, priest holes, and secret rooms. You'd think Ben would've loved them, too, since he'd built his own castle, even bringing stones over from Scotland, but to my disappointment, I found no helpful notation on the floor plan marked "secret room" or "hidden chamber."

"Forty rooms and no secret room. What a lost opportunity," I groused as I rolled my tired shoulders. I was going to put aside the plans when I found a spot by the master bedroom's fireplace labeled with familiar symbols: two thistles, two hearts, one lyre.

The symbols from Ben's heraldic crest. I'd seen them on the shield in the great room, and on the fireplaces in the dungeon and Maud's she shed. I searched the floor plan again. The same cipher appeared in the plan next to the fireplace in Maud's cottage.

Could there be a tunnel between the castle and Maud's cottage?

"Adam always takes Maud's calls," Prentiss had said. What if Maud summoned Adam to the dungeon, injected him with the venom, then returned to her cottage through a tunnel, to be alibied on the security camera footage and, as luck would have it, by Tony looking out his window at midnight? Rocky padded into my room and I scooped him up. But Maud had seemed so upset when Caroline and I overheard her telling Prentiss about the missing venom, and the shocked look she'd exchanged with Prentiss at finding the drone with Adam's lifeless body had seemed genuine.

What had Prentiss told me? There'd been a renovation and Ben's bedroom was now part of the library office.

I stroked Rocky as my eyes went out of focus and the shapes on the floor plan dissolved like ink in water. I imagined Vye sitting on her bed at the castle, scrolling through photos in her room off the attic hallway, Tony going through Ben's trunk in his attic workroom. I pictured Maud, serene, unhurried, walking from her cottage to the castle. Prentiss playing poker with his friends. Dree, wandering the castle like a ghost from Adam's past, making a detour to the darkroom to steal his work.

Were the symbols—the thistle, the hearts, the lyre—signposts to the route the killer used to get into the dungeon? I had to get back in the castle.

Chapter 44

I'd barely slept but still woke early, my body thrumming with the excitement I used to feel before taking off on a trip. I'd be back in the castle this afternoon, even if it meant I had to become the librarian for the Penniman Historical Society.

To my surprise, Vye was up and had made pancakes. "I hope you like them. It's my grandmother's recipe."

"Thank you." I was almost too excited to eat, but I dug in to the golden brown, buttery pancakes. "These are really good, Vye."

"Thanks." The compliment seemed to surprise her. "It's the only thing I can cook."

We took separate cars to Bitsy's, since Vye didn't know when she'd be done with the shoot and I had to open the shop. The only thing I could think of was my three-o'clock appointment at the castle.

Bitsy's Creative Catering office was in a white Cape Cod on the green, but Vye didn't stop there. Instead we drove five miles out of Penniman to a brick strip mall with a gym, a post office, and a repair shop. A carved pink sign that read Creative Catering hung above the door of the corner storefront. The window next to it was

covered with white paint and a large poster reading
Coming Soon, More Creative Catering! I helped Vye
carry tripods and duffels of equipment to the door, where
Bitsy greeted us, her smile broad, her pink lipstick perfect. "I'm so excited! Thank you for coming at this early
hour. We're so busy, this was the only time that would
work."

"No problem." Vye's reply was gruff, and I realized that
she was nervous, that this was her first solo job, her first
without Adam calling the shots. I gave her shoulder a reassuring squeeze.

We stepped into the interior of the shop, all black-and-
white tile flooring and pastel green and pink walls and
furnishings. "Bitsy, it's wonderful. It's so you!"

"You should see my office at the cottage on the green.
Stuffed to the gills," Bitsy said. "Most people don't realize
that it's my house and I've been working out of my living
room all these years. Barry helped me move into this new
space and we're planning to expand."

We followed her into a gleaming industrial kitchen. "This
is where the magic happens. No one's cooking now, of course,
but I got the space ready like you said, Vye, and the food's
ready to go." I'd give my eyeteeth for one of the stainless-steel
worktables in the center of the space, and I made a mental
note to buy one for the shop.

Vye was all business. "I'll set up. It'll take a couple of
minutes."

"Okay." Bitsy gave her a pat on the shoulder, also sensing
Vye's nerves. "Riley, how 'bout I show you the rest of the
building?"

Bitsy and I chatted as she led me into a storeroom
chockablock with furniture, rental chairs, folded tents, and
white lattice arbors used in weddings. In another room we

passed shelves of multicolored linens, tablecloths, napkins, and matching seat cushions, all in Bitsy's signature bright pastels.

We went farther into the back of the building, where even more tables were stored, podiums like the ones used at the Barn Gallery, and even a gazebo. A loading bay opened to the parking lot, where Barry and Travis unloaded tables from a van.

"Did you have an event this morning?" I asked.

"Not this morning, but we do breakfasts, yes," Bitsy said. "Lots of times we're done so late at night, the team unloads the next morning.

Travis jogged over and handed Bitsy a notebook. "You left this in the van." Bitsy beamed. "Thank you. Travis is becoming my right-hand man." The slender guy gave Bitsy a wry grin as I recalled that Barry said Travis lost his cell phone and that's why he'd returned to the castle the night of Adam's death.

"I remember you from the castle," Travis said. "Your ice cream was so good!"

"Thanks," I said, as I wondered if the police had checked his story about the lost cell phone. "We're experimenting with some new flavors. Come by the shop and try some."

"I will, thanks," Travis grinned.

"By the way"—I tried to make my tone casual—"I heard you lost your cell phone at the castle the other night. Did you find it?"

"My cell?" Travis' eyebrows knit together and I caught a flash of wariness, then he laughed. "Oh yeah, my cell."

"Oh that!" Bitsy gave him a playful punch in the arm. "Travis dropped it in the van. He sent us all on a wild-goose chase!"

I forced a smile. "We've all lost our phones. Don't forget to come by the shop for those new flavors."

"Will do. Gotta get back to work," he said. "We have a luncheon at the symphony club today."

As Travis turned to join his dad, I noticed a tiny mole by his jawline.

Bitsy continued talking but I didn't hear a word. The guy who tried to sell Dad the autograph book had a tiny mole by the left side of his jaw, was tall, slim, with a thin nose. Travis fit Paulette's description to a T.

"Bitsy," I said, "where did you meet Barry?"

"At a retirement party at the insurance company he used to work for. He swept me off my feet." She leaned close, her eyes shining. "He treats me like a queen. My birthday's next week and I caught him looking at a website with gorgeous jewelry . . . he closed the screen as soon as I looked, but—"

Vye joined us. "Ready, Bitsy?"

I noticed a small folding chair by the gazebo. "I need to make a call. Can I sit here? I'll be right over."

Bitsy poufed her curls and said, "Sure. Ready for my close up!" then followed Vye.

I hunched over my phone as if texting, but I kept Barry and Travis in view. I watched them carry several folding tables into the warehouse and set them on racks, but one they placed against the wall at the back of the warehouse. Why?

Bitsy ran back to me, handing me a thick photo album. "I thought you might like to look at this while Vye takes my pictures. It's my scrapbook of events. I just added photos from the art festival weekend."

"I'd love to." Keeping an eye on Barry and Travis, I flipped through the pages but stopped at a photo of a couple renewing their vows in a lakefront garden. I recognized the senator from Penniman. What had Tillie said? The senator's house had been burgled.

I flipped through the pages to a wedding shower, and recognized the elegant home of the owners of Blue Heron Farm, where I'd catered an ice cream sundae party for their eight-year-old twins.

Travis and Barry finished unloading the van. Travis drove off and Barry passed me on his way to the kitchen. I gave him a smile. As soon as he went into the kitchen, I jumped to my feet and hustled to the rear of the warehouse.

Why was this table stored separately? I pulled the table from the wall, tilting it so I could see the underside. It was covered with lumpy brown butcher paper that matched the table's wood finish. I peeled the paper away, revealing plastic bags, haphazardly affixed to the table with strips of heavy duct tape. Through the plastic I saw silver picture frames, a gold watch, jewelry, cash, and even some bottles of medication.

The sound of a car engine pulled me back. I leaned the table back against the wall and hurried into the kitchen, marveling at the simplicity of the plan. Stolen goods were carried out when the catering team left, hidden under an innocent-looking table.

I joined everyone in the kitchen and watched Vye photograph Bitsy, my anger building. Did Bitsy know that the love of her life was masterminding thefts? I recalled Paulette's description of the guy who tried to sell Dad the antique guest book. Travis. Did Travis work alone? No, Barry had to know, he must've seen the underside of the table or felt its weight as he carried it. Was Bitsy in on this or was she being used? I couldn't imagine the openhearted, effervescent woman stealing. I was certain she was being used. My heart ached for her.

I made my excuses and hurried out to the car. I had to make a phone call, but first I drove away, checking my rearview mirror for a tailing catering van. I pulled into a donut shop and called the police department.

A familiar voice answered. "Penniman Police."

"Tillie"—

"One moment please." She cut me off and put on hold Muzak. I tapped my hand on the wheel impatiently until she came back.

"Okay, Riley," she said in a whisper. "Any news on the murder?"

"Sorry to disappoint you." I did, of course, have news on the murder, but I wanted to search for the secret passage on my own. "I have something else for you."

I explained what I'd seen in the warehouse. "Plus," I said, "I think if you cross-reference these addresses, you may find other thefts."

"Cross-reference?" Tillie asked.

"Match up the addresses of Creative Catering parties with your police info on the string of thefts. You know where the thefts have been, right?" I recalled a photo from the album. "Any at Blue Heron Farm? I know there was one at the senator's house."

"Hang on." She put me on hold again and five minutes later, she came back. "How do you know this?"

I told her about the album of Bitsy's parties.

"I'll tell Jack." She hung up.

I drove back to Udderly, telling myself it was out of my hands and feeling awful for what would happen to Bitsy when the news of her connection to the burglaries broke. Who would hire a woman who had been tainted by such a scandal? Her company would take a hit, and it would be a devastating hit. I doubted she was the criminal mastermind behind the thefts but no matter what, she'd be crushed by Barry's betrayal. *Oh, Bitsy.*

Chapter 45

I drove past the town green and pulled into the lot by Penni-man's covered bridge. Needing a few minutes to think and let the flowing water soothe my spirit, I sat under a maple tree by the river. A few other cars were parked in the small lot; I noted license plates from Massachusetts, Florida, Iowa, and Rhode Island. Leaf peepers who would soon be at Udderly for a pumpkin spice ice cream cone.

I pulled my notebook from my bag, leaned back against the rough tree bark, and turned to the page where I'd written "Who Killed Adam Blasco?"

I closed my eyes, letting the water flow by and the voices of the leaf peepers fade as I considered the motives of every-one who'd been in the castle the night of Adam's murder.

Maud. Was she weary of the hold Adam had on her for years? She knew the castle better than anyone and had ac-cess to bee venom. She'd be most likely to procure the drone left at the murder scene too.

Vye. By turns so sweet, so unstable. Sprinkles sure liked her, but was that a recommendation? I'd seen her fight with Adam and now that I knew they were married, it was clear Vye would benefit financially from Adam's death. Or would she, since Adam was a bigamist? I needed a lawyer.

Dree, Adam's stalker. I'd seen her fight with Adam, but of all the people who stayed in the castle, she wanted Adam alive to write the foreword to her book. If anything, I could see Adam killing *her*. She'd stolen Adam's work from the darkroom, and she and Max were in cahoots. Didn't everyone say that artwork increases in value when the artist dies? Were they partners in murder?

Prentiss. He had an alibi. But what if he'd managed to slip away from the poker game for a while? This was the trouble with being an amateur sleuth—I didn't have access to all the witnesses. Would Prentiss's poker buddies cover for him if he did slip away? Maybe he'd tired of seeing how Maud suffered over the years because of her connection to Adam. Did he have any idea that Maud and Adam were still legally married? Maybe the self-styled major domo had lied and knew the existence of a secret passage, picking up a syringe and vial of venom in Maud's cottage and using a secret underground tunnel to the dungeon to kill Adam?

Great, Riley, now you're sure there's a secret tunnel.

Tony Ortiz. What did I know about him? Good looking, worked out, devoted to Maud, and had a degree from Rhode Island Design University, if his sweatshirt was accurate. I recalled the uncomfortable scene in the Barn Gallery when Adam had practically accosted Tony.

I replayed the scene. Adam thought Tony looked familiar, Tony left, and then Adam stood in front of *Dallas* . . .

I recalled the name of Adam's model, Dallas Whitaker. I typed her name and "Adam Blasco," into my phone. Her haunting face filled the screen, her almost geometrically square jaw, the bold arch of her nose, the wide-set eyes, the widow's peak hairline. I leaned closer as recognition dawned. Why hadn't I noticed her resemblance to Tony? Because of his distracting muscles, his glasses, and his charming but obscuring fall of hair. Dallas' eyes accused me from behind the curtain of her own long and matted hair.

I searched further and found an online memorial page for Dallas Whittaker. "Dallas loved the sea and finally found the rest she needed in it. She is survived by . . ." I scanned the list of survivors, and caught my breath at the last entry: "a brother, Anthony Ortiz Whitaker."

Vye and Dree weren't the only ones who'd changed their names.

Adam, with his keen artist's eye, had seen the resemblance between Dallas and Tony.

Did Adam understand that the cost of being his model had been too high for the young woman to bear? Did Adam realize a reckoning would come one day?

Chapter 46

It wasn't even ten o'clock and I was exhausted.

When I got to Udderly, I checked the schedule and luckily some farmhands were available for the afternoon shift. I threw myself into making ice cream, trying to keep my focus on the proper proportions of cream and sugar and vanilla extract and not on the problem with my theory of who killed Adam Blasco.

My theory hinged on the existence of a secret passage to the dungeon. From what Prentiss had told me and from the floor plan, I knew that a renovation had reconfigured the space where the library office was now, where the fireplace was marked by the rose, heart, and lyre cipher. I had to get in there.

I was so lost in thought that when Jack knocked on the door and stepped into Udderly's workroom, I didn't have time to be surprised. Flo looked from Jack to me and back again.

"I hate to interrupt you at work," Jack said. "Do you have a second to talk?"

Flo took over stirring my ice cream mixture and Jack motioned for me to join him outside. He gestured to a picnic bench away from the other customers and we took seats across from each other.

The lines around Jack's gray blue eyes were more pronounced today. He was tired. "Some information has come to my attention and I need to ask you some questions. You were at Creative Catering this morning?"

I hesitated for only a moment, thinking of poor Bitsy, but I told him everything I'd seen, everything I suspected. He took a few notes, his printing clear and easy to read, even upside down, and I noticed he underlined "Travis" twice, as if in confirmation of suspicion. If only I could read Jack as easily.

"One more thing." I told him about Dree passing Adam's artwork to Max.

"How do you know this?" Jack's hand tightened on his pen.

"I was jogging and—"

He held up a hand. "I'll take it from here."

He flipped his notebook closed and gave me a long look. "And next time, you can call me instead of my secretary."

Somehow I got through the day, and Flo and I jumped into Gerri's Lincoln Continental at five minutes to three.

"You look so serious, Riley." Gerri glanced at me in the rearview mirror as Flo bent over her phone.

"I didn't sleep well last night." *Plus, information I gave the police will ruin the life of a woman I truly liked and I was pretty sure we were on our way to play historian with a murderer.*

Should I share my suspicions with Gerri and Flo? Not yet—I didn't want them tipping my hand. What if I was wrong and Tony wasn't the killer? That would make for some awkward Penniman Historical Society meetings. I had to find that secret passage.

Flo gasped and looked up from her phone. "A friend just texted me that the cops are at Creative Catering. Tillie

O'Malley cross-referenced some police calls and parties, and the cops think the caterer was a front for a burglary ring."

"Cross-referenced," I muttered.

Gerri and Flo discussed the news, but I remained silent. At the castle, Flo turned to me. "You're nervous as a cat."

"That's what happens when you eat hot fudge sundaes for lunch." Gerri sniffed.

Zach greeted us at the back door. As we walked through the dining room and great room to the stairs, I replayed the steps the killer had taken. My theory was possible, but only if there was a secret passage.

There had to be a secret passage.

Fresh air and warm afternoon sunshine streamed through the open windows of the attic workroom. Tony greeted us with a smile as he heaved a box of clippings onto the table. "Lots to go through today, ladies."

Gerri and Flo took places next to Tony as I forced a smile and tried to act as natural as possible while keeping my distance, sure that mistrust radiated off me.

I picked up a yellowed newspaper clipping from the *Boston Globe*. The headline blared "Industrialist Millionaire Benjamin Clitheroe Dies at Opera at Age 48." I read: "Accompanied by his wife, songbird Alma de Luce, the millionaire suffered a heart attack in his box shortly after the curtain fell on a performance of *Aida*."

Aida was one of my favorite operas. Like many operas, it had a wonderfully improbable storyline but the ending, when star-crossed lovers are entombed alive in a pyramid as they sing to each other, always brought tears to my eyes.

Entombed.

The paper fluttered from my hand to the floor.

"What did you find, Riley?" Flo asked.

I cleared my throat. "Tony, what happened to Alma after

Ben died?" I retrieved the clipping and willed my expression to remain neutral.

"She moved to California and enjoyed Ben's money." Tony grinned and Gerri laughed.

I picked up another clipping, but I couldn't keep up the charade. I had to make my exit, so I pulled my phone out of my pocket and faked an incoming text. "I have to step out to take this call. Excuse me."

"Reception's terrible here," Tony said. "You can try by the window or on the balcony in the library."

"Thanks." I raced downstairs.

Once in the library, and after checking to ensure I was alone, I ran into Tony's office. I stood in front of the magnificent fireplace and mantel, grandly out of place beside modern oak book shelves on one side, a metal office desk on the other, and walls covered in bland beige drywall.

I ran my fingers over the carved stone of the mantel. What had Prentiss said? This part of the floor had been reconfigured out of part of Ben's bedroom.

Bridget Flynn said Ben brought stonemasons from Scotland to work on the castle. I bet they'd built secret passages in the fireplaces, and when they finished Ben sent them home to ensure that they'd never divulge his secret.

I traced the shapes carved into the stone mantle: thistles, entwined hearts, a lyre. The same symbols on the shield in the great room, in the dungeon, and on the floor plan. I recalled the placement of the symbols on the shield: two thistles in the upper left-hand corner, two entwined hearts in the upper-right-hand corner, both above a large gold lyre. Thistles for Scotland, hearts for Oona, and the lyre for his other love, music.

The grand fireplaces downstairs had no carving, unlike this one and the one in the dungeon. Why put such a large, grand fireplace in a dungeon—a basement room?

An idea kindled. The basement room was by an exit to the cottage outside the castle, where Alma had stayed.

Unlike the dungeon fireplace, which had a decorative arrangement of dried flowers inside the fire box, this fireplace had a heavy iron grate piled with logs. I dragged it aside, wincing as it screeched across the tile surround. I imagined that Tony, with his massive biceps, could simply lift the grate and wood, because there were no scratches or drag marks on the tile. I ducked inside the fireplace and crouched, shining my cell-phone light on the walls. They were lined by the same decorative tiles as the dungeon fireplace, plus there was a row of small black iron rings around the fireplace's interior wall. I tugged them one by one, but nothing moved, no hidden door revealed itself. I didn't expect it to. I was certain the tiles were the key.

Just above eye height, there were three rows of tiles at the back of the fireplace's interior: a row of tiles decorated with the thistle, on top of a row of tiles carved with lyres, on top of a row of heart tiles. Beginning with the top row, I pressed each tile decorated with a thistle. The second tile gave the tiniest bit beneath my fingers. I knew it! But then nothing happened. No secret door magically opened. Why?

Think, Riley. It's a pattern.

The shield had two thistles. I'd pressed the second thistle tile.

One lyre. I pressed the first tile in the row of lyres.

Two hearts. I pressed the second heart tile and heard a click. I reached up and tugged one of the rings. The side wall, seemingly crafted of a single sheet of heavy iron, gave way and a door opened with surprising ease, testimony to the skill of the men who'd built it.

The hidden door opened onto a void edged with a torn curtain of cobwebs. The shock and elation that surged in me turned to apprehension as I peered into darkness.

Chapter 47

The impossibly thick curtains of cobweb that hung from the ceiling of the narrow brick space seemed to absorb the light of my cell-phone flashlight. An offhand comment Vye had made about Tony came back to me. *"He had a cobweb in his hair and I brushed it away."* Why hadn't I noticed that detail? The attic was pristine. Tony said Maud had her cleaners there once a week.

Tony had been the first person to step through this door in decades.

Hurry. I crouched to avoid the webs, shuddering as they caught on my hair and trailed along my cheek. I aimed my beam into the dark. Another void opened just ahead of my feet, and I picked out a railing and a narrow set of stairs corkscrewing down into the dark. A spiral staircase. I placed my foot deliberately on the narrow step, sweeping the beam of light from side to side.

I descended, trailing one hand close the moist brick walls, their musty smell almost suffocating. Another spider web tangled in my hair and I bit back a scream as I flailed at the gossamer threads.

My shoulder scraped the dank wall as I squeezed down

the steps and I recoiled, hunching my shoulders, wondering how Tony had fit in this narrow space. The metal steps swayed slightly and made the softest ringing sound with each footfall. The walls were so close and the space so narrow, I had the sensation of descending into a well.

At the last twist of the staircase, I stumbled and panicked as my hand lost contact with the wall. I'd reached the bottom. I played my light on the dripping brickwork until it reflected on a narrow metal panel. A door. There was a bolt attached to the wall and I slid it to the side, pulling the door to reveal a floor of blackened brick and a rectangular opening. I stepped forward cautiously and when I put out my hand to steady myself, I felt smooth tile and the outline of a lyre. Aiming my flashlight through the opening, my beam illuminated a long table and chairs, a whiteboard, and a door.

I was in the dungeon.

Now I knew how the killer had made his escape. I squeezed back through the doorway and shut it behind me but left the bolt open. I planned to go upstairs and call Jack, and leaving the door unlocked would give him access to the secret staircase. I'd return to the attic and play it cool, so as not to let Tony know his secret had been uncovered.

As I groped toward the staircase for the climb upstairs, my flashlight caught a quick spark of reflected light on a pile of rags behind the flight of stairs. I knelt and aimed my light, revealing a tiny glass vial with a while label. *Apis mellifera.* Bee venom extract. The beam caught something else and I recoiled before my brain could fully process what I saw.

It wasn't a pile of rags, it was a dress, and my beam caught the sole of a small shoe.

I grabbed the railing and raced up the stairs, my only thought to run toward the weak glow of light at the top. *Oona. It's Oona.* My chest constricted as I pounded into the library and through the open French doors onto the balcony, desperate for a breath of fresh air.

I gasped, leaning on the solid stone rail, brushing away cobwebs. Had Oona fallen? If she'd fallen, she'd be by the foot of the stairs. She was under the stairs. My God, Ben closed her up in that awful darkness.

My hands trembled so much, my cell phone fell to the gravel parking lot three stories below. After a few breaths, I felt steadier and raised my head. Maud's white clad figure moved serenely through the garden, her back to me. I was about to call out and wave to her when I heard movement behind me and turned to see Tony stride into the library.

I jumped back behind the doorway and I heard him run into the office. Taking a deep breath, I dared a peek around the door frame. With a curse, Tony bent into the fireplace and pulled the secret door closed. Then with one fluid motion, he hefted the heavy iron grate and logs into the fireplace and jammed them against the secret door.

My heart hammered. He thought I was in there. He thought he was shutting me in, trapping me in the darkness with that unspeakable thing under the stairs.

I froze, afraid to breathe, as he pulled a book from a shelf, opened the cover, and took something out of it. I saw a gleam of metal as he stuffed it in his back pocket and reshelved the book. The key. He was going to lock the dungeon door. The walls were three feet thick—no one would hear me scream.

My body trembled as adrenaline surged and I flattened myself against the wall, watching him. As soon as he left, I'd get to the phone and call Jack.

He stalked toward the library door and relief flooded me. But he hesitated at the threshold, turned back, and walked through the space, looking down the rows of bookcases, his long legs moving impossibly fast. Looking for me. I scrunched into the corner of the balcony, tried to make myself as small and invisible as possible.

"I know you're here, Riley. You should've left it alone." His heavy footsteps barreled toward the balcony.

I popped up and looked over the balcony rail. Too far down to jump. The thought that he could throw me off the balcony flared. He was tall and strong. I'd just seen him lift the heavy iron grate as if it weighed nothing. I had only moments to move, he was heading right toward me.

I clambered onto the railing and, willing myself not to look down, reached out my hand and grabbed onto one of the jutting stones of the castle exterior. It pulled away and I felt my body tilt into thin air. I clawed at another, testing it. It held. Just as I swung off the railing Tony reached the doorway, fury in his voice. "Why didn't you leave it alone?"

I screamed. "Help!" No way I could climb up or down. But dangling here for long wasn't an option. The stones were too hard to keep hold of, the handhold too narrow. My fingertips started to slip.

Tony lunged over the rail as I flung my arm toward one of the woody, thick canes of the old rose plant. I grasped the cane with one hand, then drove my other hand through the plant to the metal arbor, shrieking as thorns pierced my hand. My feet scrabbled for purchase, for any ledge to stand on to take my weight from my burning arms. The plant pulled away from the wall and my legs swung out, pulling me down toward the ground. Somewhere I heard shouting, but I was afraid to take my eyes from my pursuer. Tony lunged over the railing again and made a grab for my leg. I felt his fingertips brush my shoe as I kicked out of his reach. He tried again as I managed to scrabble my feet against the rough stone, my hands grasping the arbor's hard metal.

For the briefest moment my terror subsided, but then Tony stepped up onto the rail and reached for the arbor.

"Stop!" Gerri's booming voice—one that had instilled fear in generations of Penniman High School students—made me raise my head toward the attic balcony. "What on earth is going on down there!"

Flo's head popped out the window, then disappeared.

"Gerri!" I shouted. "Throw me the rope in the trunk!"

Chapter 48

believe you dropped this," Jack said as he handed me my cell phone.

I sat at the long wooden table in the castle kitchen, Gerri and Flo close on both sides. Prentiss set a cup of fragrant tea in front of me and patted my shoulder. I wrapped my trembling hands around it and met Jack's eyes, finding concern there, and—was that a bit of admiration?

"Thanks." I sipped the tea and discovered that Prentiss had added a shot of whiskey.

"I heard from the state police," Jack said. "They stopped Ortiz's car at the Rhode Island border."

Flo squeezed my arm. "Riley, I felt like I was watching a scene in one of those action movies!" she gushed. "He almost got you!"

"Thank you for throwing me that rope, ladies," I said. "I don't know if I could've held on much longer."

"When I heard you scream, I ran to the house." Maud leaned over my shoulder, gently lifted my hand, and wrapped a bandage around it. I hadn't noticed the blood smearing the side of my cup.

"Thanks. I didn't have a plan," I admitted.

"That's adrenaline for you," Flo said. "That's how we were able to get the rope to you so fast. We heard you scream. When I saw you hanging onto the side of the building, I ran for the rope and tied it to the leg of the table."

"And Gerri tossed it down to me." I'd never been so happy to see Gerri in my life.

"Once a Girl Scout always a Girl Scout," Gerri said.

"Thank you, ladies." I tried to sip my tea, but my hand trembled too much to lift the cup, so I clasped my hands in my lap. "Jack, did you go in the staircase?"

He met my eye and gave me a small nod, then looked at everyone at the table in turn. "You're all to stay out of that area of the house, the library, and the dungeon"—he winced—"conference room. Don't discuss any details of the case." Jack's phone buzzed with a text and he stepped out of the room. Gerri, Flo, and I shared a who-is-he-kidding look.

We sat in silence for a moment, then everyone peppered me with questions.

"What about Tony Ortiz?"

"How could he do it?"

"Why?"

"Tony Ortiz changed his name from Anthony Ortiz Whitaker," I said. "His sister was Dallas Whitaker."

Maud's eyes widened. "The model who killed herself?"

"Is that why you suspected Tony in the first place?" Prentiss said.

I managed to take a sip of my tea. "It struck me as strange when Adam approached Tony at the exhibit opening. He was scrutinizing Tony's face, said he was sure he'd seen Tony before. He'd recognized the resemblance between Tony and Dallas."

Flo said softly, "Tony killed Adam because he blamed him for his sister's suicide?"

I nodded. "I think he's been planning this for a long time. He'd met Maud, moved into her orbit when he was in Newport, saw the connection between her and Adam. He was biding his time, and when he discovered the secret staircase, a plan came together."

"But how?" Maud said. "The entrance to the secret staircase is in the fireplace in his office. He had to get to the library without Vye hearing him leave his room or the attic."

Understanding dawned on Gerri's face. "He climbed down to the library balcony with the rope he found in Ben's trunk."

"Yes," I said. "That way Vye was his alibi. The floor squeaks and Vye has insomnia, so she'd hear him leave the attic, right? Except he'd already killed Adam and returned to the attic when he asked her to get a snack downstairs." *There was a cobweb in his hair . . .*

"What a cool customer," Flo said.

Maud said, her voice disbelieving, "So in the darkness, he climbed down the rope to the balcony of the library and then used the secret staircase in the fireplace to go to the dungeon?"

I nodded. "And he'd discovered another key, so after he killed Adam he locked the door of the dungeon from the inside." I recalled the advertisement I'd seen in the old newspaper: *Doors locked from within and without.* "He never even had to try to use the key in the security office. And when he returned up the secret stairway, he tossed the vial of venom and syringe beside—" I paused, the horror and pity I felt for the poor woman washing over me.

"Beside what?" Prentiss said. "I hate not being in on a secret."

"Riley found Oona," Flo whispered.

Maud sank into a chair next to Flo. "In the . . . secret staircase? All this time?"

"I'm pretty sure it's her," I said. "Oona never ran away with the chauffeur. Ben murdered her and left her in that stairwell so he could marry Alma."

Chapter 49

A few days later, at Maud's request, a group from the historical society arranged for the Penniman water rescue squad to drag the pond behind the castle. After a few hours, an antique car was discovered in the mud on the bottom. When the vehicle was pulled onto the shore, a skeleton was found in the trunk along with metal buttons and a belt buckle that matched the ones in the photo of Ben's chauffeur.

That night, Prentiss and I sat around the farmhouse table in Maud's cottage with Flo and Gerri. Maud and I had searched her she shed's magnificent fireplace after she had a chimney sweep and a carpenter check it. They found no secret passage. If there was one, it was so well hidden it fooled two professional and several amateur searchers. Now a fire crackled there, casting a golden glow and warmth on the gathering, doing its best to exorcise any ghosts that lingered.

Maud pulled a luscious garnet cashmere wrap around her shoulders as Prentiss served mulled cider and a charcuterie board piled high with apples, strawberries, three kinds of cheese, crackers, cornichons, and slices of summer sausage. "I asked you all here because I'd like to take control of Oona's story and put together a display about her in the house. I hope the Penniman Historical Society will help."

"Of course," Gerri preened.

"Absolutely," Flo said, misty eyed.

I sipped my cider and smiled at Prentiss.

"Riley, tell us more about what you discovered in the floorplan," Maud said.

I gathered my thoughts. "One of the things that struck me about the castle was the fact that Oona and Ben had separate but not adjoining bedrooms. Yes, it was typical in upper-class homes for a husband and wife to have separate bedrooms, but Ben had placed his wife's room on the other side of the building. I think he always wanted to have a way to, how do I put this—"

"Keep his wife out of the way while he visited his girl-friends?" Prentiss said.

"Exactly," I said. "The hotel's renovation of the house before you bought it reconfigured the floor plan of the castle, but one thing remained—Ben's fireplace, his secret staircase to the dungeon. I don't think he was meeting his songbird Alma in the dungeon—or maybe he did, but who would think of that dank space as a love nest? No, the pretty cottage right outside the back door was a perfect love nest. The back door was well away from prying eyes in the more public parts of the castle. The secret staircase was Ben's private highway."

"Get to Oona's murder," Flo said.

"I'm getting there." I took a sip of cider. "The biggest clues were the coat, the car, and Jamie, her dog. Oona supposedly ran off with the chauffeur in the winter, but she left behind a gorgeous and warm fur coat. But most strange and out of character, Oona left behind her beloved dog. I couldn't believe she'd do that, she was so devoted to him. Tony said the chauffeur took off with Oona and the car. So I thought of the pond at the back of the castle. That's been fenced off for so many years. I wondered if the chauffeur hadn't gotten very far at all."

We sipped our cider as the fire crackled. To my surprise, tears spattered Maud's cheeks. Flo, sitting beside her, clasped Maud's hand.

"That poor young girl!" Maud spoke quietly. "I feel a kinship with her. I was once so young and stupid and betrayed too."

Flo handed her a tissue and Maud thanked her before continuing. "I see it all so clearly now, but I believed Adam when he told me"—she raised her head and looked at Prentiss sitting across from her, his eyes welling too—"he'd gotten the divorce. He'd said, 'Vegas divorces are just as easy as Vegas weddings, babe.'"

Flo and I exchanged glances. Her genealogist friend had been correct.

Maud took a deep breath. "I left Vegas to go to Europe with Freddie, and my engagement to him was such a scandal—all of it. How young I was. The prince marrying a Black girl. An American, a divorcée." She shook her head. "I wanted it all to go away. I just wanted Freddie and I told him the truth: Adam told me that his lawyer had seen to our divorce. Freddie told me not to dwell on it so I didn't. Look in the envelope, Prentiss. I know you're dying to."

I sat as still as I could, afraid that if I moved I'd break whatever spell had come over Maud, that had driven her to this outpouring. Maud sobbed, and Flo pulled Maud's head onto her shoulder in a comforting embrace. The tall woman wrapped her arms around the petite senior and broke down. Prentiss opened the envelope and took out several sheets of paper. He shook his head and swore as he paged through them. "Maud, what do you want to do?"

Maud wiped her eyes and straightened her back. "What do you think I should do?"

Gerri took the papers from Prentiss, read them, then handed them to me. Flo leaned over and we read them together. Divorce papers with Maud's signature and an empty space where Adam's signature should've been. "He never signed your divorce papers?"

Maud nodded. "I was legally married to Adam Blasco until Tony killed him."

I lowered my eyes, thinking of Vye, who had declined Maud's invitation and was back at the house. Her marriage to Adam would surely come out at some point, but I didn't want to be the one to mention it here. I couldn't imagine what Maud's reaction would be. Or Vye's.

Maud continued. "All these years, when Adam said he needed money, I'd give him a job. He never used the word 'blackmail,' but I always felt under threat. He had some photos of me I wouldn't want to get out . . ." Her voice trailed.

Flo tapped the divorce papers, "Maybe we could sign Adam's name and my genealogy friend in Vegas could enter this now. Computer mistakes happen all the time, right?"

This information was dynamite. "Someone might talk," Maud said. "There's always a chance someone could discover that the information was entered now."

All eyes turned to Gerri, her back straight, her chin raised, as she intoned, "Let sleeping dogs lie."

Was the president of the Penniman Genealogical Society saying this?

"Burn them, Prentiss," Maud said.

Prentiss tossed the papers into the fire.

As Prentiss walked us through the darkened garden to Gerri's car, I turned to him. "You know, Prentiss, I'm still puzzled about something. Adam was shooting a cookbook for Maud, right? But I've never seen her cook."

Prentiss threw his head back and laughed, then leaned close. "Maud can't even boil water! But who cares? She has the style, the story, the setting! People buy cookbooks for the fantasy."

"If Maud doesn't cook, who did the recipes?" I asked.

Prentiss spread his arms wide. "Me!"

I remembered him in the kitchen, chopping vegetables. The brioche. The baked goods for the security staff.

"Who's going to buy a Prentiss Love cookbook?" He snorted. "Nah, everyone wants one by Her Serene Highness Maud of the Royal House of Terbinia."

Chapter 50

Thanks again, Caroline," Vye said.

"Any time," Caroline hugged Vye. "I can't thank you enough for what you've done for Sprinkles."

"My favorite model? I can't thank you enough for letting me play with her." Vye picked up Sprinkles, gave her a quick snuggle, then set her down with a besotted sigh.

"You're always welcome." Caroline turned to the stairs. "Now you'll have to excuse me, I have to finish packing." Jack had asked Caroline to go away with him for a weekend of hiking at his cabin in the Berkshires. It was their first trip together and I knew that Caroline had been freaking out upstairs over what to pack.

Vye threw her arms around me. "Riley, I'll never be able to thank you enough. You've been my rock through all the"— she waved her hand—"craziness with Adam and letting me stay here for the past couple of weeks. It was great to be normal and work at the shop."

"You can work at Udderly any time." I meant it.

"I still can't believe Tony killed Adam." Her face crumpled. "But I've always felt that Adam had it coming, like he was due some kind of cosmic payback from the universe, you know? He put so much ugliness and pain in the world, he used so many people and spit them out." She picked up Sprinkles again to give her an extra snuggle. "I'm going to miss seeing you every day my fluffy-wuffy magnificent queen." She put Sprinkles down and slung her duffel over her shoulder. "You're sure it's okay if I come visit, right? Even on days we're not shooting?"

"You can visit Sprinkles any time you like," I said.

Using money from the sale of the recovered *Dallas*, Vye had bought the storefront where Bitsy's Creative Catering had planned to expand. Vye decided to stay in Penniman while she decided on her next step in life, and in the meantime run a pet photography studio. Her current project was a calendar featuring the many moods of Sprinkles.

Police had seized the photos Dree had stolen, and Vye had sold them, too, all except one, an enchanting shot of Willow in the tea garden. Vye had given it to her, but I didn't know what Willow had done with it.

Of all the things that had happened since Adam's death at the art festival, there was one that puzzled me the most: On the Saturday afternoon that EMS was called to the castle after the discovery of Adam's body, Dree had appeared at the kitchen door of the castle dressed in her clothes from the night before and waved to me. Since Dree had lawyered up after leaving Max almost literally holding the bag of stolen photos, this was what I surmised.

At first I'd assumed she was making her way back from spending the night with Max. After all, I'd seen them flirting at the opening. But I'd also seen Max with his wife that night. It was possible, but I couldn't imagine that Max's wife would come to the opening and then not stay the night with Max at Loch Lomond Cottage. Then Vye and Tony told me they'd seen Dree at the castle around eleven o'clock the night of the murder. It didn't make sense that she'd come back to the castle and then go back to Max's cottage, especially with his wife there.

She'd had theft on her mind, not murder. After Adam again refused her request to write a foreword for her book, she'd resorted to blackmail—I hadn't heard exactly what she'd threatened to reveal, but I'd heard the words "money" and "darkroom." She knew he'd gone back to the darkroom. By the time she'd returned to the castle, I believed Adam was lying dead in the dungeon. She'd opened the darkroom door and had seen the photos Adam had taken that day and decided to steal them. She had Max in her pocket, and he had art-world connections where she could sell Adam's work.

The next day, when EMS was called to the castle, she saw police vehicles and assumed her theft had been discovered. She didn't yet know about Adam's death. She'd put on her dress from the previous evening, sneaked out the front of the castle, and pretended to arrive at the kitchen door, where there was a crowd. She spotted me and made sure I saw her, hoping I'd mention that I'd witnessed her "arriving" at the castle. She must've been shocked to discover that Adam had been murdered. She had his stolen property in her room. She'd waited until things quieted, then dreamed up the dead drop with Max.

She wanted me to be her alibi for theft, not murder.

As Vye waved and got in her SUV, Jack pulled up, not in his police vehicle but in his even larger personal SUV. He gave Vye a nod as she pulled away.

"Caroline, Jack's here," I called.

"I'll be down in a sec," she shouted.

"Coffee?" I said, holding the door wide for Jack. Sprinkles flipped her tail and stalked into the parlor—she still didn't like sharing Caroline with him. Rocky sniffed at

Jack's shoes, intrigued by some enticing scent, while Jack gave him a scratch.

"Sure, thanks."

I poured us each a cup and we took seats at the kitchen table.

Jack gave me a nod over the rim of his coffee mug. He looked as relaxed as I'd seen him in months. As well as being an unusual shade of bluish gray, his eyes were kind, especially when he wasn't interrogating me. "Thanks again for giving me the tips on Luca and Barry," he said.

"Yes, the words Adam yelled at Barry and Luca struck me as strange," I said. "'You shouldn't have come here.' When I realized he meant those words for Barry and not Luca, it made me think they were working together." I recalled the scene in the tea garden. "I also realized that Tony must've been the shadowy figure who watched Luca and Adam argue in the tea garden. That's why he tried to pin Adam's murder on Luca by taking the EpiPen from Adam's bag and putting it in Luca's backpack. He'd seen them argue."

Jack shook his head. "Poor Luca. Kid was always in the wrong place at the wrong time."

A thump came from upstairs and we both raised our eyes to the ceiling. I wondered what on earth Caroline was packing for a two-day trip.

Jack cleared his throat. "I thought you should know. Barry talked in exchange for a deal for his kid. He said he met Adam at a party Bitsy catered in Penniman last summer, and they cooked up the scheme for Barry to steal *Dallas* and Adam to make the claim. Then they were going to split the insurance money."

I knew that after Barry and his son were arrested for burglary, Bitsy shut down her business. Barry, despite being a thief, did have feelings for Bitsy, and had sworn she had nothing to do with his crimes.

I sipped my coffee. When I considered his awful treatment of Maud, Vye, and Dallas, insurance fraud was the least of Adam's transgressions. "Jack, how do you do it? I mean, it's awful for anyone to lose their life, but I feel some sympathy for Tony Ortiz."

He choked on his coffee and sputtered, "The guy who tried to kill you?"

"Well, not for that," I said. "He lost his sister."

Jack scratched the back of his head vigorously. "Once I had a case where, well, I can't give details, but the person who was murdered had abused his killer for years. The law takes things into account, but—" He reached across the table and picked up my copy of *Death on the Nile*. "This is a good one."

"You read it?"

"You don't think my little gray cells would like it?" Jack smiled, then grew serious. "Riley, there's one thing I'm pretty sure you, me, and Hercule Poirot agree on."

I met his eyes and quoted, "'I do not approve of murder.'"

Later, I stood on the porch, giving Caroline and Jack a wave as his SUV rolled away. Rocky threaded around my ankles and then dashed down the steps, heading off into the fields for some hunting. Conversation and laughter flowed from Udderly's packed parking lot. I breathed in the soft evening air; time for a nice, quiet evening. Maybe I'd actually finish my book. As I reached for the doorknob, Sprinkles' face loomed through the screen.

Oh no, I'd be alone with Sprinkles. Without Vye. Without Caroline. Without Rocky, at least for a while.

I looked back toward the warm light streaming from Udderly's windows. I'd just made a fresh batch of pumpkin spice ice cream. I edged through the screen door past Sprinkles' baleful look and before I could lose my nerve, called Dr. Pryce's office.

I recognized Imelda's voice and put a smile into mine. "Hi, this is Riley Rhodes. May I speak to Dr. Pryce?"

She put the call through and his warm voice answered. "Dr. Pryce."

"Hi, Liam. This is Riley Rhodes. Would you like to stop by tonight for an ice cream?"

THE END

Afterword

The story of the Weeping Lady was inspired by the Green Lady of Fyvie Castle in Scotland. There are many wonderful legends of ghostly ladies of every hue—Green, Blue, Gray—but this is one of my favorites and, like Riley, I hope to collect Fyvie Castle one day.

Fyvie Castle was already cursed when Lillias Drummond married Alexander Seton, Lord Fyvie, in 1592. After several years of marriage and four daughters, Seton blamed Lillias for the lack of a male heir, and he began an affair with Grizel Leslie, who happened to be Lillias' cousin. Some stories say that Lillias discovered the affair and died soon after of a broken heart. Some say her death was caused by starvation or poisoning by her husband.

A few months after Lillias died in 1601, Seton married Grizel. On the night of their wedding, the couple was distracted by the sound of moaning and weeping outside their window. Despite a search, no cause for the noise could be found.

The next morning, writing was discovered carved into the windowsill of the bridal chamber—the words "D. LILLIAS DRUMMOND" dug into the stone fifty feet off the ground. Ever since, it is said that the castle is haunted by a lady in green, who cries after all these years over the betrayal of her faithless spouse.

Recipe

No-Churn Pumpkin Spice Ice Cream

No ice cream maker? No problem!

Make your own ice cream in a pinch—even without an ice cream chiller. I was a bit skeptical of no-churn recipes, but I experimented and came up with one that worked like a charm.

This delicious, fall-inspired ice cream is easy to make and even easier to eat.

This makes a wonderful accompaniment for any spice cake or use it as a delicious filling for ice cream pie. Just fill your favorite pie shell and let it firm up in the freezer for six hours and drizzle with caramel sauce before serving.

Ingredients

One 14-ounce can sweetened condensed milk
¾ cup unsweetened pumpkin puree
1 teaspoon pure vanilla extract
½ teaspoon ground cinnamon
¼ teaspoon ground ginger
⅛ teaspoon ground nutmeg
Pinch ground cloves
½ teaspoon salt
4 tablespoons plain yogurt (I like Greek or Icelandic)
    at room temperature
2 cups heavy cream

Directions

In a large bowl, combine the sweetened condensed milk, pumpkin puree, vanilla, cinnamon, ginger, nutmeg, cloves, and salt.

In another bowl, whisk the yogurt, then slowly pour in the heavy cream and combine, using a hand mixer on low (or a stand mixer, if you have one). Then whip on high until stiff peaks begin to form.

Add half the whipped cream mixture to the sweetened condensed milk and whisk until completely combined. Using a spatula, gently fold in the remaining whipped cream mixture until no streaks remain.

Pour into a freezer safe container and cover. (At this point you can fill a pie shell if you'd like an ice cream pie.) You can use a loaf pan and cover with a layer of plastic wrap topped with tinfoil. Put it in the freezer until firm, at least 6 hours, and then enjoy!